A Murderer Among Us

Detective Molina appeared deep in thought. Finally he spoke. "It's quite a puzzle we have: two women, both Twin Lakes residents, argue in public. The following morning, one woman's dead, struck down by the vehicle of the other."

Lydia's hand flew to her pounding heart. "I didn't kill Claire Weill! Why should I? Besides, I wouldn't be stupid enough to use my own car!"

He gave her a sidelong glance. "That might be considered a stroke of genius."

Lydia gasped. This detective managed to twist whatever she said into a damning statement.

What They Are Saying About
A Murderer Among Us

A Murderer Among Us is a suspenseful, thoroughly enjoyable page turner. I intended to read only the first chapter, then attend to a dozen tasks waiting for my attention. Instead I kept reading throughout an entire day and finished the next morning.

Lydia is a spunky, likeable heroine, coping with widowhood and new beginnings and drawn, in spite of herself, into her married daughters' problems as she seeks to solve the mystery of the Twin Lake murders, while enjoying a late-in-life romance with the handsome policeman in charge of the case.

Ms. Levinson keeps the reader guessing up to the time Lydia is caught in the murderer's snare. This is one of those "impossible to put down" books. Let's hope we meet Lydia again in another adventure

Dorothy Bodoin
http://www.dorothybodoin.com

Free up some time, grab your favorite beverage, set your phone on voicemail and settle in to enjoy an excellent mystery novel. **A Murderer Among Us** by Marilyn Levinson is a must read. It is an absolute delight and you will find yourself captivated from page one, rushing to the end to find out what happened.

A Murderer Among Us is a page turner and thoroughly enjoyable. I highly recommend it and look forward to Levinson's next novel.

Suzanne M Hurley
www.suzannemhurley.com

Wings

A MURDERER AMONG US

by

Marilyn Levinson

A Wings ePress, Inc.

Mystery Novel

Wings ePress, Inc.

Edited by: Jeanne Smith
Copy Edited by: Joan Powell
Senior Editor: Jeanne Smith
Executive Editor: Marilyn Kapp
Cover Artist: Kathy Williams

All rights reserved

Names, characters and incidents depicted in this book are products of the author's imagination or are used fictitiously. Any resemblance to actual events, locales, organizations, or persons, living or dead, is entirely coincidental and beyond the intent of the author or the publisher.

No part of this book may be reproduced or transmitted in any form or by any means, electronic or mechanical, including photocopying, recording, or by any information storage and retrieval system, without permission in writing from the publisher.

Wings ePress Books
http://www.wings-press.com

Copyright © 2011 by Marilyn Levinson
ISBN: 978-1-61309-981-0

Published In the United States Of America

June 2011

Wings ePress Inc.
403 Wallace Court
Richmond, KY 40475

Dedication

To my critique partners: Bernardine Fagan, Myra Platt, and Marianne Tremaroli

One

Lydia Krause never made scenes, but tonight she longed to rip out the heart of the man approaching their table.

Her neighbor, Peg DiMarco, smiled as she introduced her to the monster. "Lydia Krause, this is Marshall Weill. Marshall, Lydia just moved to Twin Lakes. I persuaded her to come down to Bingo Night to meet her fellow residents."

"It's a pleasure," he said, nodding with the self-assurance of a seventy-year-old male who had retained his trim physique and handsome demeanor. Everything about him was stylish and shouted "designer," from his Italian loafers to the elegant suede jacket.

Marshall Weill? Could she be wrong? More than six years had passed. He stepped closer. Years of running her own company had sharpened Lydia's B.S. sense, and this man was sleaze with a capital S.

She hesitated before shaking his extended hand then wished she hadn't. His palm felt too smooth, almost as if it were slimed with sweat though her hand wasn't damp. She jerked free of his grasp and lifted her hand to cover a false cough. At the same time, she questioned her visceral reaction. Was she suddenly psychic—able to detect sleaze with a handshake, or was her negative frame of mind getting the better of her?

"Marshall's our HOA's financial advisor," Peg offered with pride. "He's also handling several residents' portfolios."

Financial advisor? Portfolios? A frisson ran down Lydia's spine. This couldn't be a coincidence!

The growing certainty that she faced an amoral, malevolent fiend vied with her mind's insistence that he couldn't possibly be the person she supposed him to be. To cover her dismay, she spoke disparagingly.

"I didn't realize the homeowners' association has enough funds to warrant the services of a financial advisor."

Marshall Weill gazed down at her. "Regardless of the amount, you don't want to let money lie fallow in a bank. Put it to work, I always say."

He smiled, revealing a gap between his front teeth. All doubt vanished. Lydia gasped.

"You're Warren Mannes." Suddenly lightheaded, she gripped the edge of the table.

The smile returned, but this time it was forced. "You're mistaken. My name is Marshall Weill."

The fear and anger Lydia read in his eyes empowered her. She'd recently moved to this Eden-like retirement community and felt obliged to protect her fellow residents from the serpent in its midst. She drew herself up and plunged ahead.

"You're Warren Mannes, and you've no business handling anyone's money."

Though she hadn't raised her voice, people sitting at nearby tables sensed something sensational was happening and paused in mid-conversation to gape and listen. Lydia, usually so in control, was too enraged—too outraged—to watch her words.

"You went to prison for stealing millions of dollars from people who gave you their trust. Innocent people, whose lives you destroyed. Not to mention that company you took down!"

He gripped her arm. "Stop it! You've confused me with someone else."

She jerked herself free. "Oh, no, I haven't!"

"Lydia, get a hold of yourself!" Peg hissed, grabbing her other arm. "You're spouting nonsense."

"I wish I were." Her baby sister's face flashed in her mind, causing Lydia to wince in pain. Here stood Warren Mannes, decked out in expensive clothes and a salon hair cut, enjoying a lifestyle paid for with stolen money, while Allison lay dead in her grave!

Incensed, she went on. "Six years ago I attended his trial where victim after victim testified that this man stole their life savings. I'll show you newspaper articles, Peg."

A short, stocky woman who was undoubtedly the man's wife pushed her way through the crowd until she faced Lydia. Her coiffed, stiffly sprayed hair bobbed as she exclaimed, "I hope you're pleased with yourself, exposing a man before his friends and neighbors for a mistake best left in the past."

Marshall Weill/Warren Mannes grimaced. "Thank you, my dear, for making a bad situation worse."

"It's all her fault!" his wife retorted, glaring at Lydia.

Taken aback by the woman's fury, Lydia blinked. Her silence spurred the wife on. Ignoring the pleas of friends urging her not to upset herself, Claire Mannes's voice rose higher.

"Who asked you to move to our quiet community and start trouble? We were happy until you arrived."

Lydia found her voice and her indignation. "I suggest you put the blame where it belongs–on your husband, a convicted embezzler. How dare he handle anyone's finances, here or anywhere else!"

Claire Weill/Mannes drew in such a deep gasp, for a moment Lydia feared she was about to expire. Instead, she retaliated.

"You've ruined our lives! I wish you'd never come here. Better yet, do us a favor and die!"

Furious, Lydia retorted, "Someone should put an end to you, you stupid cow! Open your eyes and face facts. Your husband destroyed lives. He's the guilty one here, only you're the loyal little wife and refuse to see it!"

A blonde woman with an incipient dowager's hump came to stand beside Claire. "Claire, honey, don't upset yourself. You know we have complete trust in Marshall."

She glared at Lydia through tortoise-shell cat's-eye-shaped glasses. "Stop badgering the poor woman!" She spun on her heels and ushered her charge away.

Lydia grabbed her parka and fled. Noting that neither Marshall nor Claire and her staunch supporter were in pursuit, she headed for the ladies' room where she leaned heavily on the marble counter until her heartbeat returned to normal.

You're losing it, kiddo, she told herself, appalled by the way she'd ousted Warren Mannes in a public display of histrionics. Maybe early retirement was having an adverse effect on her brain. As president and CEO of Krause Gifts and Furnishings, she'd contended with her share of frustration and had never vented her fury in this manner. Never! Then again, she'd never encountered the man who had deceived and ruined her sister.

Lydia splashed cold water on her face and decided to put her unit on the market first thing tomorrow morning. No matter that this would upset her daughter, Meredith, who lived five minutes from Twin Lakes.

Still, she didn't regret having exposed Warren Mannes/Marshall Weill as the embezzler he was. She'd forfeited whatever peace and serenity she hoped to enjoy at Twin Lakes. So much for the quiet life of Suffolk County!

The sound of retching emerged from the next-to-last stall, which stood ajar. As Lydia wondered if she should disturb whomever was in distress, a woman staggered out, her face as white as chalk. She lowered her face to a sink and drank greedily.

Lydia recognized Barbara Taylor, a woman she'd met the week before and had intended to call.

"Barbara, what's the matter?"

"Either the fish I ate tonight was bad or I'm coming down with a stomach virus. Argh!" She clamped a hand over her mouth and dashed back into the stall.

Lydia shuddered. "Can I call your husband?"

"No husband," Barbara managed between pants. "He died two years ago."

"Oh!"

"'S all right. I'll be all right." She turned back to the toilet and retched. When she emerged, she was shaking.

Instinctively, Lydia put an arm around her shoulders. "You're not well. Let me drive you home."

Barbara's nod was barely perceptible. "All right, but we'll take my car. In case I throw up again."

Lydia yanked paper towels from the dispenser. "We'll take these along, just in case."

On their way out, Lydia asked the woman at the desk to tell Peg, with whom she'd come to Bingo Night, not to worry about her, that she was going home. She helped Barbara out to the parking lot and slid her into the passenger seat of her car. Barbara handed her the car keys. "I live on the east side of Lake M. Number 32."

"We're on our way," Lydia said. She drove slowly down Lake Boulevard, which bisected the community of Twin Lakes. The long, manmade lakes stretched out behind houses and trees on either side. Named Lake Montaukett and Lake Nissaquage in honor of Long Island

Indian tribes, they were more familiarly known as Lake M and Lake N.

"Oh," Barbara moaned as Lydia pulled slowly onto her driveway.

Lydia stepped on the brake. "Feeling sick again?"

"No. I just realized I'll have to drive you home. Or you can borrow my car."

Lydia thought a moment about her own car, parked in her driveway. She always pulled the Lexus into the garage at night, but this was a gated community. Surely nothing would happen if she left it out one night.

"Not to worry. I can walk home."

"Certainly not! The path along the back of the complex is desolate. Oh!"

Barbara covered her mouth and ran from the car to the front door. Lydia followed her into the house.

"Don't you lock your door?" Lydia asked, shocked.

"I do when I go to sleep for the night," Barbara called from the bathroom.

Her unit was a ranch like Lydia's, but considerably smaller and decorated in Country French. Lydia called to her from the cheerful blue, yellow and white kitchen. "Do you have any cola?" she asked. "That should settle your stomach."

"In the fridge."

Gingerly, Lydia helped Barbara out of her jacket. Barbara said, "Just toss it on top of the washing machine. I'll wash everything I'm wearing tomorrow."

"Well, all right," Lydia reluctantly agreed. She was all

set to wash them now.

Barbara looked up at her. "I'll be fine. Really."

Only she wasn't. She sipped some soda then dashed into the bathroom to upchuck again.

Lydia wiped her mouth with wet tissues. She felt her forehead. "You have fever."

"My head aches," Barbara complained.

Lydia escorted her to her bedroom and helped her into a nightgown. She didn't like the sheen of sweat forming on Barbara's face. "I think I'd better stay."

"Oh, Lydia, I feel terrible!" Barbara gave a weak laugh. "I mean it both ways. I feel lousy, but I hate to make you play nursemaid."

"You're too sick to stay alone. I'll find a blanket and sleep on the den sofa."

"No need. The spare room's made up. Towels are in the linen closet."

"I'll be fine. Now get some rest."

Barbara slipped between the covers. "Thank you. I'll see you in the morning."

Lydia turned out the light and returned to the kitchen. The evening's events ran through her mind like a surreal movie. She'd encountered Allison's nemesis and blasted his cover, then ended up spending the night nursing a woman she hardly knew. She glanced at the clock. It was barely ten o'clock. She had the entire night to get through.

An hour later she was dozing off in the spare bedroom when she heard rustling, then Barbara's cry of distress.

"I'm coming," she called out.

The next time Barbara was sick, Lydia suggested she call her doctor. Barbara insisted there was no point in disturbing him; she'd call in the morning. She kept repeating how very sorry she was. Lydia, fearing dehydration, fed her tea and soda, most of which she couldn't keep down.

Lydia awoke hours later with the panicky sensation of not knowing where she was. She groaned as it all came back, confrontation and all. She glanced at her watch. It was almost ten o'clock.

She sprang out of bed, used the bathroom, then followed the aroma of freshly brewed coffee into the kitchen. Barbara sat at the table, munching an English muffin. She smiled up at Lydia.

"Good morning! I've no idea what was wrong with me, but I think it's passed, thank God."

"I'm glad," Lydia said. The sound of the dryer running in the adjacent room told her Barbara had been up for some time.

"Want some toast and coffee?"

Lydia thought a moment. "Well, okay, but then I must get going. I'd no idea it was so late."

"Do you have an early appointment? Are you expecting a workman?"

"No, but I'm usually up by seven. I've slept half the morning away."

Barbara laughed. "For good reason. You were up most of the night. You must be exhausted."

"Not really. Just discombobulated. Thanks," she said as

Barbara set a glass of orange juice before her.

They ate in virtual silence. A comfortable silence, Lydia thought. She felt free of any obligation to make the usual conversation expected of a newcomer to the community. She thanked her lucky stars when she realized Barbara knew nothing of her scene with the Weills, as they now called themselves. She wanted to put that behind her.

Barbara cleared the table then offered to drive Lydia home.

"No need. I love to walk," Lydia said. "Besides, you're still weak."

Barbara smiled. "If you insist. The car probably reeks." She chuckled. "I know spending the night here wasn't on your agenda, but I'm grateful that you stayed. More for the company than anything else. It's times like this I miss Robert the most."

"I know exactly what you mean," Lydia said.

"How long has your husband been gone?"

Gone. Yes, that's exactly what Izzy was. Gone from her everyday life. "Eight months, though at times it feels like eight days—or eight years."

Barbara rested her hand on Lydia's arm. "I wish I could say it gets easier with time, but after two years I feel the loss as keenly as ever. I keep busy and the days pass. I've good friends and a good life here at Twin Lakes. I'll call you the next time a group of us goes out for dinner and a movie. We often do that on Saturday night."

Lydia smiled. "I'd love that. If you give me a pen, I'll

jot down my phone number. It's not in the directory yet."

She left Barbara's house with the knowledge that she'd made her first real friend since Izzy's death. She appreciated the instant camaraderie she'd felt in another widow's company, of being with someone who understood exactly what she was going through. But it was more than that. Even sick to her stomach, Barbara was witty and resilient. Too bad Lydia had decided to leave Twin Lakes.

Maybe she wouldn't move, after all. Lydia considered her options as she walked along the woods bordering the rear of the development, then followed the curve of N Boulevard around to her house. There would be hell to pay for having exposed Mannes in such an open, direct manner, but eventually the furor would die down. Maybe they would move away. At any rate, she needn't act in haste. Finding the temperature surprisingly warm for November, Lydia unzipped her parka. It was a delightful morning for a power walk—if only she were well rested.

Her car stood smack in the middle of the two-car driveway. Was that how she'd left it? Out of habit, she still parked on the right side of the driveway because Izzy used to park on the left.

As she punched in her code on the pad beside the garage door, Lydia caught a glimpse of the front of her car. She moaned. No, it couldn't be! She blinked, her mind refusing to accept the sight that met her eyes.

She walked around the vehicle, shaking her head in distress. Her beautiful Lexus had been badly damaged.

The hood was crumpled, a headlight smashed, and the windshield was cracked in several places. What on earth had happened? How had it gotten in this condition?

She unlocked the door that led to the kitchen and rushed inside. Her red tom, Reggie, came meowing to demand his breakfast, which was hours overdue. Lydia set down food and water then, with trembling fingers, dialed 911.

Two

"Mrs. Krause, I'd like you to tell me everything you did, from the time you left for Bingo last night until now."

Lydia stared incredulously at the police lieutenant sitting at her kitchen table while outside the crew of CSIs scrutinized her car and the taped-off area of her driveway. She could only imagine what her gawking neighbors must be thinking.

"What does it matter what I've been doing? I called the police to report that someone vandalized my car."

Unperturbed, Lieutenant Detective Solomon Molina looked up from his note taking. He was good looking, Lydia noted. Dark rather than fair. Nice, even features set off by a full head of salt and pepper hair. She judged him to be a few years younger than her fifty-eight years.

"We have reason to believe your car was involved in a serious accident involving a pedestrian."

Ice water coursed through her veins, momentarily rendering her incapable of speech. "Oh, how awful!" Images flit across her mind, turning her horror to fury.

"I think I know who's responsible, Lieutenant, though I'm shocked that even he would harm an innocent person to get back at me." She swallowed. "Was the pedestrian badly injured? Will he or she be all right?"

"Who do you think took your car, Mrs. Krause?"

"Warren Mannes, a convicted embezzler. Last night in the clubhouse, my neighbor introduced him as Marshall Weill. When Peg said he was the homeowners' association's financial advisor, I told him I knew who he was and expressed my outrage that he was handling other people's money."

"Did this exchange take place in public?"

Lydia paused, recalling the shocked expression on residents' faces, the awful exchange with Mannes's wife before she fled to the ladies' room. "Oh, it was very public."

"Were you angry?"

"Furious. The thief stole the life savings of several of his clients. I didn't want a repeat at Twin Lakes."

Molina's green eyes, bright as emeralds, studied her. "Were you or someone close to you one of his victims?"

Lydia grimaced. "My youngest sister, Allison."

He nodded, his face softening with compassion. "You have my sympathy."

Lydia looked away so he couldn't see the tears welling up in her eyes. Taking Allison's money had been the least of it. The unscrupulous predator had seduced her sister then threw her away like a used condom. Depressed by Mannes's rejection, the last in a series of failed relationships, Allison had swallowed all the pills in her medicine cabinet and ended her life at thirty-eight.

"How do you think Mannes, or Weill managed to drive your car?"

Lydia dreaded having to explain her stupidity. "I left it in the driveway, the key magnetically affixed to the underside of the fender. I thought it was safe, here in a gated community. Anyway, I intended to park it in the garage when I came home last night. Only I didn't come home until just now."

"Where were you, Mrs. Krause?"

"I spent the night at a neighbor's house because she'd taken ill." Lydia described her encounter with Barbara in the ladies' room.

"How very kind of you, Mrs. Krause."

Was he commiserating with her? Mocking her? Lydia couldn't be certain what he intended as his remarkable green eyes fixed on her like tines piercing her soul. The effect was sobering but somewhat exciting, as these days men gave her as much attention as a piece of furniture.

"Especially since Mrs. Taylor can't be a close friend of yours," he continued in a reasonable tone. "You moved to Twin Lakes less than a month ago."

"What does that matter? Last night she needed looking after." Lydia glared at Molina. "It was the decent, humane thing to do."

He ignored her implication that he was a heartless bastard and asked, "Did you get much sleep last night?"

"Very little"

"What time did you leave Mrs. Taylor's house this morning?"

Lydia twirled a strand of curly hair as she thought. "Almost ten-thirty."

"You arrived home when?"

"About seven minutes later. I saw the damage to my car and called nine-one-one."

"Did you meet anyone as you walked home from Mrs. Taylor's house?"

"I don't think so. Oh, yes—I passed Sally Marcus speed walking just before I turned down Nissaquage Boulevard. I know she saw me, though—"

"Though?" he prompted.

Lydia felt her face grow warm. "She looked the other way."

He jotted down what Lydia had told him then asked, "See anyone else?"

"No."

"And why would Mrs. Marcus choose not to greet you?"

"She's a board member. I assume she resents me for outing someone she's worked with on Twin Lakes business."

He wrote in his notepad, then said, "We'll see what Mrs. Marcus has to say."

Lydia stiffened. Lieutenant Molina was treating her as a suspect! She gave a nervous laugh. "Why? Do you think I'm lying? That I ran down a pedestrian last night, left the car in the driveway, then called the police?"

He shrugged. "Why would you do that, Mrs. Krause?"

Lydia had had enough. "Who is this person I'm supposed to have hit? Is he young? Old? A man or a woman?"

When he didn't answer, she glowered at him. "I have every right to know since my car was involved."

His cell phone rang. "If you'll excuse me."

Lydia watched him stride through the dining room to hunch over his cell phone in the far corner of the living room—a trim, well-built man just under six feet, who carried himself as though he hadn't a fear in the world. He stood beside "Family," her favorite of Izzy's large sculptures. One of his less abstract works; it represented four figures meant to be their family when the girls were young. The detective spoke for some time, too softly for her to make out the words. Then it was his turn to answer—two yeses and a no.

He ended the call, glanced at his notebook, and punched in a phone number. Was he calling Sally Marcus, whom she barely knew? Barbara? Lydia's heart thundered as she wondered just exactly when her Lexus had been taken and used to run someone down. Did this happen in Twin Lakes? Was the person dead? Lydia prayed the victim wasn't a child. Her breath came in gasps as her anxiety grew intolerable. She had to know what was happening.

She was about to interrupt Lieutenant Molina's conversation and insist he answer her questions, when he returned to the kitchen.

"I'm sorry to have kept you, Mrs. Krause. You must have things to do. I'm afraid your car will be impounded for several days while the crime lab people run various tests. Whoever drove it struck a pedestrian. We've yet to determine if the death was an accident or murder."

Death! Murder! Lydia's hand flew to her mouth. "How awful! Who was killed, Lieutenant?"

"Claire Weill. According to her husband, she was taking her usual run right outside the Twin Lakes community. A young fellow on his way to work spotted the body on the side of the road. He called from his cell phone. An ambulance and a police car went out immediately. The body was still warm, so death must have occurred shortly before he arrived."

Lydia sank back against the kitchen chair. She had to swallow a few times before she could speak. "Claire Weill, Marshall Weill's wife," she said wondrously, as if speaking the woman's name would help her comprehend the fact of her death. "When did he find her?"

"Eight-twelve this morning."

"Oh." The sound came out as a moan.

"Did you know Mrs. Weill?"

Lydia shook her head. Though she made every effort to speak calmly, her voice came out an octave higher than normal.

"No. She came over to our table while I was talking to her husband." The blood rushed to Lydia's cheeks as she recalled the short, pudgy woman in elegant clothes, her stiffly sprayed hairdo bobbing like a helmet during their heated exchange. "Claire Weill lashed out at me, and I'm afraid I lost my cool."

"What exactly did you say to her?"

"She accused me of bursting her bubble of happiness, and I told her to put the blame where it belonged, on her husband. That fueled her anger even more. She said I'd ruined their lives and should do them a favor and die."

"And?" Molina prodded.

Lydia frowned. "I reminded her that her husband had ruined the lives of many people by stealing their life savings and—I can't remember what else I said."

Detective Molina turned pages and read, "And someone should put an end to you, you stupid cow."

So he'd known all along! Lydia's ears burned with shame. "It was stupid of me, but I had to expose Mannes before he duped more people out of their money. Then hearing his wife blame me for telling people what kind of man they'd asked to be their financial advisor—it made me see red."

Oh God, she shouldn't have said that!

"How is it that you knew about Mr. Weill's criminal past and no one else at Twin Lakes did?"

"He was tried in Chicago six years ago. My sister, Samantha, is an Assistant D. A. there. I watched part of the trial." For Allison's sake.

"Seeing him here on Long Island must have been a shock."

"Oh, it was." She added wryly, "I'm usually the calmer-downer, Detective Molina. The voice of reason. I regret having lost my cool last night. I should have gone about it differently."

"How so?" he asked, curious.

"I should have informed the Board of Directors, had them inform the community instead of confronting Warren Mannes at a Twin Lakes event."

Molina gave her a half smile. "Don't beat yourself up. You probably would have ended up with the same results."

"What do you mean?"

"Regardless of how you presented the facts, some residents would have been outraged on Weill's behalf. His wife still might have attacked you verbally."

Lydia shook her head. "I felt morally obliged to expose that man. I never considered the fallout that would follow."

Detective Molina appeared deep in thought. Finally he spoke. "It's quite a puzzle we have: two women, both Twin Lakes residents, argue in public. The following morning, one woman's dead, struck down by the vehicle of the other."

Lydia's hand flew to her pounding heart. "I didn't kill Claire Weill! Why should I? Besides, I wouldn't be stupid enough to use my own car!"

He gave her a sidelong glance. "That might be considered a stroke of genius."

Lydia gasped. This detective managed to twist whatever she said into a damning statement.

"And you left the ignition key magnetized to the car,"

he went on casually as if they were discussing the weather, "accessible to anyone."

'Anyone' included her. Lydia felt the blood rush to her ears.

"Mrs. Taylor vouches for you," Molina murmured. "She claims she was up most of the night and that you tended to her each time she awoke." He allowed a small smile to brighten his face. "She places you somewhere between Mother Teresa and an angel."

Lydia brushed the compliment aside. "You've been checking up on me."

He raised his eyebrows. Now his eyes appeared darker—light brown with flecks of green. Of course! They were hazel, not green, and changed color according to his mood.

"Despite her good intentions, Mrs. Taylor can't account for your actions when she finally slept–from about five-thirty until a few minutes before nine."

So, she was a suspect.

"What about the guard on duty at the gatehouse? Didn't he notice my car coming or going?"

"I'm afraid not."

"What do you do next?"

Her question caught him by surprise, but he covered it quickly. "We continue to question everyone who knew Claire Weill."

"I suppose you'll focus on people who live at Twin Lakes, since they had easy access to my car."

"Who knew of your habit of leaving your key under the fender?"

She shrugged. "I've no idea. I found the magnetic key chain about ten days ago when I was unpacking. Anyone might have noticed where I put the key whenever I parked near the clubhouse. Or no one."

Lydia bit her lip, wishing the last three words hadn't slipped out. "Never offer information," Samantha always said. Not that Lydia had ever needed such advice before today.

Molina shrugged as though her last comment were of no importance. "It's a common if unwise practice to leave a car key where you did. It's like leaving a house key under a planter. Actually, some people can start up a car without a key, though that's getting more and more difficult, with all the safety features they're installing."

Was he trying to make her feel better or was he pretending? Did he want to put her at her ease so she'd confess?

Reggie sauntered into the kitchen. He rubbed his tawny body against her legs, purring loudly.

"Excuse me. I have to feed my cat."

"Don't let me stop you." Lieutenant Molina bent down to stroke Reggie's back. To Lydia's immense surprise, the cat rolled over and waited to have his belly rubbed.

"He doesn't do that with anyone but me!" she exclaimed, ashamed of the note of injured pride that had crept into her voice.

"I have three of my own," Molina said.

She'd no sooner set a plate of treats down on Reggie's place mat when her phone rang.

"Lyddie, it's me," her sister said. "What's up? I'm due in court in five minutes but your message frightened me. You sounded absolutely frantic."

Lydia eyed Molina as he headed for the living room corner he favored, already deep in conversation on his cell phone. She drew in breath and began. "Warren Mannes is living here at Twin Lakes. He's changed his name, and he's the HOA's financial advisor."

"In which case he's breaking the law and a condition of his early release. He lost his license to advise and handle another party's finances for ten years and a day. He can reapply, of course, but not for four years."

"Sammy, listen to me!"

Detective Molina turned from his own conversation and eyed her curiously. Lydia lowered her voice and explained why Detective Molina was questioning her.

"Oh, Lydia, how awful! Don't say another word to this cop. I have a friend in Manhattan–a brilliant criminal lawyer. Take his number and call him ASAP."

"Okay." She reached for a pen and pad. "Shoot." Too late, she realized that wasn't the best expression to use, given the circumstances, but Molina was talking too intently into his cell phone to look her way.

Samantha rattled off the name and number. "Jack's a good friend from law school. Call him any time. They must be a bunch of fools if they think you could do anything like vehicular homicide."

Lydia sighed. "I can't help thinking she's dead because I spilled the beans about her husband's past. Mannes is handling some residents' portfolios, too. Could be he's been skimming money, and the victim decided to pay him back."

"I doubt anyone would go after his wife for his thievery. It doesn't make any sense."

"Why did the murderer use my car? Even if he noticed I kept the key under the fender, he took a chance being seen."

"Oh, Lyddie, you're not doing that again!"

"Believe me, I'm tossing that magnet key chain in the garbage—as soon as the police finish checking it for fingerprints."

"But it explains why he took your car."

"Which makes me feel guilty." Lydia sighed deeply. "Any way you look at it, I helped cause that poor woman's demise."

"You didn't, Lyddie! Get a hold of yourself!"

"The only way I can get a hold of myself is to find out who killed her." Lydia gave a snort of disgust. "Suspect Number One is always the husband. In this case, for good reason. Mannes is a thief and a runaround."

"Leave the investigating to the police. Promise me you won't get involved!"

"I'll just talk to residents. Learn what I can about the Mannes/Weills." She glanced at Detective Molina still on his cell phone. "I bet I can find out more than some male cop trying to sniff out secrets."

"Don't, Lyddie! Asking questions is dangerous. I couldn't bear it if anything happened to you. I love you more than anyone in the world!"

"Nothing will happen to me," Lydia said firmly, touched by her sister's unusual burst of emotion.

"Keep your doors locked and don't go anywhere alone in the dark."

"I'll be careful. Speak to you soon."

She hung up as Detective Molina returned to the kitchen. Talking to Samantha had bolstered her confidence and enabled her to ask what she'd been dreading to put into words.

"Are you considering me a suspect, Lieutenant Molina?"

Molina raised his eyebrows. "How can I answer that, Mrs. Krause? We've yet to determine whether this was a hit-and-run or an intentional murder. If it was, in fact, your car that struck Mrs. Weill." He shrugged. "But if this case turns out to be a homicide, you had a motive of sorts, the weapon, and an alibi a good prosecuting attorney could rip to shreds."

"Well!" Lydia exclaimed, her confidence evaporating like rain drops on a hot summer day.

He nodded to her. "That's it for now. Thank you for your cooperation. I'd like to know you'll be available the next few days. In case I have more questions."

"I'll be here. You took my car, remember?" she said, trying for levity.

"So we did." He turned to leave.

"By the way, that was my sister on the phone. She told me Mannes lost his investment advisor's license when he went to prison. He's violating that with impunity."

"It sure sounds that way." Molina pulled out his notepad and wrote a few lines. When he was finished, he said, "Good-bye, Mrs. Krause. We'll be in touch."

Fatigue washed over her like a giant wave. Lydia went into her bedroom. She longed to crawl under the covers and sleep the day away. But she couldn't. She had to make sense of what was happening. Claire Weill had been killed, accidentally or on purpose. And if it proved to be murder, Detective Molina had made it clear that she was a suspect.

Who killed Claire Weill? As an executive, Lydia had become adept at finding solutions to complex problems. Solving a murder couldn't be that different, could it? What she needed were facts, information. Who hated Claire? Who hated her husband? Who wanted Claire dead? Did Warren/Marshall do it?

Lydia reached for a pad of paper and a pen, and was about to jot down her ideas, when the doorbell rang.

"Damn!" she exclaimed. "What now?" She considered ignoring the intrusion when the bell sounded more insistently. She peered through the glass panel and groaned when she saw her next-door neighbor. Peg noticed her and waved.

Reluctantly, Lydia cracked open the door. "Hello, Peg. I really can't talk. I've been up all night."

Peg's rabbity eyes gleamed with excitement. "I stopped by to make sure you're okay." She lowered her voice. "I saw the police car in your driveway. I knew it was that detective. His men are questioning practically everyone in Twin Lakes."

"Did you see anyone take my car this morning?" Lydia asked.

"No—sorry. I went outside for my newspaper about eight-thirty, but didn't so much as glance at your driveway. I told all that to the policeman who just left my house. Poor Claire."

"Yes, poor Claire," Lydia agreed.

Peg reached out to touch her arm. "I hope the police don't think you had anything to do with this tragic accident."

"Actually, I believe I'm one of their chief suspects."

Peg gasped. "How awful!" A sly expression crossed her features. "It was eerie, how you recognized her husband after all these years."

Lydia pressed her lips together. "I wasn't likely to forget his face."

"Really? Why?" When Lydia didn't explain, Peg went on. "People are upset about the way you broadcast his past history. You can't imagine the to-do after you left last night."

"Unfortunately, I can," Lydia answered wryly. "Sally Marcus, who was all smiles and good cheer when I first met her, gave me the cold shoulder this morning."

Peg shrugged. "Friends of the Weills think you should have kept what you know to yourself. I'm sure Marshall learned his lesson and put all those shenanigans behind him."

"That's being naive, Peg. For all we know, he killed his wife."

Peg looked at Lydia as if she'd accused the Pope of

going out on a date. "How ridiculous! Marshall's not capable of hurting anyone, much less Claire. They were deeply devoted to one another."

Lydia stiffened. "The man's a Lothario—as deceitful as they come."

"How can you say that? You hardly know him!"

"I've no idea if he killed his wife or not, but I intend to find out."

Peg blinked. "What do you mean?"

"Exactly what I said. Someone made a big mistake when he used my car to kill Claire Weill. I won't stop till I find out who he is. Good-bye, Peg. I have work to do."

Three

Now that she was finally alone, Lydia found she was too restless to do much of anything. Last night's encounter with the Mannes/Weills followed by Claire's death had shocked her system. Though thoroughly exhausted, she was much too agitated to nap. If she closed her eyes, she feared she'd see herself in prison garb, sitting on a thin mattress in a cell. God, what had she gotten herself into?

She made herself a cup of tea, then settled down at her desk in the den to pay bills. The phone rang. "Hello?"

No answer. It happened again. Disgusted, Lydia disconnected the phone. She reconnected it fifteen minutes later. Immediately, it started to ring.

"Hello!" she thundered.

The caller identified herself as Viv Maguire, a good friend of the Weills. Lydia recognized the raspy voice of Claire Weill's staunch supporter.

"You killed a wonderful woman. I'll see that you pay for it!"

Shaken, Lydia hung up. She had to get away from

Twin Lakes. She opened the residents' directory and dialed Barbara's number. When Barbara answered, Lydia gave a gasp of relief.

"Barbara, it's Lydia. Lydia Krause."

"Just a minute. I'll be right back."

Barbara was gone for such a long time, Lydia was beginning to think she had no intention of speaking to her. She was about to hang up when Barbara came to the phone sounding breathless.

"Sorry, Lieutenant Molina just left. How awful, Lydia, that someone took your car and killed Claire while she was out jogging."

"Yes." Lydia's heart pounded like a jackhammer. "What did he want?"

"To talk about you, about last night. I don't know why, since I told the other policeman all I knew. But some of his questions were a bit different."

Lydia heard herself panting. She was hyperventilating. "How different?"

"For one thing, he found it odd that I knew nothing about the incident between you and the Weills in the ballroom. I explained I was too sick to discuss anything and you were too busy looking after me."

"Did he ask anything else?"

"Let's see—was I sure you'd spent the night. I told him you most certainly did. I knew since I was up most the night."

But not early in the morning. Molina was right. Barbara gave her a partial alibi at best. "Barbara, I was wondering. Are you busy right now?"

"I was going to run to the supermarket, but that can wait."

Suddenly an ordinary trip to the supermarket was as appealing as a weekend in Paris. "Would you mind if I came along? I could use a few things."

"Of course, Lydia. I'd be happy for your company."

"The truth is I've received some unpleasant phone calls. I'd like to leave the house, but the police impounded my car to examine it for clues." She shivered. "Not that I want to set foot in it ever again."

"Poor Claire, killed—for God knows what reason. And poor you—to be embroiled in this mess when you've just moved in."

"Thanks, Barbara."

"I'll come by in half an hour."

A shower did much to revive Lydia's spirits. She got dressed and decided to wait outside for Barbara. An old Cadillac slowed down as it approached her house. Lydia jumped out of the way as the driver swung erratically onto her driveway, partly missing it, cutting a deep rut in the lawn.

Was someone out to kill her? Lydia wondered, about to dash back into the house and phone Molina. She paused as a woman with short, iron-gray curls peered out at her from the driver's window.

"Are you Lydia Krause?" the woman asked, her voice barely above a whisper.

"I am." No longer afraid, Lydia moved closer to the car.

The woman looked over one shoulder then the other. Satisfied, she spoke in the same low voice. "I want to commend you for exposing Marshall Weill. You did a mitzvah, putting a stop to his shenanigans. Now he won't dare fleece any more people of their life savings."

Lydia nodded. "I'm glad you see it that way, Mrs...."

"My name's Doris—Doris Fein—and I've good reason to thank you." She paused, obviously debating if she should go on. "And I'll tell you something else."

They both turned as Peg DiMarco pulled into her garage.

"We'll talk another time," Doris whispered.

She revved the car's motor and jerked the car backward until it was once again on the road. Lydia watched her slow progress down Lake Boulevard. Someone should tell Doris Fein her driving days were over.

Lydia's cell phone rang, giving her no time to puzzle over Doris's cryptic message. It was her daughter, Meredith, sounding frantic.

"Mom, are you okay? I heard someone took your car and ran down a woman on Bellewood Road."

"I'm fine, Merry, really I am," Lydia said, not wanting to frighten her daughter by saying how shaken she really felt. "How did you find out about it so quickly?"

"It was on the radio. I think you'd better come here and stay with us until the police find the person who did this terrible thing."

Lydia bit back her exasperation. Ever since Izzy died, Meredith treated her as if she were ready to enter a nursing home. "I'll be fine."

"Really, Mom. We'd love to have you."

"That's not necessary, Merry."

"But, Mom—"

"I have to go. My friend's picking me up to take me shopping."

"Oh." Meredith paused, then asked, "Can you still watch the girls on Sunday? I have that baby shower in the afternoon."

"Of course I can. Good-bye, dear. Please don't worry so much."

A dark gray BMW pulled into the driveway. Barbara waved from the passenger seat. "Hi, Lydia. I brought Caroline along. She's great company in times of crisis. Caroline Lieberman, Lydia Krause."

A tall, stately woman with rosy cheeks and curly brown hair stepped out of the driver's seat. "Hello, Lydia, pleased to meet you," she said with a broad smile.

Lydia put out her hand to greet Caroline. Instead, she found herself enveloped in a bear hug. She shut her eyes and, for a moment, allowed herself to take comfort in Caroline's exuberant warmth.

"I'm so sorry for all you've been through," Caroline said when they were on their way. "At any rate, you can forget about it for the next few hours."

Barbara and Caroline took Lydia to a nearby town for an early lunch and regaled her with amusing stories about themselves, their families and other Twin Lakes residents. Caroline's husband, Benny, was on the Board of

Directors, and their two married children lived in California with their families. Barbara entertained them with tales of her teaching-high-school-English days. Claire and Marshall Weill were never mentioned.

They stopped at a specialty supermarket some distance from Twin Lakes, where they shopped at a leisurely pace. At four o'clock they headed for home. Lydia sank against the back seat's soft leather cushions and sighed.

"Thank you both. I never could have made it through the day without your company."

Barbara turned around to give her a smile. "We wanted to show you most of us at Twin Lakes are good people. We didn't want you to put your house up for sale."

How had she guessed? Lydia wondered.

"Oh, yes," Caroline agreed. "Most of our fellow residents are gems. I, for one, am relieved you blew the whistle on Marshall, or whatever his real name is. I told Benny he was a conniver. My soft-hearted husband didn't see it."

"Frankly, I was leery of him, myself," Barbara said. "There's something about him that made me keep my distance. A few times I sensed he was about to come on to me, and would have if I gave him half a chance."

"How many residents did he talk into letting him handle their finances?" Caroline asked.

"My sister said he lost his license to manage anyone's money," Lydia said.

Caroline glanced at her over her shoulder. "You did everyone a favor—outing a rat like that!"

Lydia frowned. "Maybe, but my neighbor, Peg, said some residents feel I shouldn't have said anything. Viv Maguire called to tell me I wasn't going to get away with killing her friend."

"What a lame brain," Barbara said.

"I had to take similar action some years ago." Caroline let out a wry laugh as she drove up to the gatehouse and waited for the security arm to lift. "Only in my case the man with sticky fingers was a family member."

"That must have been difficult for you," Lydia said.

"Trust me, it was. I was cussed out by relatives I didn't even know I had. And here I was trying to help people I loved. In the end, some went along with Cousin Al and lost a bundle for being loyal to the wrong cause."

And I lost a sister, Lydia thought bitterly. As much as she appreciated Barbara and Caroline's caring support, she couldn't bring herself to talk about Allison.

"I wonder who killed Claire," Barbara mused. "And why?"

"Me, too," Caroline said. "I know she mouthed off to you last night, Lydia, but I always knew Claire to be a kind woman. She was devoted to her husband and her family, and as meek as the proverbial lamb."

Some lamb, Lydia thought. She'd come at her more like a lioness protecting her own.

"Who could possibly have a grudge against her, enough to want her dead?" Barbara asked.

Caroline turned around and gave Lydia a meaningful look. "Or why someone chose your car as the murder weapon."

I don't know either, Lydia thought, *but I intend to find out.*

~ * ~

At home, Lydia fed a hungry Reggie then put away her groceries. She stretched out on a living room sofa to consider her plan of action. She needed to figure out the best way to learn everything she could about Claire Weill. Yes, Claire Weill, she told herself, because that was how people at Twin Lakes knew her. Claire's husband and best friend, Viv, could help her the most. Unfortunately, they both would probably slam the door in her face if she stopped by to ask questions.

Had either of them murdered Claire? Marshall might have been after money. And Viv? Could be she was after Claire's husband? Lydia shrugged. A bit far-fetched, but so was murder. At any rate, until she learned more about Claire and her nearest and dearest, everything was pure speculation.

She must have dozed off, because when she awakened she found herself in a darkened house. "Izzy!" she called out before she remembered. Except for Reggie, she was alone.

A wave of desolation threatened to drag her down to the lowest depths of despair. She'd pulled up stakes to live among strangers in unfamiliar surroundings. She was a suspect in a murder case because a woman she'd met and argued with the night before had been killed with her car.

Lydia blinked back tears as she switched on lights and closed the verticals along the sliding door that led to her small patio.

Reggie appeared from wherever he'd been sleeping and meowed for a second dinner. "You're too fat," she told him, but obliged him anyway before unloading the dishwasher. She turned on the TV and flicked it off. From her den window she noticed a twinkle of light coming from Peg's house. She dialed Peg's number. The line was busy.

The line was still busy fifteen minutes later. Feeling the need for human companionship, Lydia decided to pay her neighbor a visit. She slipped into her parka and stepped outside. The icy wind stung her face as she dashed across the lawn to Peg's tiny porch. Loud voices emerged from within and stopped her from pressing the doorbell.

Fear rippled down her back. A murderer was on the loose! He could be inside Peg's house this very moment, claiming another victim.

What to do, what to do? Lydia turned to dash home and call the police when she decided to first find out what she could. She pressed her ear to the door and gave silent thanks that she hadn't jumped to a hasty conclusion.

Peg was shouting at someone. She sounded angry rather than frightened. The other person spoke in fainter, less animated tones. Though Lydia couldn't make out words, she was certain Peg's visitor was a man. He sounded as though he was trying to calm Peg down. Lydia covered her mouth to stifle her giggles. Her neighbor wasn't in danger. Nor was she in any position to play hostess. She had a guest—possibly the longstanding lover she'd once hinted at. Lydia shook her head and returned home.

She made herself a tuna fish sandwich, then read in bed and watched the ten o'clock news. Afterward, she turned out the lights and watched the colorfully-lit fountain spray water onto the darkened lake. She'd miss the fountain when it was shut off the first week in December.

She was about to lower the blinds when she heard a door open and murmuring voices, then Peg's laughter. Her visitor was leaving. Lydia opened the window and stuck out her head in hopes of catching sight of him. No luck. She couldn't see the man who had aroused her neighbor's fury then remained to calm her down.

~ * ~

Lydia awoke on Sunday morning, feeling rested and more like her optimistic self. Surely, the police would come to their senses and start investigating other people—if they hadn't already—as possible suspects. Regardless, she decided to undertake an investigation of her own. She'd make use of her brain power and people skills to find out who killed Claire Weill.

But first she'd go for her morning swim. She put on her bathing suit and outer clothing, then groaned as she considered the two bags of garbage she had to shlep to the refuse area on her way to the pool. After feeding Reggie and drinking a mug of coffee, Lydia set out, bags in tow. She was about to toss them into an almost-filled bin, when she noticed a ripped paper bag lying on the ground. Spilling from it were ceramic pieces—no doubt of a figurine—that had been smashed to smithereens. Curious, she extracted a fragment and detected the delicate feathers of a bird. There was the beak! A larger piece—the base—slipped free of the bag. The writing on the bottom was an inscription: "For Magpie, now and forever."

Magpie? Which of her neighbors was Magpie? Lydia shrugged. Another Twin Lakes mystery, though this one seemed innocuous and fated never to be solved. She disposed of her garbage and slammed the lid shut.

Barbara was kind enough to drop her off at Meredith's on her way to her son's house. Merry opened the door to her spacious colonial home and pressed her mother into a tight embrace.

"Mom, I'm glad you're here! Maybe you'll reconsider and stay with us a few days."

"No, dear. The police are on top of the case," Lydia said to allay her daughter's fears, if not her own.

She stood back to admire her tall, slender daughter. Merry was dressed up and wearing makeup for a change, her dark hair perfectly angled to frame her heart-shaped face. She'd put on a black leather pants suit, white silk blouse and high-heeled black boots.

"Don't you look stunning—as though you were off to a rendezvous instead of a baby shower."

"Oh, Mom, what a ridiculous thing to say!"

Lydia would have agreed it was a frivolous comment if not for the flush that colored her daughter's cheeks."

Was Meredith having an affair? She'd been very moody lately. But Lydia had no time to ponder this latest concern. Meredith was issuing instructions.

"The girls are watching TV in the den. Let them sit

quietly for a few minutes. They've been running wild all morning. I want Brittany to have enough strength to play well this afternoon."

Meredith handed her a sheet of paper. "I've written out everything I can think of. Brittany's soccer game starts at two, but please get there at least twenty minutes before. I've got tuna fish and turkey for lunch."

Always micro-managing, Lydia thought as she shrugged off her jacket and sat down in a kitchen chair.

Merry spoke as she disappeared into the bathroom to fuss with her already perfect hair. "If Jeff finishes early at the office, he'll come straight to the game and drive you home while one of my friends watches Greta. I have to warn you, he might not walk into the house until five."

"On a Sunday?"

"Oh yes. His new firm considers Sunday another work day."

Lydia was dismayed by the anger simmering beneath her daughter's words. Meredith knew Jeff would have to work longer hours when he'd changed jobs to one that put him on the partner track. He did it to earn more money to pay for their new home.

"Is everything okay between you two?" Lydia asked, but Merry didn't hear her over the running water. It was just as well. Her daughter would take offense at the question and never share what was in her heart. Hadn't she always been like that? Not always, but for almost as long as Lydia could remember.

Satisfied with her appearance, Meredith sat at the

kitchen table and faced her mother.

"Mom, our friends invited us to play bridge next Saturday night. Do you think you could watch the girls? It won't be a late night since we're all helping set up for the elementary school's fall festival the following morning."

Lydia hesitated. "I'll have to let you know."

"Why? It's Saturday night I'm talking about."

"Yes, I know." Lydia bit back the retort she longed to toss at her daughter. "Some of the single women go out for dinner and a movie most Saturday nights. But if you need me, I suppose that takes precedence."

"Mother!" Merry touched her cheek as if Lydia had slapped her. "I'm glad you're making new friends. That's why I suggested you move to Twin Lakes."

Lydia stared levelly at her daughter. And not so you'd have a baby sitter at your beck and call? she wondered silently. In the month since she'd moved to Twin Lakes, Merry had her watching the girls at least two afternoons a week and most weekends. Lydia was repelled by the thought she was being used as a baby sitter so her daughter could meet her lover for afternoon trysts.

Tears glistened in Merry's brown eyes, driving away Lydia's ugly suspicion.

"Jeff, the girls and I are happy to have you close by. Don't you remember how Greta cried the first few times you watched them? Now she asks for Grammy all the time."

"I love spending time with the girls and watching them grow up." Lydia hesitated, trying to put things as diplomatically as possible. "Frankly, I'm not ready for retirement and a life of leisure."

"Then maybe you should consider getting a part-time job," Merry said, her tone a bit too snippy for Lydia's liking.

"Maybe I will," Lydia said.

Merry blinked, startled by her mother's response. "I have to go or I'll be late." She paused, then asked, "Can you still watch the girls tomorrow afternoon?"

"Of course."

"Thanks, Mom." Merry sounded relieved. "If you want to go out with your friends Saturday night, I'll see if I can find a sitter, though they're so damn expensive." She gave Lydia a peck on her cheek and went into the den to say good-bye to her daughters.

Lydia welcomed her moment of solitude. She felt drained. Why did every conversation with Meredith turn into a battle of wills? Meredith strode through life, assuming people and events would bend to her expectations. That included Lydia, now that she was widowed.

She never fought with Abbie. Lydia smiled as she thought of her younger daughter. But then she'd given up trying to tell Abbie what to do when she was very young. In exchange, Abbie respected her mother's life choices. How different her two daughters were. Why, they were as different as she and Samantha!

Nodding at this insight, Lydia went to the sink to make herself a fresh carafe of coffee. She was startled when

Merry reappeared in the kitchen, a large, beautifully-wrapped gift in her arms.

"Mom, I want you to know your living five minutes away makes everything more—complete somehow. The way things were before you took over the company."

The old familiar guilt flushed through her body. Merry had never adjusted to being left in the care of baby sitters—all fine and caring women, except for the college student who once had been too busy talking to her boyfriend to notice that her older charge had wandered off. That had been at the beach, and to this day Meredith refused to take an island vacation.

"You're thirty-four now, Meredith. You have your own family."

"Right, and I'll only leave the girls in the charge of someone I completely trust."

Lydia's head sank to her chest, her daughter's parting words reverberating in her head like a life sentence.

Four

As soon as their mother departed, her granddaughters traipsed into the kitchen, saying they wanted Grammy to take them to the playground. Lydia obliged. She sat Greta in her stroller, and the three of them set off for the playground a few blocks away, where the girls played for an hour. Lydia fed them an early lunch, after which Greta fell asleep on the den couch. Lydia straightened up the kitchen, then helped Brittany change into her soccer clothes. Parkas zipped up against the November chill and Greta once again in her stroller, they set out for Brittany's game.

Why was she panting? she wondered, as she chased after her two-year-old granddaughter for the fifth time in the past half hour.

"Greta, honey, stay here beside me."

"I'm bored, Grammy," Greta protested.

"I know, sweetheart, but I have to watch Brittany play. It won't be for much longer."

Shortly after halftime, she was delighted to see her son-in-law striding toward them.

"Daddy, Daddy!" Greta shouted as she flew into his arms.

Jeff grabbed her up then bent down to kiss Lydia. "How's my favorite mother-in-law?"

"Fine. Brittany assisted on a goal."

"That's my girl!" He went to the sidelines to wave to Brittany, who waved back.

"I'll ask one of our friends to keep an eye on Greta while I drive you home," Jeff said.

"Well, all right," Lydia agreed, thinking how nice it would be to stretch out on her den couch for a cat nap. "I am kind of wiped out. I didn't sleep well last night."

"I don't blame you. Not with a murderer in your midst. Any new developments?"

"Nothing I'm aware of."

"They'll catch who did this. Just keep your doors locked."

"Oh, I will."

Jeff buzzed her cheek. "Thanks for looking after the girls. I'm glad they have a grandma who dotes on them."

Lydia was fond of her son-in-law. She gave him an extra squeeze. "Your mother would have doted on them, too."

Jeff nodded. "Don't I know it." He shook his handsome head as though to rid it of sad thoughts.

As they got into his car, Jeff said, "Did Merry tell you she'll probably be working again?"

Lydia stared up at him. "No, she didn't mention it."

He drove slowly out of the school parking lot. "Her school called to see if she would fill in on a maternity leave starting in February, even though her own extended leave isn't over."

"What did she say?"

"That she's seriously considering it but wants to give it more thought."

"Really?" She met Jeff's eyes as a sinking sensation settled in her stomach. "You mean Meredith's willing to hire a woman to take care of the girls?"

He gave her a wry smile. "Not exactly."

"Oh. She wants me to watch them."

"I told Merry she had no right to ask it of you. Certainly not on a daily basis."

Lydia's nostrils quivered as they did when she was truly agitated. "I love your daughters and I enjoy spending time with them, but..."

Jeff put his hand on her arm. "You needn't say another word. I don't know where she gets her sense of entitlement with you."

"I think I do."

He looked at her questioningly, but Lydia didn't explain. Instead, she said, "Hiring a capable woman is costly. I'll be more than happy to contribute toward that expense."

"That's kind of you, but we can manage, especially if Merry's working again."

~ * ~

Monday morning Lydia arose early and spent twenty minutes on the same aerobics and yoga routine she'd been following for the last thirty years. It kept her limber and slim, except for the small belly she decided all women over fifty toted around. Instead of swimming laps, she decided to walk over to the arboretum across Bellewood Road. She spotted the site of the murder immediately. It was set off with yellow tape and signs were posted to keep people away. No one was there, not even a police officer to guard the area.

Lydia glanced around then stepped over the tape. The brutal evidence spoke for itself—three sets of car tracks rutted the ground like furrows. A rhododendron bush lay crushed to the ground from the impact. Lydia shuddered. Whoever did this had gone over the body more than once. The proverbial lamb had stirred up strong emotions.

Shuddering, Lydia turned and headed for home, thinking as she walked.

Someone had hated Claire Weill—hated her with enough passion to kill her, consciously and deliberately.

Someone who lived at Twin Lakes.

~ * ~

Caroline called as Lydia stepped out of the shower, to see how she was holding up.

"All right. I walked over to the arboretum to see where Claire was killed. Someone had it in for her, all right."

"I took a peek there, too," Caroline admitted. "Benny thinks I'm being gruesome. I called to see if you'd like to attend a Women's Club meeting tonight. I forgot to mention it Saturday, which I should have as I'm the president. Anyway, Shari Morgan's going to give a talk on when she lived in Italy and show slides."

"Sounds great, but I'm not sure I can make it. I'm babysitting today."

"Again?" Caroline asked. "Not that there's anything wrong with that," she added quickly. "Both my daughters live in California. I'd give my eye teeth to get to see the grandkids more often."

Merry was taking advantage, Lydia decided, and now was as good a time as any to break her of the habit. "Yes, I will come. What time?"

"Seven-thirty. I'll pick you up."

She took her time getting dressed, and was just putting on her lipstick when the doorbell rang, startling her. Lydia glanced at the clock. She didn't expect Merry until one. She opened the front door and felt her heart race at the sight of Detective Sol Molina standing before her.

"Good morning, Mrs. Krause. Sorry to be barging in on you like this."

"That's all right." Lydia felt a stab of pleasure as he eyed her discretely and seemed to like what he was seeing.

"More questions, Lieutenant?"

He raised the leather attaché in his right hand. "I came to bring you a copy of your statement. I'd like you to read it and sign it if it's accurate."

"Now?"

"If you don't mind." He offered her a real smile. "I'm

caught up on my paper work, and I'm trying not to fall behind."

"All right." She led Molina into the living room and they resumed the places they'd taken during their first interview. Molina reached into the attaché case and handed her a stapled report. She read through it, surprised that it was concise, well-written, and—except for two slight changes which she made—exactly what she'd said. How on earth had he managed that with pen and note pad?

She looked up, disconcerted to find him studying her.

"Yes, it's basically what I told you on Saturday. But why don't you use a tape recorder?"

"Old habits die hard."

"Yes, they can."

She signed the three copies in the places he indicated and handed back the papers. "Have you found out anything new about the case? Anything," she quickly amended, "that you can share with me?"

He shook his head. "Nothing conclusive, though judging from the site of impact, it does appear that whoever struck Mrs. Weill did so intentionally. The point of collision is several feet beyond the road."

"Yes!"

"Oh?"

Lydia bit her lip, wishing she'd kept quiet. "I walked over there before and saw the damage done to the shrubs and the ground." She shuddered. "Who would do such a thing?"

"People do some awful things to one another."

"How much longer will you need my car?"

"The crime scene people work pretty fast. You should have it back by the end of the week."

"Not that I'll ever drive it again! I'll trade it in for a new Lexus—if they'll take it." She looked at him. "Or do you think that's too awful of me, letting someone else buy a car that killed someone?"

He shook his head. "Once it's repaired and cleaned thoroughly, it's just another car."

He stood. Lydia felt an opportunity slipping past her. Determined to find out what she could, she blurted out, "Do you think Claire's husband took my car and ran her down?"

Detective Molina shrugged. "I couldn't say. Seems he had a breakfast meeting at the local diner at eight forty-five."

"Eight forty-five? Then he could have killed his wife, right?"

"It's possible, though he was on time for his meeting." He followed her to the front door. Relieved that he hadn't asked her any more questions, Lydia put her hand on the door knob when he spoke again.

"By the way, Mrs. Krause, I find it odd you never thought to mention that your sister had been involved with Warren Mannes."

Lydia froze. "I—I didn't think..."

"Didn't think it was important for me to know?"

She turned to face him. "No, I didn't," she said softly. "How did you find out about Allison? We don't have the same last names."

She struggled to hold back her tears, but they spilled down her cheeks. She allowed Molina to lead her back to the living room.

This time he sat beside her on the same sofa. Despite the few feet between them, he was close enough for her to feel the warmth radiating from his vibrant body.

"I'm a detective, Mrs. Krause, remember?" he said gently. "I sent for the transcript of the trial, called all my Chicago connections to find out about Claire and her husband. Along the way, I learned a bit about your sister, the assistant D.A."

"Samantha?"

"Yes, Samantha. I heard what a hotshot litigator she is. That she would have been the prosecutor to try Warren Mannes, but she had to recuse herself because her sister, Allison, was one of his victims."

Lydia buried her face in her hands. "He stole her hard-earned money. But the worst was he took her as his play toy. My poor, foolish Allie. She thought she'd finally found a man who knew how to love. Instead, he was a thief. A villain of the worst kind. She was devastated. She went berserk, swallowed all her medicine. Everything. Bottles and bottles of pills. They couldn't revive her."

~ * ~

Lydia washed her face and put on fresh lipstick. Reggie rubbed against her legs, then jumped up to the bathroom counter to keep her company. Lydia stroked him and kissed him between his eyes. Cats were affectionate and attentive to their owners, despite their bad rep.

She was glad Molina had let himself out without further ado. She had no idea if he considered this latest revelation further proof that she might have killed Claire Weill or what. The truth was, she was relieved he'd found out about Allison. Now she had nothing to hide. And his knowing seemed to forge a bond between them, God only knew why.

She was calm by the time Merry came to pick her up. Her daughter had on skin-tight jeans and a cashmere sweater. She was bristling with energy.

"Your hair never looked better," Lydia said. "Why on earth are you going to the salon?"

"Oh, Mom, it needs a cut. Badly." Meredith flashed her mother an annoyed look, but Lydia caught the high color on her cheeks. What was churning in that overactive mind?

They rode the rest of the five-minute trip to her daughter's house in silence. Meredith carried a sleepy Greta up to her room for a nap. Then she ran through her list of instructions as she slipped into a leather jacket. Lydia noted it was new and had a fur collar. Jeff was doing well, but Meredith, who loved to shop, often bought expensive items without thinking. Were Meredith's extravagances the reason Jeff was working so many hours? Were finances becoming a problem in their marriage?

Was Meredith carrying on an affair?

"I called the school to tell them you'll be picking up Brittany. Do you still want to walk over?"

Lydia nodded.

"Then make sure you wake Greta at two-thirty the latest. Otherwise you'll have a whimpering child on your hands every step of the three blocks. Take the stroller, regardless of what she says. Brittany may watch TV for half an hour. If she asks, please help her with her homework."

"Of course I will. That's what grandmas are for."

Merry was at the door leading to the garage when she turned. "I should be back at six the very latest."

"That late?" Lydia stared at her daughter. Since when does a trim and blow out take so long?"

"Why, is there a problem?"

"I've a meeting tonight and was hoping to be home by five."

Merry's eyes blinked, as they did when she became flustered. "You're welcome to eat with the girls and me. We're having macaroni and cheese, which Jeff hates. But he's taking a client out to dinner."

Lydia grimaced. Like her son-in-law, she detested macaroni and cheese. "Thanks, I'll make myself an omelet when I get home. Run a few errands if you must, but try to be home by five-thirty."

"Sure, Mom." In an uncharacteristic gesture, Merry threw her arms around her mother and squeezed tight. "I appreciate having you here more than you'll ever know." She let go as suddenly and flew out the door.

She is having an affair, Lydia thought, but dare I bring it up?

~ * ~

Merry was good to her word and arrived home at five-thirty sharp. "Here I am, an on-time Cinderella."

Greta came dashing in. "Mommy! Mommy!"

Merry swung her around so that Greta's outstretched legs almost knocked over a vase. This wasn't like her daughter. My God, she's glowing, Lydia thought. As though she's just come from her lover's bed.

"Have a good time?"

"Mmm, yes," Merry answered and carried Greta into the kitchen. "It was nice to be out, now it's nice to be home."

"Mmm," Lydia echoed, her tone skeptical, but her daughter was singing nonsense to her child and didn't hear.

Lydia brooded as Merry drove her home, but her daughter was too engrossed in her own thoughts to notice. She told herself she had to be wrong. Merry would never cheat on Jeff. Jeff was a wonderful husband. He was attentive to Merry and to the girls when he was around. True, he worked late most nights and often on Saturday, but that was to pay for their lovely home and two cars. Even if Meredith occasionally felt lonely, it didn't give her license to find another man to amuse herself.

As Lydia sautéed onions, mushrooms, and green peppers for her omelet, she tried to remember how Merry and Jeff had related to one another lately. Then realized she hadn't seen them together in weeks.

"Meaning what?" she demanded in exasperation, and

poured the beaten eggs into the sizzling pan.

She was forced to admit she hadn't the slightest idea which issues, if any, were causing discord in her daughter's marriage.

~ * ~

Two hours later, Lydia followed Barbara and Caroline into the library where the Women's Club was meeting. It was a cozy, book-lined room, warmed by a fire in the gas fireplace. Caroline went to see to the refreshments while Barbara introduced Lydia to the few women already seated in the plush chairs set up for the evening's activity.

A trio of older women latched on to Lydia and bombarded her with questions: How did she know about Marshall Weill's past? Wasn't it terrible about poor Claire? She answered as diplomatically as she could and was grateful when Barbara shepherded her away to meet Shari Morgan.

More women arrived. Caroline came to stand before the screen. A hush fell over the room as she introduced Shari. Shari spoke about the years she'd lived and worked in Italy. She told a few anecdotes, then walked back to the setup of slides. Someone dimmed the lights and the show began.

Lydia hadn't realized how engrossed she'd been in the presentation until the lights came on again, causing her to blink. Almost an hour had passed.

"That was wonderful, Shari," Caroline said. "Let's break for refreshments, then we'll have a short question-and-answer period."

Too soon it was over and Lydia was back in Barbara's car and on her way home.

"Well," Caroline asked, "what do you think of our Women's Club?"

"I think it's wonderful. A far cry from Bingo."

They all laughed. Barbara said, "We think so. It was Caroline's brilliant idea, so she gets to be president until she's sick of the job."

"Though everyone helps plan new events," Caroline said.

"Shari's presentation kept me from thinking about things," Lydia said.

"Claire's murder?" Caroline asked.

"Yes." And the state of my daughter's marriage, Lydia thought.

"That's why I wanted you to come."

As Barbara pulled into her driveway, Lydia said, "I'm afraid Detective Molina considers me a suspect."

"That's ridiculous!"

Lydia's heart warmed to her new friends' outrage on her behalf. "Of course it is, and I intend to prove it by finding out who did it." She turned to face Barbara. "I need to find out everything there is to know about Claire and I'd like both you to help me."

"I'll help you," Barbara said.

"Me, too," Caroline seconded. "Come for lunch tomorrow at one and we'll brainstorm."

Five

Lydia sat in the Liebermans' Southwest-style dining room, a platter of fresh bagels and bialys and four kinds of salads spread before her, and felt as though she'd reentered the world of normalcy. Surely, Claire Weill's death and her damaged Lexus were parts of a gloomy nightmare. Conversation remained light as they ate. Caroline brought out a chocolate babka and replenished everyone's mug of decaffeinated coffee.

She sat down. "Now," she intoned, "let's get down to business."

"The question is, did Warren Mannes-er, Marshall Weill kill his wife?" Lydia said.

Caroline sipped her coffee. "Why would he? People in their late sixties are past the stage of passionate adulterous affairs. They're happy to live in relative peace with a loving spouse."

"That was Claire to a tee," Barbara commented. "She was sweet and kind. Always deferring to her husband."

"Oh, yes. She adored him," Caroline agreed.

"I wonder if he adored her," Lydia said, trying to keep her tone light. From her own take of the man and from what she knew of his whirlwind affair with Allison, she figured he'd had plenty of adulterous affairs. But she was here to get Barbara and Carolyn's impressions and whatever information they had.

Caroline took a bite of babka as she considered. "Marshall seemed attentive enough to Claire at our summer party, though I don't remember seeing them together very often. He spent most of his time talking business with the men."

"Or flirting with other women," Barbara added. "Though maybe that was in the service of drumming up clients."

"I wonder if he's low on funds," Lydia mused, "and stood to inherit a good deal of money when Claire died."

"I heard they paid cash for their unit when they moved here about a year ago," Barbara said. "I don't think money was an issue."

Something to ask Detective Molina, Lydia thought. Aloud, she said, "This was a brutal crime. What do we know about the murderer?"

"I think we can assume he lives at Twin Lakes," Caroline said.

"Or she does," Barbara threw in. She shuddered. "Lovely to think there's a murderer among us." She turned to Lydia. "Could anyone have seen you leave the car key under the fender when you parked near the clubhouse?"

"It's possible," Lydia said.

"Then anyone might have seen you and figured your car was for the taking when looking for a murder weapon," Barbara said.

Caroline stood and went into the kitchen. "Yes, they happened past your house and saw your car outside. Figured you might have left the key magnetized to the fender and took it."

"Using your car might have been a coincidence," Barbara said, "but Claire wasn't a random target. Whoever killed her knew she went running along Bellewood Road every morning at seven-thirty."

"Most residents knew that," Caroline said as she carried a platter of cookies to the table.

"Oh, Caroline, my favorite!" Lydia said, biting into a tiny chocolate chip cookie.

Then she asked, "Why did Claire go running every morning?" Lydia asked. "It's cold and dark that time of day, and women of her age don't usually run—not when we have a fully-equipped gym."

Barbara said, "Doris Fein mentioned once that Claire had a personal trainer years ago, before they moved here. This fellow believed in running and Claire worshipped him as her guru."

"Doris Fein," Lydia echoed. "I met her—briefly."

"Doris lives around the corner from Benny and me," Caroline said. "She and Claire often went shopping and out for lunch."

"Interesting that Doris and Claire were friends," Lydia

said, "because Doris stopped by to thank me for informing the community about Weill's past." She thought a moment. "What about Viv Maguire?"

Caroline shrugged. "I don't know her very well. She was very friendly with both Claire and Marshall."

They talked about other residents, but nothing Barbara or Caroline told her seemed relevant. Lydia got to her feet. At least she had one lead to follow.

"I'll speak to Doris and see what I can find out. Thanks for lunch, Caroline, and thank you both for your support and your help." Lydia hugged them good-bye and set out for home.

Doris Fein was delighted to hear from Lydia, though she made no mention of their previous meeting. Over the phone, she struck Lydia as a pleasant woman in her late seventies. No whispered admissions. No fearful hesitations.

"My mah jongg game played here today and they're just leaving. Why don't you stop by in fifteen minutes? Do you have my address?"

"Yes, it's in the directory."

"Of course. Silly me. See you in a bit."

Doris's home, the smallest model in the development, had *tchotchkes* on every available surface—tables, wall shelves, window sills, curio cabinets and baker's racks. She welcomed Lydia into her living room and chuckled as Lydia's eyes darted from one collection of small ceramic figures to another.

"I can't resist figurines of people, animals, fish, birds.

You name it, I've been collecting them these past fifty years." She sighed. "But like all good things, my buying days are over."

Lydia suddenly remembered the broken figurine she'd seen in the garbage the other day and wondered if it had belonged to Doris.

"How about a nice piece of carrot cake and tea while you tell me what's on your mind?" Doris said.

"That would be lovely," Lydia said, though she was anything but hungry.

She followed Doris into her small kitchen—all white but for the border of red and yellow tulips running along the walls just below the ceiling—and felt a rush of nostalgia as Doris sat her down and fussed about her as her Aunt Irene always had when Lydia came to visit.

"I want to ask you about Claire Weill."

Doris put on the kettle then placed a mug and plate before Lydia. "Terrible business, Claire dying like that. We spent most of the afternoon talking about her instead of playing mah jongg. I understand someone took your car and ran her down."

Lydia nodded. Maybe that explained why Doris had seemed so frightened when she'd stopped by the other day. "The police have taken the car to search for clues. Frankly, they aren't too pleased I have no witness to prove I was fast asleep when Claire may have been hit, so I'm trying to piece together who could possibly have wanted her dead."

Doris nodded. "So it's murder you think. Poor, poor

Claire. She deserved a better life."

"You mean her married life, or in general?"

"I'm talking about Marshall, of course," Doris said with asperity. "Out in public he was the perfect gentleman—praised her cooking, helped her on with her coat. When they were alone, he put her down every chance he got."

Lydia wasn't surprised. "You must have been a good friend, for Claire to tell you something as personal as that."

Doris paused in her ministrations to meet Lydia's gaze straight on. "We were good friends until a month ago."

"Did you have an argument?"

Doris served Lydia a generous piece of carrot cake and a small one for herself. "Claire took offense when I told her Marshall lost me a lot of money by investing in risky stocks. She stormed out of here when I added he no doubt made himself a pretty penny in the deal." She met Lydia's gaze. "From your outburst the other night, I gather this was how he conducted business. A *goniff* through and through."

Lydia nodded. "I'm sorry, Doris."

"Not as sorry as I am."

Lydia bit back her disappointment. The fact that Doris and Claire had quarreled meant that Doris couldn't possibly know anything relevant about Claire's last days. Still, she was eager to hear whatever Doris might tell her.

"What was Claire like?" she asked.

A beautiful smile wreathed the older woman's face.

"She was a wonderful person—caring, warm." She gave Lydia a knowing look. "Claire's first husband left her a very wealthy woman, but she never threw her money in your face, if you know what I mean. And she could buy and sell half the people here."

"Do you think Marshall married her for her money?"

Doris frowned as she shook her head. "That *nishtgutnick*—I wouldn't be surprised. Our investment advisor pulled the wool over everyone's eyes, including mine. If you want my opinion, that man's capable of anything."

Lydia stared at her. "You mean—murder?"

At that moment, the kettle whistled. Doris attended to Lydia's tea. "Who knows? Taste the cake. I made it this morning."

Lydia did as instructed and, despite her large lunch, was glad she had. "Mmmm, it's delicious."

"My mother's recipe. Let your tea steep a bit. It's green tea. Good for what ails you."

Obligingly, Lydia left the tea bag in her mug. She ate another forkful of cake.

Doris said, "All I know is Claire was besotted by that husband of hers. She knew he had affairs over the years, but instead of throwing him out like any other woman would, she'd pamper him. She insisted the extra attention worked to bring him back to her. They moved here and everything was hunky-dory."

Lydia nodded. She was familiar with that type of wife.

Doris continued. "A few months ago, Claire got it into

her head that Marshall had a hussy on the side. Frankly, I had my doubts. The man's pushing seventy, and he has a few medical problems like we all do. I told her he was busy with clients, but she carried on how she was going to win Marshall back by making herself more appealing. She'd lose weight, become more youthful."

"More youthful? Is that why she ran every day?"

Doris hesitated and the frightened look came over her. For a moment, Lydia thought she was going to clam up, but she continued speaking. "Claire heard about this miracle supplement that makes you look and feel thirty years younger."

Lydia wondered if she'd missed something. Some vital pages of the story were missing. "Is that what you and Claire argued about? Her taking the miracle capsules?"

Doris frowned. "Good heavens, no. I told Claire her husband had lost me a bundle of money, and she wouldn't believe me."

~ * ~

Lydia walked home slowly under the darkening sky, reviewing all that Doris had told her. Claire had been madly in love with her husband, despite his adulterous affairs and the fact that he treated her badly. Instead of divorcing him, she'd set out to regain his affections and was doomed to fail. No wonder she'd gotten angry when Doris criticized Marshall and turned her wrath on Lydia for exposing his past misdeeds.

Was Marshall up to his old embezzling tricks? And what to make of the miracle supplement Claire had started taking? That couldn't have anything to do with Claire's murder, could it? And who was supplying her with this hush-hush wonder?

The wind rose, sending dry leaves rattling along the street. Lydia sensed someone was following her, but when she spun around, no one was there. It gave her little comfort. The many trees and shrubs provided adequate cover for someone lurking in the dusk. Shivering, Lydia quickened her pace, and didn't relax until she stood safely locked inside her home.

Lydia spent a good part of the evening reviewing all she'd learned about Claire Weill. Despite her own unpleasant encounter with the woman, she was forced to concede Claire had been a loving wife and caring friend, evoking the affection and loyalty of at least two female friends. No one seemed to dislike her.

From every angle, Marshall Weill presented himself as the likely candidate. The police had to consider him their chief suspect. No doubt, he had any number of motives for killing his wife. Maybe he wanted all of her money. From what she'd gathered, Marshall was bored with Claire, which was probably why he'd had an affair with Allison. As for opportunity, Weill had been at the clubhouse the night before and might have seen Lydia place her key under the fender. Her blood pressure rose as she imagined him congratulating himself for creating a murder scenario that included a way to get back at her. He'd use her car to kill his wife. Who better than Weill knew his wife's jogging routine?

But proving his guilt was another matter.

Lydia turned off her reading lamp at eleven-thirty, then tossed and turned for two hours as her fears and anxieties rose to the surface. Her breath came in deep gulps. What if the police charged her with the murder? They had no proof, but she had no alibi. She and Claire had fought. Her car was the murder weapon. Lydia trembled, imagining her trial. She finally took herself in hand and swallowed a sleeping pill, vowing to call Samantha's criminal lawyer friend in the morning.

When she did, it was to learn that Jack Campbell would be out of the country for another two weeks. Did Mrs. Krause care to speak to anyone else in the office?

Mrs. Krause didn't. With a sigh, Lydia put down the phone. If she got arrested, she'd call Samantha. Her sister would know what to do.

Lydia spent the next few days discussing Claire's murder with whomever she happened to meet out walking or in the clubhouse. No one had much to add to what she already knew. The only interesting piece of information came from a widow named Audrey Fuller, whose husband, Frank, had died the previous May.

"He loved to birdwatch, Frank did. All spring and summer. He kept an accurate record of every bird he saw. Wrote it down in his diary."

Lydia was about to cut the conversation short, then was glad she hadn't when Audrey added, "That morning he went to his favorite spot—the arboretum across Bellewood Road. You know where it is?"

Lydia nodded. The older woman's eyes filled with tears.

"The police said he must have fallen and hit his head on a rock, but I don't believe that for a minute." Audrey shook her head. "Not my Frank. He was always cautious where he stepped."

Frank had a digital camera, one she'd given him for his last birthday. He loved taking photos and always carried it with him. Audrey was certain he'd brought the camera with him the day he died, though it wasn't on his person and never turned up. The police didn't think this was important. They told her someone must have stolen the camera, or Frank must have lost it.

Interesting, Lydia thought, but not relevant to Claire's death. Much as she disliked the idea, it was time to call on both Claire's husband and best friend, Viv Maguire. She'd do that tomorrow.

She woke up after ten on Wednesday morning, discouraged and grumpy. Swimming laps would be just the thing to get her motor running properly again. The indoor pool was a godsend, she thought, as she brushed her teeth. Except for the two men who swam every morning from seven-thirty till eight-fifteen, hardly anyone used it, so often she had the pool to herself. No need to watch out for wild elbows or splashing as other swimmers passed by. Most residents loved the card room, but the pool was her haven.

She nodded to the few people she met in the clubhouse, and made her way down the steps to the women's changing room. She took off her outer clothing, grabbed a towel and entered the pool.

The water, several degrees cooler than tepid, always shocked her system. But she was willing to endure the brief unpleasantness for the wonderful benefits that followed. Once her body adjusted to the water temperature, Lydia floated on her back and let herself drift. Her mind emptied of all thought, her body released every tension. *Ah, if heaven exists, it must feel like this,* she thought. Relaxed now, she began her crawl across the length of the pool.

She managed to complete eight laps before her arms grew tired and she switched to the side stroke. She could continue for hours, she decided, if she were ever tossed off a ship and had to remain afloat. This and other inane thoughts flittered through her mind as she turned from the deep end of the pool.

The sound came from behind—a mechanical type of noise, as if an awning were being raised or lowered. She glanced over her shoulder and saw that the pool cover—she hadn't even known there was one—was moving toward her. Terror rose in her throat. She jerked forward, arms and legs flailing, so that she was splashing instead of making headway. Water entered her mouth, went down her trachea. She coughed.

Mustn't panic! She began swimming in earnest, kicking as hard as she could. The noise grew louder as the metal cover inched closer to her. It was six inches above the water line. Once it covered the pool, she wouldn't be able to breathe. How on earth...?

Don't think. Concentrate! Swim fast. Faster! The steps were before her. Awkwardly, she scrambled to her feet and up the first step as the metal pushed against her hips. She took the second step, then the third, finally standing on the rim of the pool as the cover slammed shut behind her.

"I'm safe," she murmured, sinking into the nearest chair. She wrapped herself in her towel, attempting to soothe the tremors that racked her body. It was minutes before she could walk. She reached for the intercom phone and asked whoever was at the desk to please send the office manager down to the pool because there'd been an accident.

Margie, the efficient, forty-something manager, came immediately. "The pool's closed! Who on earth activated the cover?" she asked.

"That's what I'd like to know," Lydia said. "I was in the pool when it happened."

"Oh, no! You could have been killed!"

"I know."

Margie sat down beside her. "What's happening to this place? It used to be so—peaceful."

"Until I came to live here," Lydia said.

Margie patted her hand. "Don't be silly. You didn't close the cover. The mechanism's inside the men's locker room. Someone must have..." She faltered.

"Wanted to kill me."

"Don't say that! I'm sure it was an accident."

"Did you see anyone come down here in the last hour or so?"

"No. I've been busy in the office." She looked at Lydia. "Would you like me to wait here while you change into your street clothes?"

"I'd appreciate it. Then I'm going home to call Detective Molina."

~ * ~

He arrived at her front door half an hour later, looking handsome in a tweed blazer and grey trousers.

"Hello, Mrs. Krause. You've had yourself one hell of a morning."

"So it seems."

She led the way into the living room and sat on a sofa. He sat facing her. "I've just come from the pool. The mechanism appears to be in perfect working order."

"Any idea who closed it?"

"No. I spoke to Stefano, your head of maintenance. He told me they almost never use the cover. I spoke to two other workers, Ralph and John. They don't know anything, either." He pressed his lips together. "They're going to place a small metal cage over the switch, so this will never happen again."

"Thank God."

"Did you see anyone while you were down there?".

Lydia shook her head. "Whoever it was knows I rarely miss a morning swim. He was waiting down there to kill me." A tremor ran through her body. "Maybe it was Marshall Weill, angry because I exposed him as a felon.

Maybe he waited to ward off suspicion, then tried to kill me."

"Days after his wife was killed?"

Lydia shrugged, suddenly confused. "I—I'm not sure."

The smile he offered was filled with kindness. "I'm wondering if someone meant this as a warning, Mrs. Krause."

"A warning? Why?"

"You tell me."

She hesitated. Was Detective Molina clairvoyant? It was the only explanation she could think of that explained how he knew she'd been asking questions.

"For your information, I did speak to a few people about Claire Weill."

"Uh huh. Just as I thought! Either the murderer's worried you'll discover some detail he overlooked, or he—or someone else—fears you'll uncover a secret from the past."

Lydia was indignant. "Of course I asked questions! Did you imagine I'd sit here twiddling my thumbs while you consider me a homicide suspect?"

Molina smiled, showing white, even teeth. "No one's accusing you of killing Mrs. Weill. In fact, I came to tell you the ME strongly believes Mrs. Weill died at seven at the outset."

Lydia shrugged. "I don't see how that takes me off the A List."

"I never told you—and I asked Mrs. Taylor not to discuss this with you—but she was certain she threw some clothes in the dryer at a quarter to seven, looked in on you, then read until she fell asleep about half an hour later. That puts you in the clear."

Lydia sighed with relief. "Thank God!" She thought a bit. "That was fast. I thought tests like that take time."

"I pressed for a fast result—at least regarding time of death—and I'm glad to pass along the good news, so far as you're concerned."

"Thank you," she said with heartfelt ardor. "One less problem to be concerned about." She thought a bit. "Do you think the murderer was trying to frame me?"

"Could be."

"That doesn't give me any comfort."

He blinked, revealing that his eyes were closer to hazel today. "I would be remiss if I gave you false comfort, especially after this morning's incident. Looks like you got someone angry, Mrs. Krause."

"The only person who comes to mind is Warren Mannes, aka Marshall Weill. I hope you're checking out his whereabouts this morning."

"We already have."

"Oh." Lydia's felt her ears grow warm and knew they must have been blazing red. Damn, it wasn't like her to tell a professional how to do his job. She'd lost all sense of propriety because Claire Weill's murder had involved her in a deep and personal way.

Lydia frowned. "Maybe if I hadn't exposed him, this never would have happened."

Detective Molina stood. "Mrs. Krause, don't start

blaming yourself. You might have been the catalyst for something we know nothing about—yet. You were right to bring Weill's past actions to the attention of your community. Who knows what else will come to light? We've only begun to look into every aspect of the Weills' lives, past and present."

"Thank you," Lydia murmured. "You've been very kind."

"For a police detective, you mean."

She laughed, admitting to the thought. "Would you like a cup of coffee?"

"I'd love it. By the way," he said, pointing to the statue of "Family" in the corner, "that's one beautiful work of art. So are the sculptures in the hall and the dining room."

"Thank you."

"Are you a collector?"

"My husband was a sculptor. I have five of Izzy's pieces. My daughters each own one. The rest are in museums and galleries."

"Oh. Is he...?"

"Yes. He died earlier this year. Which is how I ended up living here at Twin Lakes."

"I'm sorry."

In the kitchen, Molina sat at the small round table and stretched his arms overhead. They made small talk as Lydia ground coffee beans and filled the carafe with water—about life in Suffolk County and Lydia's recent retirement. Detective Molina said little about himself and nothing of the incident that had brought him to Twin

Lakes. Lydia felt at ease in his company. She liked the way he listened to what she said. Really listened, as he drank from his mug of coffee and ate several of the tiny delicious white chocolate cookies from Trader Joe's she always kept on hand. Listening was a trait very few people possessed.

As he stood to leave, Lydia felt a moment's panic and the urge to detain him.

"I almost forgot to tell you what I learned when I spoke to Doris Fein yesterday afternoon."

He pulled out his notebook and pen. "Who is Doris Fein?"

"A resident here. A friend of Claire Weill's, or was. I believe Marshall may have given her some bad financial advice. Doris told me Claire was obsessed with her husband even though he ran around. She said Claire had started taking herbal capsules to make her look and feel younger. The way she said it—kind of hush-hush—made me wonder if this supplement was legal."

"Interesting," he murmured.

She watched him jot all of this down.

"Anything else you remember?" he asked.

Lydia thought. "Just that Claire thought her husband was having an affair, though Doris didn't know if that was true or simply that he was busy handling people's finances. Though Doris did say Marshall was a flirt." She gave a humorless laugh. "But we already know about that side of him."

He nodded, his expression gentle, his eyes now apple

green. "Do you have Mrs. Fein's address and phone number handy?"

Lydia went to get the Twin Lakes telephone directory. As Molina copied down the information, she had a sudden thought. "Do you want me to contact you if I hear anything else about Claire Weill?"

He shook his head, but he was smiling. "Please don't start playing detective like that woman Angela Lansbury used to portray on TV. What was her name?"

"Jessica Fletcher," she supplied. Thank God he hadn't compared her to Miss Marple.

"Right. My wife used to watch that program."

His wife. Of course he had a wife. Her disappointment was as keen as a child being told there'd be no birthday party after all. "I suppose you're not interested in hearsay." Something perverse, a desire to rile him, made her add, "Though I should pay a shiva call and offer Marshall Weill my condolences."

"What!" He frowned at her. "Have you already forgotten what happened to you this morning? I suggest you send him a card."

"So, you think he murdered his wife and had a stab at killing or warning me."

"It's too early to say in either case, but the circumstances and evidence point to someone in this community."

"And the spouse is always the first suspect," she murmured, remembering the case she'd built against Marshall Weill last night as she tried to fall asleep.

"Yes, and please keep that and everything else we've spoken of to yourself," he said as he turned to leave.

So they were back where they'd first started.

"Of course I will. I'm not a gossip!" She skirted past him to unlock the front door.

"I'm sure you're not." They stood close enough in the small entrance hall for her to catch a trace of his Davidoff aftershave.

"The thing is, I don't want to have to worry about your welfare while we follow through on this investigation. You were attacked this morning. Your vehicle was taken and misused." He gave her a half smile. "But if you should happen to hear something relevant to the case, by all means, pass it on to me."

He withdrew a card from his sport jacket's breast pocket. "Here are a few numbers where you can reach me. Call if you learn something relating to the case. Please, no more interrogations, though. That's our job."

She took the card. "Of course."

"We'll talk again."

Lydia nodded, savoring the words as though they were a promise. She watched Lieutenant Molina get into an unmarked car and drive away.

Six

Claire's funeral was held the following afternoon. Lydia heard Marshall Weill had pressured local rabbis and politicians to get the autopsy done ASAP so the body could quickly be laid to rest as Jewish law required. Caroline, who attended the funeral with her husband and the Linnetts, called Lydia later that evening.

"We just came from paying a shiva call at Marshall's daughter's in Smithtown. Lots of Twin Lakes people were there. I've never seen anything like it! Widows and divorcées—even married women like Sally Marcus—swarmed around Marshall as if he were Hugh Hefner or Bob Guccione. In a matter of days, he's gone from Man with a Scandalous Past to Bachelor of the Hour. Makes you wonder if he bumped off Claire for all this female attention."

Caroline giggled. "Oops, you didn't hear that! And coming from a board member's wife."

Lydia laughed as her friend intended her to. "Who knows how deep his criminal tendencies run, but since the police have no evidence connecting him to the crime, he's free to go about as he pleases."

"Oh?" Caroline asked coyly. "Have you gotten a private update on the case from that handsome detective?"

"Of course not!" Lydia denied, though Lieutenant Molina had said as much last night when he called to see how she was feeling after her ordeal in the pool.

Caroline laughed. "Have it your way. But keep us informed if you hear anything more about the case."

"If I happen to," Lydia said carefully.

She wondered why both Barbara and Caroline spoke of the detective as though he were interested in her. He had to interview her since her car was the weapon used to kill Claire Weill and she was halfway to being a suspect. After that, he came by to let her know he'd found out about Allison. Then there was the swimming pool cover incident and a brief follow-up call. Every communication concerned Claire Weill's murder. Besides, Lieutenant Molina had mentioned his wife, which meant he was happily married. No doubt, with a slew of grandchildren who visited every Sunday.

"I'll send Marshall a sympathy card," Lydia said. "Somehow I feel I'm partly responsible for his wife's death."

Caroline's tone changed from that of a teasing friend to a scolding mother, "Now that is absolutely ridiculous. Barbara and I have told you a dozen times—your car was chosen because someone noticed you put the key under the fender and for no other reason. You've nothing to blame yourself for."

Lydia gulped back a lump of emotion. While she couldn't shake her sense of culpability, she appreciated their concern. "Thanks for your support, Caroline. I feel as though I've known you and Barbara for years instead of days."

"That's how it goes in a place like Twin Lakes when people click. Good night. See you tomorrow."

Lydia put the phone down. A fragment of one of their discussions resounded in her mind. Marshall Weill must have had many adulterous affairs during his marriage to Claire. What if he were conducting an affair here at Twin Lakes and it had gotten out of control? What if the woman wanted him to marry her, and when he said he couldn't she decided to take matters into her own hands?

Lydia shook her head in disbelief at the lengths to which her thoughts had taken her. At their brainstorming session, she, Barbara and Caroline had agreed most of the Twin Lakes residents were well past the age of passion. Certainly past the age when one died—or killed—for love.

Of course there was the possibility that Marshall was involved with someone considerably younger.

Someone who lived outside Twin Lakes and had access to the community. Someone like Allison.

She changed into her nightgown and robe, and was about to turn on the TV when Barbara called. "Don't forget we're going to the supermarket tomorrow. I'll pick you up at ten-thirty."

Peg also called—to tell her about the funeral and to rave about Marshall's daughter's gorgeous home. "It's huge and chock full of antiques and modern paintings. She and her husband own a multi-million dollar antiques business. Elinor's smart as a whip and as beautiful as a movie star—takes after her dad."

"He is a nice-looking man," Lydia agreed. She remembered what Caroline had said about women swarming around Marshall at the shiva. "How did Marshall seem to you?"

"How do you think he seemed?" Peg snapped. "He was awfully upset by Claire's death but touched that so many friends and neighbors came to pay their respects."

Was this a barb because she hadn't gone to the funeral or paid a shiva call? Or was Peg annoyed at her for making Marshall Weill's criminal record public knowledge? Probably the second, Lydia decided.

"By the way, your detective friend—what's his name?—came to the service and to the cemetery."

Lydia's heart began to race. "It's Lieutenant Molina, and he's not my friend."

"Right, Molina." Peg let out a derisive laugh. "He stood in the distance, the way they do in the movies, no doubt expecting to identify the murderer by his guilty expression."

"The murderer could have been at the funeral," Lydia said, her irritation with Peg making her forget the promise she made to herself not to discuss the subject with anyone but Barbara and Caroline. "He probably lives right here at

Twin Lakes, since he used my car to kill Claire."

When Peg said nothing, Lydia mused, "I wonder who stands to gain financially from her death."

"Claire was wealthy, all right. Her first husband left her a fortune that never stops growing. It's being handled astutely."

"By Marshall, no doubt."

"By her first husband's team of investment advisors," Peg retorted, almost defensively. "It was a cleverly drawn-up trust. Now that she's dead, most of the money goes to Claire's son and daughter from that marriage—if you're so interested."

Lydia ignored Peg's hostility because yes, she was extremely interested. "Oh? Marshall receives nothing?"

"Not all that much. Claire handed over quite a chunk of her money to Elinor and her husband when they started their antiques business. Why do you ask? Do you think Marshall ran Claire down?"

"Frankly, I don't know what to think."

"Because he wouldn't! He's not that type of person."

"Peg, how do you know so much about the Weills' finances?"

Peg gave a little laugh. "When you get friendly with Twin Lakes' people, they talk freely—about their children, their health and their money."

"What about their love affairs?"

"What love affairs?" Peg sounded shocked.

"I've no idea. Doris Fein told me Claire was worried her husband was running around again."

"Really? Whom did she suspect?"

"She didn't tell Doris. I suppose that's a secret she kept in her diary."

"Claire kept a diary?"

Lydia let out a breath of exasperation. "It's just an expression, Peg." Then she gave voice to the bitchy thought that had crossed her mind. "What about Sally Marcus? Do you think she and Marshall were having it off?"

"I wouldn't know." Peg said good-night and hung up.

Lydia waited until the following afternoon, after food shopping and lunching out with Barbara, to call Detective Molina. She was told he was on another line and asked if she could hold. When he came on, he sounded rushed.

"What's up?" he asked.

She repeated her conversation with Peg and felt a twinge of guilt when she told him Caroline's observations at the shiva.

"Interesting." He sounded wistful when he added, "That spread of food must have been something awesome to behold. I bet she served really good belly lox and a mean white fish."

"Oh!" Lydia exclaimed. "You like bagels and lox and—all that stuff?"

Detective Molina laughed. "Why not? It's my heritage, at least the Solomon half."

"Oh!" Lydia repeated, surprised. "You're half-Jewish."

"And my mother saw to it that my daughter was a Bat Mitzvah."

And your wife? Lydia wanted to ask. What's her part in all this? What's she like? But there was no time. Detective Molina had changed the subject.

"Getting back to the case, your neighbor's on target regarding Mrs. Weill's finances. We've checked out the terms of her will."

Curious, Lydia asked, "How long were Claire and Marshall Weill married?"

"Thirty-two years. They have one daughter, Elinor Weintraub. She of the beautiful house." He paused, as though debating whether or not to tell her something else. Lydia held her breath, then exhaled when he continued.

"Claire's son and daughter from her first marriage flew in from California and Michigan to attend the funeral. A taxi drove them from the cemetery to Kennedy Airport."

"No shiva call for them," Lydia commented. "Which leads one to assume they have no use for Marshall Weill or their half-sister."

Molina laughed. "Actually, they're very fond of Elinor and her husband, but they think Weill's the lowest of the low. He married their mother two years after their father's death—when they were thirteen and eleven. A difficult age to acquire a stepfather. According to both of them, their worst fears proved true. He turned out to be a thief and a runaround."

"Kids have good antennas about people." Lydia remembered the creepy-crawly sensation she'd felt when she'd shaken hands with Weill at Bingo. Of course, she might have picked up negative vibes because, on a visceral level, she knew immediately who he was. "It sounds like he cheated on Claire all through their marriage. Do you think he married her for her money?"

"Could be he assumed she had more money at her disposal and only found out about the trusts after the marriage. Harry Kleinfeld was a successful businessman, considerably older than Claire. Knowing he had a bad heart, he set up trusts for her and the children. Most of Claire's money goes to her children and five grandchildren."

"So, Marshall didn't stand to gain from his wife's death."

Molina laughed. "I wouldn't say that. Just under a million dollars, the home in Twin Lakes and one in Florida are nothing to sneeze at."

"I suppose," Lydia agreed.

She heard noises in the background. "Gotta go," Molina said. "Talk to you soon."

Lydia felt forlorn. She'd hoped to find out when she would see him again. Which was silly. If she happened to see Detective Molina, it would be because she had something vital to tell him that might shed light on the murder. There was no sense fooling herself that he would share sensitive information with her. No doubt what he'd just told her was common knowledge to half the residents of Twin Lakes and was being bandied about in the clubhouse this very minute. If she didn't watch it, she'd turn into one of those pathetic widows who cooed and fluttered at the smallest sign of attention from any virile man.

The phone rang. She beamed when she heard Detective Molina's voice again.

"I forgot to say—the SCI people have finished checking out your car. You're free to come and collect it, or tomorrow someone from the station could drive it over to your place."

Lydia sighed. "Could someone meet me at the Lexus dealer instead? I'm trading it in, remember?"

"Sure thing. I forgot. Give me the dealer's address, and if nothing urgent comes up on any of my cases, I'll drive the car over myself. Around one-thirty good?"

"Sure. I'll get there around one—to fill out the paper work for my new car."

But it was Officer McKlusky who pulled up at the dealership as the salesman was showing Lydia the small improvements in her brand-new Lexus. She stepped out of the shiny red car, which only minutes earlier had made her feel as giddy as a kid with a new toy, and swallowed her disappointment as she greeted the policeman.

"The lou's sorry he couldn't make it himself, but something came up."

Lydia ignored his grin and said she was almost finished with the transaction. If he could wait a few minutes, she'd drive him back to the station. She averted her eyes from the smashed up grille and was glad when the salesman said he'd get someone to drive the car to the body shop in back.

"First, you'll have to sign a few releases," McKlusky told Lydia.

He handed them to her through the open window. Lydia glanced through the forms and signed where xes had been highlighted for her. She was about to follow the salesman inside, when McKlusky said, "Don't forget to clear out the glove and center compartments and the trunk. And check under the seats. People always find stuff under the seats."

"Oh, right," she said, and gathered up the personal articles, surprised at how many she found.

Twenty minutes later, she was behind the wheel of her new car, edging into the flow of traffic on the main boulevard.

"This is one sweet car," McKlusky said as he ran his hand along the car seat's soft leather. "I like my Altima, but everything about this car is pure luxury."

Lydia grinned. "At one point, I was tempted to chuck the sedan look and buy a sports car, only my daughter would disapprove. And she's right. Grandma needs a big, safe car to drive her granddaughters around."

He laughed. "That's for sure. We have a van for our kids."

They drove the rest of the way in companionable silence. As they approached an intersection, Officer McKlusky said, "This is the short cut to the station—hang a left at the corner, follow the windy road through the development, then turn right at the light."

Lydia waited for the oncoming traffic to pass. She made her turn then casually asked, as though it were part of their previous conversation, "What's Mrs. Molina like?"

"The lou's mom? I met her once. She's one spunky lady. Lots of fun."

Lydia nodded. "That's nice, but I meant his wife."

"Let's see—if I remember correctly, she was a pretty woman—light brown hair, good figure. Looks enough like you to be your sister." Now he was grinning broadly.

She felt her face heat up with embarrassment, but it didn't stop her from asking, "You say she *was* a pretty woman. Did she—die?"

"Not that I've heard. I think she moved to Maryland after the divorce two, three years ago."

"Oh!" Lydia accelerated.

"Slow down, Mrs. Krause!"

"Sorry. I was just wondering—does Detective Molina happen to have a lady friend?"

Officer McKlusky shrugged. "I can't say."

"Of course you can't," Lydia mumbled, feeling the heat rise to her ears. She was losing control, speaking her thoughts out loud. Maybe it came from living alone.

What a dumb thing to ask a police officer! Possibly the dumbest question she'd ever asked in her life.

Lydia pressed her lips together, determined not to allow another thought to take on a life of its own. Well, the boys down at the station house would get a good laugh out of that! Mortified, she drove in silence. The next five minutes felt like fifty. Finally she arrived at the police station.

"Here you are!" Lydia announced with false cheer, "safe and sound."

Officer McKlusky opened the passenger door and unfolded his large frame. "That's for the ride, Mrs. Krause."

"You're welcome. Thanks for driving my car to the dealership."

"No problem." He turned and gripped the door handle, about to close it. Instead he ducked his head inside the car. "The lou said if you happen to hear anything important, to give him a call." He grinned. "And don't feel bad about asking about his personal life. It happens all the time."

So, women asked about Molina's personal life all the time! Lydia passed a slow-moving SUV and cut ahead of it. That could mean one thing only. Sol Molina was a flirt! He encouraged women to go after him. That had to be against the law. Which law, she wasn't sure. Harassment? Disturbing civilians? Whatever—just some law she was positive had been drawn up and passed to keep police and civilians on opposite sides of the road.

She turned into Twin Lakes and waited for the gate to rise and allow her to pass. A wave of reality spilled over her, turning her fury into shame. Detective Molina had done nothing more than show her civility and friendliness. It was she, in her state of heightened sensitivity since Izzy's death and intensified by her connection to Claire Weill's murder, who had misinterpreted his behavior and turned the detective into a larger-than-life romantic figure.

She drove slowly along N Boulevard, cringing as she recalled her conversation with Officer McKlusky. How could she have questioned him about Molina's marital status? At best she came across as a yenta, at worst a love-starved crone. Which, aside from being totally untrue, made the situation sound—so gauche. So blatantly childish. She would not indulge her silly attraction to Detective Sol Molina one minute more.

Seven

Lydia felt stymied. After speaking to more Twin Lakes residents, she learned little more about the Weills than she had two days after Claire had been murdered. She wasn't making headway. She had no way of knowing if the police were either, as Lieutenant Molina hadn't stopped by or called in over a week. She blushed to think he was keeping away because Officer McKlusky told him she'd been making personal inquiries.

Merry remained an unsolved mystery as well. Lydia didn't know if her daughter was having an affair or if she intended to return early to her teaching position. Finding herself without a direct purpose in life, Lydia decided to get herself a job.

"Not a demanding job," she told Barbara as they shared an Indian dinner after an afternoon of shopping. "Something part-time."

"Something to take you away from Twin Lakes—and from your baby-sitting responsibilities," Barbara said slyly.

"Exactly."

She found what she was looking for a few days later, while glancing through the local paper. Carrington House, one of the old manor houses built in the early 1900s for wealthy industrialists, was now used as a banquet hall for parties, weddings, bar mitzvahs and the like. Overlooking extensive grounds and a small lake, there was talk of adding a building with forty or so rooms, where guests might stay overnight. The ad said the establishment required a three-day-a-week employee to do booking, bookkeeping, liaise with the food staff, the wait staff, show potential clients around, and whatever else was needed.

Len Montardi, the manager, was a tall, balding over-forty hyper conniver. He recognized Lydia's multi-talents immediately and offered her the job on the spot at a ridiculously low salary. She demurred, asked for double the sum. After he gasped and did some figures on a piece of paper, he offered her close to the sum she'd requested. Before offering her hand, Lydia said she hoped she'd made it clear she had no desire to work more days or more hours. Len gulped, lied that he understood, and they shook hands. Lydia drove home from the meeting singing along with the radio.

Now that she was working Tuesday, Thursday and Friday from ten till five, she found herself organizing her "free" time more efficiently. The days Meredith didn't need her to babysit, she shopped for furniture. She ordered two beige sofas for the living room. Barbara pointed out they were almost identical to the sofas she already had, but Lydia said those were old and worn. Besides, she wanted something new.

On Monday morning, two and a half weeks after Claire Weill's murder, Lydia rode the train in to Manhattan. After climbing the cement steps to the street, she paused for a nostalgic whiff of the city air. She stared, enchanted by the hordes of pedestrians, the zooming traffic, and wore a smile as her taxi zigzagged its way uptown to the antique shops in the Seventies. *I must look like a tourist,* she thought. She splurged rashly on a country French armoire she no more needed than a trip to the moon.

After lunch, she wandered in and out of galleries and bought an oil painting that caught her eye. *I'm becoming quite the spendthrift,* she thought as she arranged to have the painting delivered. When she glanced down at her watch, she was surprised to see it was five-thirty. She'd barely enough time to cab down to Soho to meet Abbie for their prearranged early dinner.

At the restaurant, a narrow, high-ceilinged room half-filled with young diners, Lydia sank gratefully into her chair and sipped water while she waited. Twenty minutes later, her younger daughter beamed as she approached, late as usual. And, as usual, she sent heads turning. Abbie's colorful poncho—made of God knew what—set off her long blonde tresses, which tonight she wore in two braids Indian-style, hanging down the front of her chest.

"Hi, Mom, what's up?" Abbie kissed Lydia's cheek, then sat down beside her at the small table.

"For starters, I've spent half your inheritance," Lydia joked in a way she never would with Meredith. "I bought an antique armoire and a large oil painting to hang in the living room. They cost the earth."

"Good for you. Meredith will be pleased. She thinks you should toss everything—except Dad's sculptures, of course—and furnish your new place from scratch."

"Oh, you've been speaking to your sister!" Lydia exclaimed, pleased. Her daughters were as different as two women could be and rarely contacted one another.

"Merry's worried about you. She insists you were traumatized because your car was used to kill that poor woman."

"I'm recovering from the shock," Lydia said, glad that neither daughter knew about the pool closing incident.

"How do you like your new job?" Abbie asked.

"I love it. It's mindless, I work with young people, I get a change of scenery, then I go home."

"I'm glad, Mom. I can't see you playing tennis all day."

"I don't play tennis, Abbie."

"Whatever. Meredith thinks you're doing too much, but I told her you love to work."

Lydia's heart started racing. "Did she say anything about returning to work before her leave is up?"

"No."

"Anything about—anything?"

"No." Abbie's gray eyes studied her carefully. "Why? What's wrong?"

"Nothing."

The young waiter approached and they ordered. They chatted companionably, about Abbie's new job and her present boyfriend."

Over tea and dessert, Lydia commented, "It sounds as though you're settling down, at least for the time being."

Abbie shrugged. "For the next nine months, at least."

"What happens then?"

"Todd has to return to England. I might be going with him."

She said it lightly, but Lydia heard the earnestness beneath. "Nine months, eh? That sounds like a long time off to be making plans."

For a moment Abbie didn't answer. Then she said, "Todd's different."

Only two words, but they told her that her daughter was in love. "When do I get to meet him?" Lydia asked.

"One day soon, when he's not swamped with work. We might even drive out to the wilds of Suffolk County for a visit—that is, if you promise not to drag us off to Meredith's."

Lydia swallowed the lump that had formed in her throat. "I'd be delighted. Let me know when you'd like to come."

They said good night shortly after that. As Lydia rode home on the Long Island Railroad, she realized she'd forgotten to ask what type of work Todd did. She sighed. It was just as well. Abbie was like her older sister in one way—totally resistant to prodding. Sweet as she was, she gave up information piecemeal, and in her own good time.

~ * ~

It was close to midnight when the train pulled into the Ronkonkoma station. Tired but exhilarated, Lydia noted the small crowd exiting the train. Proof positive that for many people the trip into Manhattan was an everyday occurrence. She headed for her car, determined to ride into the city again soon. Maybe she'd take in a show or visit a museum with Barbara and Caroline. Or perhaps she and Meredith would meet Abbie for dinner.

As Lydia drove through Twin Lakes, she noticed many of the homes were dark, their owners either asleep or wintering in Florida. A man and a woman stood in Peg's driveway beside a low-slung sports car. Were they embracing? As she turned into her driveway, the man waved and called out her name. Surprised, she saw it was Marshall Weill.

Given their history, she had trouble understanding his friendly greeting. She wanted nothing to do with him. Still, they resided in the same small community and he'd just lost his wife. She waited while he crossed her lawn and lowered the passenger window to find out what he wanted.

"Hi there, Lydia!" In the street light his shrewd eyes took in her leather jacket, glanced down at her skirt and boots. "Looks like someone was out on the town."

"I went into the city and met my daughter for dinner," she said.

"Oh? Not for a romantic rendezvous?"

His comment grated on her nerves. "Did you want

something? I'm tired and I need to go inside."

"Of course. I want to thank you for your kind note," he said, his tone now serious and sad. "It means a great deal to me because you know what it is to suffer the loss of a beloved spouse."

Despite herself, she was moved by the emotion behind his words. "As I wrote, I'm sorry someone used my car to kill your wife so soon after..." she halted as she searched for innocuous words "the blow up in the clubhouse."

He gave a low laugh. "You mean, after you exposed my past to our friends and neighbors."

She stiffened. "That I don't regret! You have no business handling our HOA funds. Or anyone's funds, for that matter—something I don't expect you to understand."

"Oh, but I do! Once my head cleared, I realized your motives were for the good of the community. But I was wondering—have I somehow offended you personally?"

When she didn't respond, he went on, "If I have, I'm sincerely sorry for whatever pain I've caused you."

She glared at him. "The pain you caused will never go away. Allison Shaw was my sister."

"Was she?" He nodded as he remembered. "Poor thing, so sweet and terribly needy."

"Easy prey, wasn't she? You moved right in—took her savings and seduced her, while you were at it. Drove her to..."

Lydia stopped in mid-sentence as Peg came to join them. She placed a hand on Marshall Weill's arm as she greeted Lydia, her tone far from friendly.

Lydia nodded, too agitated to speak. She pulled into the garage and clicked the garage door remote on her visor.

Reggie was extremely vocal in expressing his annoyance for having been left alone all day. As she scooped cat food into a plate, Lydia took deep breaths to regain her equilibrium. What was the point of that scene? she scolded herself. Getting yourself all worked up, and for what? Even if that man—that monster—threw himself down on the ground, it wouldn't make up for the damage he'd caused.

She sat and sorted through her mail. The phone rang.

"Hello, Lydia. This is Marshall. Don't hang up, please," he said quickly. "I need to tell you something."

"What is it?"

He drew in a shaky breath, then spoke. "I swear to you, I never meant to hurt your sister. She was sweet, and the truth is, I fell for her in a big way. I told Allison from the start I'd never divorce Claire, but she called me constantly and said it didn't matter. That she needed to be with me."

Lydia made no attempt to mask her bitterness. "And you obliged. How kind."

"It wasn't kindness," he said, sounding annoyed. "I told you, I cared for Allison."

"What about her savings? She was devastated when she learned you'd lumped them together with other investments and put everything in your name."

"That was stupid, I agree, but I told her in a few months she could have the money back with a gain of twenty thousand dollars. All she had to do was wait it out.

And then—"

"Then you were indicted, and all your shenanigans came to light."

"With all that was happening, I told Allison to sit tight. I'd get her money back for her just as soon as I could, but she thought I was lying. She grew more and more frantic, because I couldn't spend any more time with her. I practically lived with my lawyer at my side."

"So Allison swallowed her meds and never woke up," Lydia said harshly.

"I'm sorry, Lydia. I don't know what else to say."

She gave a sniff of a laugh. "I believe those are the first honest words I've heard you utter."

"I'll send you a check for the amount of Allison's money and then some."

Lydia opened her mouth to say she didn't want anything from him, but that was foolish. The money he would be giving her belonged to her sister, not to Marshall.

"All right."

"I'll take care of it right away. And Lydia?"

"Yes?"

"I know you don't want to be friends with the likes of me, but I hope now that you've aired your issues we won't have a scene every time we cross paths."

"I won't be making any scenes, as you put it."

"Much appreciated, Lydia. Good night."

Lydia returned to the task of reading her mail. She felt melancholy but strangely at peace—as though she'd closed the cover on a particularly sad book. She'd told Marshall Weill why she despised him, and he, in turn, had explained things from his perspective. While he hadn't treated Allison right, he'd tried to make amends, and Allison—Allison couldn't cope.

A truth, one she'd been suppressing for as long as she could remember, forced its way through and demanded to be heard. Her sister had been fragile. Too fragile to live out in the world without the protection of loving family. She'd chosen independence and suffered the consequences. Marshall, for all his sleazy behavior, hadn't caused her suicide. Allison had made the decision to take her own life.

She'd been born when Lydia was twelve and Samantha was eight, a beautiful blonde baby whom they treated as their doll. For the first eight years of her life Allison was as pleasant and obliging as a doll, but then she turned finicky. She suffered from stomach aches, and though their parents took her from doctor to doctor, no one could determine the cause of her pain. When she was in fifth grade, one of the boys in Allison's class—a child from a dysfunctional family with severe emotional problems—beat her up as she was walking home from school. Allison went into a decline. She was afraid to leave the house and refused to go to school. Her parents had to enroll her in a private school, where she fared well under the careful auspices of alerted administrators and teachers. There was another setback when she turned sixteen, and another at eighteen. But she managed to graduate with her class and insisted on going to an out-of-town college. Her parents agreed to a small college in Chicago because Samantha was already in law school at the University of Chicago. It took Allison six years to complete her undergraduate degree and several more until she got her M.S.W.

Each time, it was a disastrous male-female relationship—a short, wrong-from-the-start marriage and two affairs—that threw her into a black depression. After years of therapy and a job that promised to bring her joy, Allison was finally on firm ground. Until she happened to attend a seminar led by Walter Mannes and fell under his spell.

Later, as Lydia was brushing her teeth, she wondered what Marshall had been doing at Peg's house. Was he handling her finances, or had she invited him for a widower's dinner? Or was it something else entirely?

"They can't be involved," she said aloud. "It's only been a few weeks since Claire died." Unless, despite his rock solid alibi, Marshall Weill had been responsible for his wife's death. There was always the possibility he'd hired someone to do the deed.

Because of an affair? Were Peg and Marshall having an affair? If so, when had it begun?

Lydia yawned as the emotional and physical demands of her day drew her to slumberland. She closed her eyes, as all speculation regarding Marshall Weill and Peg DiMarco faded from her mind.

Eight

Meredith called her at seven-thirty the following morning, waking her from a deep sleep.

"Hello," Lydia croaked into the receiver.

"Sorry, Mom!" Meredith apologized. "I thought you'd be up for your usual swim."

"I should be." Lydia propped herself up on an elbow to see the clock. "I suppose traipsing all over Manhattan wore me out."

"How's Abbie?"

"She's fine. Happy. I think she has a serious boyfriend."

"That's nice. Listen Mom, I know you've been watching the girls a lot lately, but do you think you could come over and stay with them for a few hours this afternoon?"

Lydia felt her irritation rising. "I can't, Meredith. If you'll remember, I have a part-time job, and today happens to be one of the days I work."

Meredith let out a heartrending sigh. "I was up all night

with Brittany. She must have caught a stomach virus because she kept throwing up. She's fine now, but I kept her home from school."

"Poor little thing. She must have gotten what my friend Barbara had a few weeks ago. Can I speak to her?"

Brittany sounded more subdued than usual. "Hi, Grammy. I'm eating apple sauce for breakfast."

"How are you feeling?"

"Better, but I'm sleepy. Are you coming over later?"

Lydia thought quickly. She had nothing pressing to deal with this afternoon. Len wouldn't mind if she left early and made up the hours on Thursday.

"If you want me to."

"Oh, goody!"

"I'll bring a little surprise to cheer you up."

"Please bring something for Greta, too, or she'll carry on."

Lydia smiled at her wise granddaughter. "Of course I will. Now let me speak to Mommy again."

When Meredith got on the phone, Lydia made it clear she'd leave work at three and could stay no longer than two hours. "There's an open board meeting tonight, and I don't want to miss it."

"Of course, Mom. Thanks so much!"

Lydia turned on the shower in her spacious bathroom and wondered about her daughter. Meredith hadn't mentioned where she was going and Lydia didn't ask. Could it have something to do with her returning to work before her extended maternity leave was up? So far,

Merry hadn't mentioned the subject to Lydia, though she was quick to complain that Jeff would be working late again.

Lydia felt a twinge of unease as she stepped into her bathing suit. Meredith struck her as being more tense and restless than usual. Jeff was working long hours. Was he working hard to get ahead and provide for his family, or was work his way of distancing himself from a disapproving Merry? Or was he having an affair?

She burst out laughing as she realized lately she'd been wondering whether many people were having affairs: Meredith, Jeff, Marshall, Peg. Were there really that many people driven by love and lust these days, or was she beginning to feel deprived of male company herself? Which made her aware of just how many days had passed since her last chat with Detective Molina.

Lydia shortened her swim time so she could buy Brittany a book at Barnes & Noble on the way to work. She had a little cloth doll for Greta, which she'd bought weeks ago, one of many toys and small gifts she now kept on hand. As she stopped for a red light, she realized she should have put the doll in the car. No matter, she'd pick it up on her way to Meredith's later.

A change in Saturday's wedding menu and the death of a ninety-year-old man scheduled to celebrate his birthday in the Linton Room on Sunday afternoon kept Lydia on the phone for most of the morning. Then her immediate boss—a pretty young woman named Jessica Holland who, age-wise, could have been Lydia's middle child—required her assistance. At two forty-five Lydia was clearing her desk when Len appeared and asked her to confirm arrangements with all outside vendors for that evening's business conference.

Lydia frowned. "Len, you said there'd be no problem if I left early today."

"You will leave early, Lydia. I promise. Make these calls and you needn't make up the two hours tomorrow. It won't take you more than half an hour at most."

Her glance swept past Jessica frantically riffling through papers to Len's outer office where his secretary and the clerk worked. "Can't Ginny or Mabel take care of this?"

"Sorry, they're busy with other things. Please, Lydia."

She gave an exasperated sigh. She was annoyed with Len for not keeping his word, with Meredith for being so demanding, and with herself for agreeing to babysit on a day when she was working. It wouldn't happen again.

"Okay, Len. Give me the phone numbers, etcetera."

He handed her a sheet of paper with everything neatly printed out. "This is a time-sensitive business. Problems crop up when we least expect them."

"So I see."

It was three-twenty when Lydia finished all she'd been asked to do. She raced to her car then took a minute to call Meredith on her cell phone to say she was on her way. Her daughter hadn't been at all happy with the delay.

Meredith flung open the door before Lydia had a chance to ring the bell. She was wearing her new leather coat and had put on plum-colored eyeshadow and liner that accentuated her lovely eyes.

"Don't you look lovely!" Lydia exclaimed. "Where are you off to?"

Meredith offered a tight smile. When she spoke, her words sounded stilted. "I'm meeting a friend in crisis at the mall."

Lydia felt rebuked for prying. Damn it, she was only making small talk!

Greta ran into the hall and grabbed Meredith around her knees. "Good-bye, Mommy." She cocked her head to look at Lydia. "Hi, Grammy. Brittany said you brought us presents."

Meredith gently freed herself from her daughter's grasp. "Greta, what did I tell you about asking for presents?"

"Not to ask for them. But Grammy's different, aren't you, Grammy?" Greta flashed her adorable smile.

She should be in TV commercials, Lydia decided with a grandmother's pride. "Of course, I am," she said, smiling back, then opened her mouth in dismay. In the rush of hurrying from one place to another, she'd forgotten Greta's doll. Flustered by her omission, she paid scant attention to Meredith's litany of instructions.

"—Brittany fell asleep on my bed watching TV. Let her sleep. I'll be back by five."

Meredith air-kissed Lydia's cheek then departed. Lydia led her little granddaughter into the den and took her hand. "Greta honey, I have a present for you, only Grammy's getting forgetful. I left it at home."

"Oh." The large blue eyes cast down at the floor. "I want to get the present at your house."

"We will, only we can't right now because Brittany's asleep."

"Then let's wake her up." Greta pulled away, ready to put deed to words, but Lydia stopped her.

"We can't, do that, honey. We have to let Brittany sleep because she's been sick. We'll get your present."

"When?"

Lydia hesitated. "When she wakes up."

The usual sunny Greta turned truculent and whiny, insisting every five minutes that Brittany had slept enough. A few times Lydia caught her halfway up the stairs, intent on waking her sister. She tried reading to Greta, but she wouldn't sit still. She slipped a favorite movie into the DVD, but Greta had her mind on one thing only—getting her present.

At her wit's end, Lydia asked, "Why do you want your present so much if you don't know what it is?"

Greta shot her a brilliant smile. "Because you always give good presents."

"Now we're going to play a game about your present," Lydia said, making it up as she went along. "It's a guessing game."

"Oh, goody!" Greta clapped her hands.

"You have to guess what it is. I can only nod my head 'yes' and shake it for 'no.'" Lydia moved her head both ways as she spoke. Greta giggled. Lydia sighed with relief. At last she had Greta's attention.

It took her granddaughter, whose mind was on animals and elves these days, some minutes to guess that her present was a doll. "Now, what kind of doll it is?" Lydia asked. As Greta tried her best to figure it out, Brittany crept slowly down the steps. She was wearing a nightgown.

"Hi, Grandma, where's Mommy?" she asked.

"She went out for a while. Want something to eat?"

"Some juice, please."

Lydia smoothed Brittany's hair, then felt her forehead. She had fever. "Sit down on the den couch and I'll bring you some."

"Apple juice, Grandma. Oh, Grammy, thank you!" Brittany shouted when she spied the book Lydia had placed on the couch.

Lydia smiled and brought Brittany her apple juice. "You're welcome."

Brittany was already reading the first page.

"Now we can get my present," Greta said as she kicked the den table.

"Don't do that!" Brittany and Lydia said in unison.

"Let's get my doll. I can't wait any longer," Greta complained.

Lydia peered at Brittany. She appeared wan and listless, certainly not on her way to recovery as Meredith had described in her phone call this morning.

"Do you feel up to taking a ride to my house to get Greta's doll? You can stay in the car while I run in and get it."

Brittany sank back into the couch. "I don't want to go."

Greta stamped her foot. "I've been waiting and waiting, and I didn't wake you up."

Brittany scowled. "I can't help it if I'm sick."

"Of course you can't," Lydia soothed. She turned to Greta. "And you've been a patient little girl," she fibbed. "Now we have to figure out what to do."

"Take Greta, Grandma," Brittany said weakly. "I'll be okay."

Lydia pursed her lips. Brittany was a sensible little girl. She would be eight years old in March, and, as far as Lydia was concerned, capable of staying on her own for the fifteen or twenty minutes it would take to get the doll. When Meredith was that age, Lydia occasionally ran out for milk or some necessary item. Meredith never minded because she always brought her back some little treat.

Now times were different. People hesitated about allowing their children to walk home alone from the neighborhood elementary school until they were about to graduate fifth grade. They hired baby sitters for twelve-year-olds. She shuddered, imagining her daughter's wrath were something to go wrong while Brittany stayed alone in the house.

But nothing would, and Greta was tugging at her sleeve urging her to hurry. Lydia studied Brittany. "Are you sure you don't mind staying alone?"

Brittany shrugged. "It's okay."

"Don't open the door to anyone."

"I won't."

Lydia tried to think what else to warn her about, when Greta said, "Let's go, Grammy."

She bent down to kiss Brittany's forehead. "We'll be

right back. Stay here and read, and everything will be perfectly okay."

Lydia belted Greta into the new car seat she'd bought over the weekend and drove quickly but cautiously to Twin Lakes. She made two green lights and, after stopping and checking that no cars were coming, turned right on a red light. Cheerful because she was finally getting her present, Greta chattered about the children in her morning nursery school class.

Lydia drove past the gatehouse and was about to turn right, onto N Boulevard, when she noticed the two cars facing each other. Their owners were gabbing away, oblivious to the fact that they were blocking traffic. Preferring not to disturb them, she continued straight on Lake Boulevard.

"I'm going to name my new doll Annabelle," Greta said.

"That's nice, honey."

"Yesterday my teacher, Nancy, read us a story about a doll named Annabelle."

Lydia couldn't respond. The sight of her daughter's SUV parked in a driveway beside a red Jaguar made her heart leap into her throat.

No, that couldn't be Meredith's, but another green vehicle the same make, the same model. Lydia slowed down and read the license plate number. It was Meredith's car, all right!

"Grammy?"

What on earth was she doing at Twin Lakes? She'd said she was going to meet a friend at the mall. Lydia remembered her daughter's reluctance to discuss her plans, her eagerness to leave. Obviously, Meredith didn't want her mother to know where she was going. Which meant she was here for a surreptitious reason. Lydia's worst fear was confirmed. Meredith was having an affair.

"Grammy, what's wrong? Why aren't you talking to me?"

"Nothing's wrong, honey," Lydia managed. "I'm sorry I wasn't paying attention. I just remembered something I have to take care of."

She drove slowly home and retrieved the doll, which she'd left on the hall table.

"Here you are, sweetie: Annabelle."

"Ooh, she's so pretty!"

Lydia was buckling her own seat belt when Greta called to her. She turned around and smiled at the sight of her granddaughter's outstretched arms. They shared an awkward but heartfelt hug.

"Thank you, Grammy. I love Annabelle already."

"I'm so glad." She shifted into reverse and backed out slowly, the warm feeling of child love spreading through her body.

Then she remembered. She turned right and drove slowly past the house on Lake Boulevard again. Meredith's SUV was still there. This time Lydia noted the number above the garage: 78. She'd look up 78 Lake Boulevard in the Twin Lakes telephone directory as soon as she came home.

Nine

Barbara was grinning like the Cheshire cat when Lydia got into her car to drive to the board meeting. "I've hot news."

"What is it?"

"My neighbor saw our boy, Marshall, with Viv Maguire in the diner this morning. She said they looked cozy—all giggles and grins."

"Viv Maguire? I remember she played mother hen to Claire that night she screamed at me."

"One and the same. She was Claire's best friend. I suppose, being a widow, she's been comforting Claire's grieving widower."

Lydia nodded, forcing herself to pay attention to what Barbara was saying instead of mulling about Meredith. "The next thing you'll tell me is she's loaded."

Barbara laughed. "Naturally. Viv's not much to look at, with those crooked teeth and dowager's hump. Not to mention her fifties glasses."

"Now, now," Lydia mock-scolded, "we can't all be

gorgeous like you."

"And you," Barbara returned, "though, if Marshall's after money and eye candy, I wonder why he's not hitting on you."

"Who says he isn't?" Lydia said archly, and felt a stab of satisfaction at Barbara's astonished expression.

"He's not really," she relented, "though last night he made it clear he didn't want bad blood between us." Lydia decided she would tell Barbara about Allison, but now wasn't the time. "He came over to thank me for my condolence note as he was leaving Peg's house."

"Peg DiMarco," Barbara mused. "Now there's a strange duck, even weirder than most of our fellow residents."

Lydia turned to study her expression in the light emitting from the fountain and the clubhouse. "Why do you say that? I mean, she's not exactly my type, but she's been a good neighbor."

Barbara shrugged. "I suppose because she's so unpredictable—friendly and helpful one day, distant and touchy the next. She was very kind to me after Robert died, then suddenly it was like she'd crossed me off her list. When I asked if I'd done something to offend her, she gave me this peculiar look and told me not to be silly, she was simply preoccupied with her own problems."

"You're right. She runs hot and cold. I thought she was angry with me for blowing the whistle on Weill."

"Could be she was. They're pretty good friends, always nattering away about stocks and bonds and investments."

"Good friends, eh? Not lovers?"

Barbara shook her head as they drove into the parking lot. "I don't get that feeling."

There went that theory.

"But maybe he and Viv are an item," Barbara said.

Lydia felt a rush of excitement as she realized Detective Sol Molina might find this bit of information relevant. She envisioned calling him, no doubt getting his tape, and leaving a message saying when she'd be home. Maybe he'd stop by. No, she told herself firmly. She would not use some third-hand observation and Barbara's speculations as a ruse to contact him.

They were about to get out of the car when Lydia asked, "Who's John Trevor?"

Barbara thought a minute. "He's a widower, about seventy-five. As round as Humpty Dumpty and a real chatterbox—not your type at all. He plays poker with Benny and George on Wednesday nights when he's here."

"Does he drive a red Jaguar?"

"I have no idea. We can ask Caroline. Why all the questions about John? I'm quite sure he's gone to Florida for the winter."

Lydia hesitated. She disliked discussing her children's personal lives with anyone, but she needed information. And Barbara, she knew, was discreet.

"Because my daughter had me leave work early and babysit so she could spend the afternoon at 78 Lake Boulevard, which is where John Trevor lives, and it scares the hell out of me."

Barbara's mouth fell open. "There must be some explanation."

"I'm sure, but whatever it is, I'm not going to like it."

Barbara nodded. "I gather you didn't ask Meredith when she came home."

"I was afraid to," Lydia admitted.

"I would be, too," was her friend's discomfiting remark.

Though the meeting wouldn't start for fifteen minutes, many residents had already arrived, filling the room with chatter and laughter. Barbara nudged Lydia.

"There's Marshall, sitting next to Peg."

Lydia smiled. "Does that mean he's given up on Viv?"

"Are you kidding? Peg's just a pal. Besides, she has no money. Viv's husband was CEO of a large corporation and left her sitting pretty. Oh, there's Caroline."

They made their way to where Caroline stood talking to a group of residents. She caught Barbara's gesture and joined them a minute later.

"Big crowd," she said, kissing them both on the cheek. "And no wonder. The walls are going to shake tonight."

Barbara grinned at Lydia. "Your first homeowners' meeting, right?"

Lydia nodded.

"Here's where everyone lets their hair down. Kind of like the bumper cars at a carnival." She turned to Caroline. "Lydia needs some information."

"Do you know who's staying at John Trevor's house and drives a red Jaguar?"

"That must be his nephew, Steve. A good-looking guy? Always wears sunglasses?"

Lydia's heart sank to her stomach. "I wouldn't know."

Caroline shot her a puzzled look and Barbara answered instead. "We'll explain later. Now tell us all you know about this Steve."

"Well, okay, though it's not much. He works for a pharmaceutical company and flies down from Boston every few weeks for business. Sometimes he stays in Manhattan. Other times he stays with John, who adores him. The son he never had."

"I wonder how they met," Lydia murmured.

"John and Steve?" Caroline asked. "I told you, they're related. Steve is John's sister's son."

A call to order saved Lydia from having to explain.

"Talk to you after the meeting," Barbara told Caroline, and led Lydia back to their seats.

Lydia glanced down at her copy of the agenda without seeing the words. Nor did she pay attention to the heated discussion about whether or not the HOA should purchase three more treadmills or one multi-purpose exercise machine. She was trying to swallow the idea that her older daughter—the daughter who had wanted a husband, children and home ever since she could speak—was putting everything in jeopardy for an affair with a good-looking man.

Where had she met him? The question, though inconsequential, plagued Lydia almost as much as the affair itself. Had they met at a local shop? The diner? The library? How long had it been going on? What would Jeff do when he found out? If he found out. What if Meredith wanted a divorce?

This last possibility caused her stomach to heave and sent her dashing off to the bathroom.

Lydia splashed cold water on her face and told herself not to rush to conclusions. It was possible that Meredith and this Steve were merely friends. Someone she could pour her heart out to. Lydia shook her head. She refused to be deliberately obtuse and pretend Meredith wasn't emotionally involved with this man, regardless of the extent of their physical relationship. The last few times she'd watched the girls, her daughter had returned home positively glowing.

Should she confront Merry? Tell her what she knew? Advise her to stop seeing her lover before it was too late? Before she destroyed the wonderful family she and Jeff had created? Impossible. Meredith would resent her interference. Bringing up the subject would only make matters worse. She could only hope and pray that Meredith would come to her senses and stop this affair before it got out of hand.

Lydia returned to the meeting room amid screaming and shouting.

"What's happening?" she asked Barbara.

"The board just announced a fifty dollar increase in our monthly payments."

"Really? I didn't see that on tonight's agenda."

"New business," Barbara said. "They didn't spell it out for us because they knew it would cause an even bigger hullabaloo."

Fifty dollars added to their $350 maintenance monthly fee was an annoyance, but no biggie, as far as Lydia was concerned. A new community might easily miscalculate the amount of money needed to cover all expenses. Most Twin Lakes residents could well afford the increase, which didn't mean they would accept it without a fight. A tall man in his sixties with the trim, fit build of a whippet raised his hand.

"Yes, Andrew?

"Our HOA monthly dues went up $25 in March, only eight months ago. At this rate, we'll be paying five, six hundred dollars a month in no time. And for what? Where exactly is this money going?"

Voices rose in agreement as George Linnett did his best to quiet everyone down. Then he said, "We've explained all that. The problem with both lakes not draining properly incurred a larger expense than expected. So is the cost of the property we're buying for a putting green, small clubhouse and miniature golf course."

Cries of "What do we need them for? Who needs that expense?" came from every corner of the room. Again, George had to quiet down the irate residents before he could speak.

"The land purchase is non-negotiable. The original HOA members voted to buy the property within five years if our original offering price went up no more than ten per cent. The owner died, and his sons have agreed to sell just under our limit. It's our misfortune that felling trees and leveling the land has risen quite a bit, as has construction. But we can manage it if we build a modest—and I mean modest—clubhouse."

Several hands shot into the air. George turned around to Roger Patterson, the treasurer. "Roger, you've been doing all the research. Would you do the honors and read off the costs?"

A woman stood and shouted, "I'm against spending all that money. This isn't a golfing community, though some try to force it down our throats. Why should we go ahead with these highfalutin' plans?"

George shook his head wearily. "Because they were voted on and passed."

"That's not fair!" the woman retorted. "I wasn't living here at the time so I didn't get the chance to vote against buying that piece of property. Besides, only the putting green was mentioned, not a miniature golf course, or a clubhouse."

Andrew stood up. Without waiting for George to call on him, he began to speak.

"Muriel has a point. The proxies regarding the miniature golf course and the clubhouse went out in February and were voted on in March. Many Twin Lakes residents are away those months and have their mail held so they never had a chance to express their views."

The rumble of angry agreement surged through the room. Lydia wondered if it would be terrible if she left right now. She'd heard about condo and homeowner association meetings—how they often turned into shouting matches where residents lost all social restraints and screamed out whatever came to mind—but she hadn't expected this!

A compact, wiry man, his shirt sleeves rolled up to his elbows, rose from his seat on the dais where the board members were seated.

"Perhaps I can explain the situation." His booming voice silenced all comments and asides. "The putting green, miniature golf course and small clubhouse were in the original plans for Twin Lakes. The builder was in the process of acquiring the lot when the owner, an elderly man close to ninety, withdrew it from the market. His two sons informed the builder they would sell the land to Twin Lakes once it was theirs. With this understanding, those of us who lived here the first year signed an agreement that we would have the amenities built within two years of acquiring the property.

"The owner died last winter, and the board was informed the HOA could buy the property no later than December of this year. We got estimates of costs, then sent a letter and a proxy to every resident asking if a. they were in favor of clearing and leveling the ground and only laying down the putting green immediately or b. agree that we'd have all three done ASAP, as this would prove cheaper in the long run. The majority approved doing it all. Therefore we break ground in the spring."

Marshall Weill stood. "Roger, I've no quarrel with the new additions, though I wasn't living here when all this was decided. I think they'll enhance our community and increase the value of our homes when any of us decides to sell. My question is how did the board go about choosing the contractors for the various projects?"

"The way we go about hiring any company—we get estimates from three or four companies of good reputation and choose the one that's reliable, does good work and charges a reasonable fee."

"That's very interesting," Marshall drawled as he leafed through some papers, "because I contacted three demo and excavating companies. All three gave me an estimated figure varying from eight to fifteen percent cheaper than the company you selected to level the house and grade the terrain. There was even a greater discrepancy among the landscaping and construction companies."

The room fell silent, all eyes on the two men. Roger Patterson nodded, to all appearances, unperturbed by Marshall Weill's accusation.

"No doubt you failed to factor in certain hidden costs. For example, the company we hired to clear and level the land will be filling in a small pond."

Marshall smiled, revealing the space between his two front teeth. "Trust me, I factored in everything, using the figures the board mailed out to homeowners. We're being overcharged every step along the way, and I'd like to know why."

Before Roger could reply, Doris Fein stood up.

"Marshall Weill, you have some nerve accusing the board of ripping us off when that's your specialty! I let you invest my savings and half my principal's gone." Her voice trembled. "How could you do that to me?"

The color drained from Marshall Weill's face, leaving it a chalky white. "My dear, Doris, I'm sorry your stocks went down, but I warned you they were volatile and bound to fluctuate. It's the state of today's market."

"So you say! I say you robbed me like you robbed those poor people in Chicago!" Tears streaming down her cheeks, Doris headed for the doorway.

"Doris, wait! The worst thing you can do is panic. In time those stocks will soar again. You'll have the big gain you're after." His voice turned shrill. "They're good stocks. I'd have my own mother buy them!"

Doris shook her head and exited the room. Marshall stared after her, stunned that she paid him no mind. He bent down to whisper something to Peg then set off after Doris. The other residents were exchanging glances when Roger spoke.

"To return to the matter at hand. Let me reassure you, the board made a careful study of costs and quality of work before choosing the companies we did. I saw photographs of their various projects, of golf courses and greens and small but utilitarian clubhouses that would suit our community's needs."

He droned on, spouting more details and figures, until a shout interrupted.

"Someone call an ambulance!"

Lydia and everyone else turned to Marshall Weill standing in the doorway.

"What happened?" voices asked.

"Doris fell down the pool steps." He shuddered. "I'm afraid she's dead."

Ten

After a moment of shocked silence, pandemonium broke out. Residents leaped up, intent on finding out if Doris was indeed dead. To Lydia's amazement, George Linnett whipped out a whistle from God knew where and blasted it three times.

"Everyone remain seated! We can't have a stampede."

His wife, Katherine, stood up. "George, I'm going to see to Doris. She may be dying this very minute for want of attention."

He made no pretense of debating the matter. "Good idea, Katherine. Go and help her if you can." He turned to Benny Lieberman. "Benny, call nine-one-one. Tell them we need an ambulance and the police."

"Roger's on the line with them now," Benny said.

Andrew Varig made his way to the exit. "She'll need a physician in any case."

Shaken by another death—this time that of someone she'd known and liked—Lydia stumbled to her feet. She'd help Doris if she could. And if Doris was beyond help, she intended to make sure the scene of death wasn't disturbed.

"Lydia, please stay here," George pleaded, but she ignored him and continued to squeeze past agitated residents to reach the aisle. Other people got up, ready to follow her example. George blew his whistle again and stopped them in their tracks.

"Please sit down," Lydia heard Roger address the crowd. "The police and an EMS crew will be here any minute."

Lydia followed Katherine and Andrew into the hall. The doctor pulled open the glass door leading to the indoor pool. Doris lay sprawled face down on the half-landing. Her neck was twisted in such a way that Lydia knew she was dead.

Katherine gasped. "The poor thing! Andrew, do you think she's...?"

"I'll check her pulse and see if she's breathing."

He started down the steps. Lydia followed after him. "I think it's best not to touch her," she said softly. "In case this was no accident."

"You mean, in case Weill pushed her?" Andrew let out a gruff laugh. "You have a point. Women around him are dying like flies."

Lydia nodded. "First his wife and now poor Doris. I visited her the other day. She gave me carrot cake and tea. Now she's dead."

"And I have the distinction of being the fool who brought Weill to Twin Lakes."

"Oh?" Her tone turned chilly. "You knew he'd gone to

prison for embezzlement and said nothing when he started investing HOA monies?"

Andrew's steely gray eyes bored into hers. "I knew nothing about the man. It was a casual encounter while playing golf at my friend's club. Weill was a guest there, too. He mentioned he was looking to move to this type of community and I told him where I lived." He sighed. "We get older and take people at face value. A mistake."

He crouched down next to Doris and gazed into her face. Then he reached for her outstretched wrist. He knelt closer to reach her chest to listen for a heartbeat. He shook his head and stood. "She's gone."

He glanced down at Doris one final time. "We'll leave her to the authorities."

"Is she dead?" Katherine asked as soon as they joined her on the main level.

"I'm afraid so." Andrew's voice was gentle.

Katherine sniffed and blew her nose. "Doris was terribly upset this past week. She said her investments were taking a nose dive. She was afraid she'd have to sell her house and move in with her daughter, something she dreaded."

Andrew rested a hand on her shoulder. "Doris was in a state of agitation. There's the possibility she tripped and fell down the steps."

Katherine's sorrow turned to fury. "Running away from Marshall! Any way you look at it, he caused her death. Doris never would have bought those risky stocks if he hadn't convinced her they'd practically double her income. Doris, being so desperate, believed him."

Andrew narrowed his eyes. "The man has caused more trouble than he's worth. Maybe one of these days someone will close his eyes for good."

~ * ~

"So, have you arrested Marshall Weill for killing Doris Fein?" Lydia asked. It was Wednesday afternoon, and once again Detective Sol Molina sat at her kitchen table discussing a dead woman.

He let out a hearty chuckle. "Get right to the point—don't you?—when I've come to ask you questions."

Lydia smiled. "This is my day off. Now that I'm working again, every minute counts."

"Can't give it up, can you?" he teased.

"I enjoy it. Besides, it's safer at Carrington House," she quipped back. "More coffee?"

"Sure, thanks."

Lydia reached for his mug. She felt his eyes—hazel at present—follow her as she walked the few feet to the coffee maker on the counter. She was glad she was wearing a trim baby blue sweater and black jeans that flattered her figure.

He added milk from her small Italian creamer and drank. "Ah, great coffee. A welcome change from the vile stuff down at the station."

"I'm beginning to think that's why you come around."

"One of the reasons," he said. Lydia blushed.

"As for Weill, we haven't charged him because we've no evidence or witnesses who claimed he killed Doris

Fein. We're not even certain Doris Fein's death was a homicide. Believe me, the county crime lab's hard at work."

"What kind of evidence are they looking for?"

"For one thing, they can determine if she suffered a stroke or a coronary at the time of death. Unfortunately, this will take a while. Probably a week."

"It sure looked to me like her neck was broken."

"The break might have been the result of her fall."

"Did she fall or was she pushed?" Lydia murmured.

"I don't know," Sol Molina acknowledged, "but Weill swears up and down he never touched her because he never caught up with her."

"How did he explain the fact that Doris fell down the steps leading to the indoor pool?"

"He assumed she ran there because she was determined not to talk to him. He claims he reached the glass door as Mrs. Fein tumbled down the steps."

Lydia sipped her coffee and considered. "As Dr. Varig pointed out, the women around Marshall Weill are dying like flies."

"How soon after Doris Fein left the meeting did Weill follow her out in the hall?"

This was an important question. Lydia closed her eyes and thought back to the meeting.

"He stood by his seat and watched her leave. She wasn't gone half a minute when he started after her."

"How long was he gone?"

"About five minutes."

The detective nodded. "That seems to be the general consensus. Could anyone else have come into the hall before you, Mrs. Linnett and Dr. Varig went to check on Mrs. Fein?"

"I didn't see anyone. I suppose the girl at the desk last night could tell you."

Sol Molina's barely perceptible nod let her know he'd already interviewed the receptionist.

"Did the three of you leave the meeting together?"

"Yes."

"How did that come about?"

Lydia told him, thinking Detective Sol Molina had a very slick way of finding out exactly what he wanted to know. Well, she had one or two surprises of her own.

"Did you know Marshall Weill came to Twin Lakes through Andrew Varig?"

"No, but I expect you'll tell me about it."

This wasn't the reaction she'd hoped for, but she told him what Andrew had said just before he examined Doris. "He made a comment that maybe someday someone would close Weill's eyes for good. I got the feeling he held a grudge against Mr. Popularity, though it could be because he feels responsible for bringing him to Twin Lakes. Everyone here is loaded with secrets."

"It's the story in every case," Sol said.

"And I was no exception," Lydia murmured, aware that she still hadn't told Barbara and Caroline about Allison."

"Poor, Lydia. This can't be easy for you."

"I've had to face the reality of Allison's life," she said,

doing her best to ignore the rush of warmth spilling over her because he'd used her first name. "Marshall Weill is scum. He took advantage of Allison, and he stole from her."

She breathed deeply. "The truth is, Allison was fragile and reckless—a deadly combination. I think it was only a matter of time before something or someone pulled her down to the depths of despair where she couldn't cope. I don't hold him responsible for Allison's suicide any longer."

Sol stood and rested a hand on her shoulder. "I admire you, Lydia Krause. For daring to face issues people run from all their lives."

"Thank you." She reached up and covered his hand with hers. After a moment, she shook her head as though coming out of a daze and rose to her feet.

"I have a doctor's appointment in half an hour." Then she remembered why he'd come. "Aren't you going to ask me more questions?"

"Nope, but if you remember something from last night, if anything occurs to you, please let me know. You still have my numbers?"

"Yes, I do." At the front door, she said, "Have a good Thanksgiving," though it was two weeks away.

"Thanks. You too."

"I will. I'm going to my daughter's house. Where are you going?"

"To my brother's. My daughter, Heather, will be spending the long weekend with me."

She smiled as she watched him walk to his car and wished she could call him back to offer another nugget of information. But there was nothing more she knew.

~ * ~

Marshall Weill and the deaths of his wife and Doris Fein were all Twin Lakes residents could talk about for the next several days. The fact that two women had died suddenly was a blight on their community. The cause of it all, most residents agreed, was a man who had joined them under false pretenses. A convicted felon who had broken the law yet again by investing HOA monies and doling out financial advice, which resulted in dire consequences.

Sunday morning after swimming laps, Lydia climbed the stairs to find several residents heatedly discussing a letter Andrew Varig had posted on the bulletin board. She edged her way through the crowd to read what Andrew had written. In very strong language, he stated his view that, for the safety and well-being of the community, Marshall Weill should leave Twin Lakes until the police discovered who had murdered Claire Weill and Doris Fein.

"They can't do that!" Despite her dislike for the man, Lydia found herself outraged on Weill's behalf. She knew first-hand the awful feeling of being a murder suspect. The police had found no evidence that Weill had killed either woman.

The white-haired, pot-bellied man next to her growled, "Andrew's right. We have to protect our womenfolk. Who knows? If you're not careful, you might be next."

Lydia glared at him and went home.

Caroline called a few hours later to say the board members were receiving phone calls demanding they do something about the dangerous ex-con left free to roam Twin Lakes. She finished by saying, "You'd think they'd have enough sense to know the board has no power to order Marshall to leave his home."

"They're frightened," Lydia said, "and turning to the only authority we have to protect them."

"Well, the board can't ban Marshall from Twin Lakes," Caroline said. After a moment, she asked, "Do you think he killed Claire and Doris?"

"The man has the morals of an alley cat. But as for killing them? I wish I knew."

Lydia hung up and spent the next few hours wondering, like many of her neighbors, if Marshall had killed the two women. And if he hadn't, who did?

Tuesday morning, Lydia took full advantage of her day off—a day free of work and babysitting—to do as she liked. She practiced yoga for an hour and a half instead of going for her regular swim. As she stepped out of the shower, she heard someone knocking at the front door. She slipped into her terrycloth robe and wrapped a towel around her head, wondering who it might be. Barbara or Caroline? Peg? Or—her heart beat faster—Sol Molina! She peered through the glass panel and unlocked the door.

"Hello, Marshall. What can I do for you?"

"Good morning, Lydia. Sorry I caught you at a bad time."

The near-arrogant grin was in place, but the eyes were bloodshot, the lids puffy. For the first time since she'd met him, Marshall Weill looked his age.

"Yes, it is a bad time," she answered coldly.

"Lydia, I need to speak to you. Please."

She thought quickly. No doubt he meant to come inside, but she didn't want the likes of him in her home. "Fine. I'll meet you in the diner in an hour."

"I'd be happy to drive you there."

"As I said, I'll meet you."

He gave her a sad smile. "You needn't be afraid of going in the car with me."

When she said nothing, he said, "Would you mind meeting instead at the coffee shop in the strip mall on Hensen Street? I know it's a hole in the wall, but I need to speak to you in private."

"All right. I know where it is."

She watched him drive off, then went upstairs to get dressed. Her hands trembled from both excitement and apprehension as she did up the buttons of her blouse. She was about to learn vital information regarding Marshall and the two dead women!

She gasped as it occurred to her that she might very well be the next victim. How ridiculous! she scolded herself. Marshall had no intention of harming her, certainly not in broad daylight. Still, to be on the safe side, she telephoned Barbara and left a message on her tape saying where she was going and why. She called Caroline and left the same message. If anything happened, Weill would be implicated and held accountable.

He sat waiting for her in the back booth of the dark, dingy coffee shop. He waved as she walked toward him and thrust back his shoulders. Though he sat erect, his face seemed to sag, weighed down by the events of the past few weeks. He gave her a wan smile.

"Thanks for coming, Lydia. I need to speak to you."

"Why, Marshall? We're hardly acquaintances, much less friends."

"True, but I know you well enough to recognize you're both intelligent and fair-minded."

She slid into the seat opposite him, unwilling to let on that his compliment filled her with a warm, rosy feeling.

He leaned forward, pressing his palms into the peeling Formica table top. "I did not kill my wife, and I had nothing to do with Doris Fein's death. I swear it!"

The intensity of his denial struck a nerve, urging her to believe he was telling the truth, but she refused to make a decision regarding his guilt based solely on emotions.

"Why are you telling me this? The police haven't accused you of murder."

"Not yet, they haven't. Which doesn't mean they're not looking for something—anything!— connecting me to the deaths. Only there's nothing to find."

"Then why worry?"

A waitress appeared and took Lydia's order of coffee and a donut. When she left, Marshall Weill continued.

"It's very unpleasant being Suspect Number One in everyone's eyes. I'm appalled by what's happening in our little community. People are stupid enough to lump the two deaths together. They treat me like a pariah. Some actually want me to leave Twin Lakes, and I've no intention of doing that."

Lydia nodded, recalling Andrew's letter posted on the bulletin board. "I sympathize, but if you're innocent as you claim, there's little they can do."

Marshall shook his head, a slight smile on his lips. "Lydia, don't act naive. It doesn't suit you. Claire and I went to great lengths to find our Utopia. I love Twin Lakes and want to continue living here, only I can't under a cloud of suspicion. I intend to regain my good name." He winked. "Or what remains of it. I hope, given your part in all that's happened, you'll help prove I didn't kill Claire or Doris."

She flinched at the guilt he'd flung at her, and replied defensively, "I don't see what I can do."

"Peg tells me you have the ear of Detective Molina."

"Peg's a busybody!"

He ignored her outburst of vexation. "Use your female wiles to find out what the police know. Keep your eyes and ears open for what they're missing. You're good with people. You ran a company. I have faith in your investigative skills."

"But I'm not a detective!" she protested. "And Lieutenant Molina tells me very little about the case."

His hand rested on her forearm. She shrugged it away, but he seemed not to notice that he'd put it there in the first place. Instead, he hunched over the table and lowered his voice to a confiding tone.

"Something weird has turned up. The crime lab found a powerful substance in Claire's bloodstream. As I told Molina, I've no idea what it is or how Claire got hold of it."

Lydia nodded. The toxicology report had included this information because of her input in the case. "Your wife was taking an herbal supplement in capsule form."

Weill's eyes gleamed. "How do you know? Where did she get these capsules?"

"I don't know where she got them, but Doris told me Claire took them to look and feel younger. She wanted to regain your attention."

"Oh, my God!" He buried his face in his hands. "Claire darling, I'll find out who did this to you!" When he looked up, Lydia saw tears in his eyes. Marshall Weill was grieving for his wife.

He cleared his throat and shifted back to his clever, man-of-the-world persona. "When did Doris tell you about these capsules?"

"A few days after Claire died."

"And now Doris is dead." Marshall's voice rose with excitement. "See the connection? Someone killed them both because of those damn pills."

"That's ridiculous. Doris fell down..."

"Whom did you tell—what Doris said about the capsules?" he asked urgently.

"Let me think. Detective Molina, Barbara and Caroline. Why?"

"Because I bet the capsules are dangerous and illegal. Which accounts for why Claire told no one else about them, including her best friend. For some reason Doris knew, word got out that she knew, and the drug supplier killed them."

Appalled, Lydia stared at him. His logic was as screwy as a Marx Brothers film. "You can't believe those capsules have anything to do with Claire's death. She was run down by a car. My car."

"Why? By whom? I've just told you the only theory that makes any sense. Please, Lydia, help me find the person who killed my Claire. Talk to the other residents. See what you can find out. They all think I'm guilty and turn away when I go into the clubhouse."

Though she didn't agree with his theory, she wanted to find Claire's murderer almost as much as he did. "All right," she said. "I'll do what I can, though I can't promise any results."

He grasped her hands in his. "Thank you, Lydia! I am eternally grateful."

She pulled her hands free. "I've one question, Marshall. Did you activate the pool cover when I was swimming laps the Wednesday after Claire died?"

His eyes widened. "Of course I didn't! You have to believe me."

Oddly enough, she did.

Eleven

Though Thanksgiving Day started out gray and gloomy, the sun made an appearance around noon. Lydia hardly noticed; she was too busy preparing a sweet potato casserole and three different desserts. It would be only the five of them for dinner, since Abbie and Todd were spending the day with his relatives in Connecticut, though Meredith had invited friends to join them for dessert.

At two-thirty she set out for Merry and Jeff's house. Brittany opened the door for her, and Lydia was assailed by the delicious aroma of roast turkey.

"I helped Mommy make the stuffing," she announced.

"She sure did," Jeff said. He kissed Lydia's cheek, then relieved her of the two shopping bags filled with food. He peeled back the tinfoil of one cake. "Mmm, looks yummy. I can't wait to dig my fork into everything." He strode toward the kitchen. "I'll put these away. Sit down and relax in the den."

Lydia ignored his suggestion and followed him into the large kitchen. Her daughter was cutting up salad amid a counter piled high with various foods and cooking utensils.

"Hi, sweetie. Anything I can do to help?"

Meredith turned, her face strained with tension. "Hi, Mom. You can finish the salad while I clear off some space to get to the appetizers and soup."

"Appetizers and soup?" Lydia wondered aloud. "You certainly have gone whole hog."

"It's Thanksgiving, isn't it? I want to set family traditions the girls will look back on and remember."

Lydia gritted her teeth, remembering that she, Izzy, and the girls had often eaten Thanksgiving dinner in restaurants.

The puff-pastry appetizers, squash consommé, turkey and accompanying vegetables were well-prepared and tasty. Lydia complimented her daughter, hoping to bring a smile to her lips, but Meredith remained tense. Once she snapped at Brittany for acting silly. The child's face reddened as she reached for Lydia's hand.

As for Jeff, Meredith rarely spoke to him except to give directives. At one point, he paused behind her chair on his way to cutting up more turkey in the kitchen.

"Relax, Merry," he joked, "this is supposed to be a fun day, remember?" He massaged the nape of her neck. She leaned back, relishing the comfort he offered, then, as though suddenly remembering something, she jerked forward. Jeff seemed puzzled as he headed for the kitchen.

Meredith's mood lifted as soon as everyone finished the main course. She turned talkative, almost hyper, Lydia thought, as she helped her daughter clear the table. Maybe she was simply relieved that the meal was over and everyone had eaten well.

In the kitchen, Lydia started putting leftovers into plastic containers.

"I'll call my friends and tell them to come for coffee in half an hour," Merry said. "Be back in a jiffy."

She dashed upstairs, leaving Lydia to wonder why she hadn't made her calls from the kitchen. She probably needs a few moments to herself, Lydia decided, and continued with her task.

Lydia was stacking the dishwasher when her daughter reappeared, a broad smile on her face. She'd freshened up her lipstick and eye shadow.

"Everyone will be over in half an hour." She kissed her mother's cheek. "Thanks, Mom. I didn't mean to leave all the scut work for you. I'll finish up. Go relax in the den with Jeff and the girls."

"Shall I set the table for coffee and dessert?"

"No, I'll take care of that. You've done enough."

Pleased to see her daughter in good spirits, Lydia followed the sounds of a football game. Jeff was comfortably ensconced in his recliner watching the game while the girls played with their dolls on the sofa. They made room for her to sit and included her in their conversation. Impulsively, Lydia hugged Brittany and then Greta. Meredith had a wonderful family and a wonderful life. She'd be a fool to put everything in jeopardy for the sake of a little excitement.

Lydia leaned back against the sofa's cushions and basked in a wave of contentment. Moving to Twin Lakes hadn't been a mistake, after all. She adored having a close relationship with her granddaughters, and looked forward to years of their company as they grew and developed into young women. If Meredith wanted to return to work early and asked her to babysit, she'd rearrange her work hours and watch them for as long as she could.

She was almost sorry when the doorbell rang, announcing that visitors had arrived. The girls stopped what they were doing and flew to the door. Jeff followed after them. Lydia brought up the rear and joined the now crowded center hall as Merry's family greeted the child and couple who had arrived.

"Mom, this is Cerilla and Jim," Meredith said."

Lydia greeted the couple she'd chatted with at Brittany's soccer game.

"This is Mandy," Brittany said, bringing the blonde little girl, a replica of her mother, over to meet her.

"Hi, Mandy," Lydia said. "I'm Greta and Brittany's grandma."

"Nice to meet you. My real name is Amanda," Mandy offered.

Before Lydia could respond, the doorbell rang again and a young woman and two children entered the house. To give them enough space to take off their jackets, the party spilled into the living room. Jeff made the introductions.

"Jen, Timmy and Cassandra, meet my mother-in-law, Mrs. Krause."

Lydia smiled and exchanged greetings with the mother over the heads of the five excited children, all talking at the same time. The children raced up the staircase and their parents moved into the dining room.

Meredith was assigning seats when the bell rang a third time. She stopped in midsentence. "I'll get that!" she announced.

"I'll go," Lydia offered, since she was closest to the door.

"That's all right, Mom," Meredith said, edging around the table.

But Lydia was already in motion. She opened the front door and stared openly at the handsome young man facing her. He had a square-shaped face, wavy black hair, and a winning smile. God, he was gorgeous! He wore no outer jacket, but a blue and gray tweed blazer and a pale gray shirt open at the neck.

"Hello," he said in an even, modulated voice. "Is this the home of Merry and Jeff Rothman?"

Lydia nodded, and stepped back to let him enter. She nearly tripped over her daughter, as Merry rushed forward to take the man's outstretched hand, which she clasped between both of hers.

"I'm glad you found the house."

"Your directions were perfect."

Their eyes locked with an intensity that blocked out everything else. Lydia grew alarmed. What if Jeff or any of their guests were to notice? She cleared her throat and placed a hand on each of their shoulders.

"Meredith, dear, aren't you going to introduce me to your friend?"

Meredith blinked as if she were emerging from a darkened theatre. "Of course. Mom, this is Steve Thiergard. Steve, my mother, Lydia Krause." She gave a little laugh. "Actually, the two of you are neighbors, in a way."

~ * ~

Lydia sat before her untouched cup of coffee and marveled at the way her daughter and Steve Thiergard performed like veteran actors in front of the others. Merry had introduced him as an old college friend she'd run into a few months ago. For all she knew, that part could be absolutely true, though she didn't remember Meredith ever mentioning having met up with an old friend from Lehigh. No one, least of all Jeff, found his presence unusual. The other adults greeted him, then turned to each other, eager to catch up on news about their children and neighborhood gossip. Was she the only person who saw the sparks flying between them?

How dare Meredith bring this man into her home! How dare Steve Thiergard invade another man's inner sanctum and openly devour his wife with hungry eyes!

Lydia was about to claim a headache and make excuses for an early departure when Steve, who had already said he was a pharmaceutical rep, mentioned that his territory was being changed to the Island and he was considering buying a townhouse nearby. Lydia's heart raced as she considered all this implied. Was her daughter's marriage in serious trouble? She'd have a talk with Meredith very soon, and this time she'd give her a piece of her mind. But right now she needed to listen and ask questions to learn as much as possible.

Steve proved to be an entertaining guest. He participated intelligently in the conversation, turning frequently to Jen on his right for her opinion, which she was more than happy to express. The subject turned to medicine then to herbal supplements. Cerilla said she was a great believer in natural supplements and asked what Steve's take on them was, given that he dealt with lab-made medicines.

The endearing smile Steve bestowed upon Cerilla made Lydia wonder if she'd imagined the connection between him and Meredith earlier—until she realized that his passion was for his subject and not her daughter's intense friend.

"You've just touched on the subject closest to my heart. I believe the right supplements add longevity and health to the average person's life."

Jen nodded vigorously. "I agree. Even doctors are recommending them now. Everyone knows all women should take calcium."

"I take CoQ 10 on my doctor's recommendation," Cerilla added.

"Glucosamine chondroitin has worked wonders for my arthritic pain," Lydia chimed in.

"Sure, those are all great," Jim said, "but others are downright dangerous. How many people died after taking ephedra? I think it's a damn good thing the FDA finally stepped in to regulate the industry."

"You think so, eh?" Steve asked.

"Sure," Jeff chimed in. "People are too quick to try anything that promises eternal youth and vitality."

"Well, I have news for you," Steve answered belligerently. "The FDA doesn't know its ass from its elbow when it comes to natural supplements. Sometimes they're heavy-handed and ban a substance that works miracles when taken in small doses."

"You mean like arsenic or belladonna?" Meredith said.

"Everything in moderation," Jim joked.

Steve wasn't amused. "Supplements can do amazing things—like reversing the aging process."

"Oh, sure," Cerilla scoffed. "Monkey glands. The Fountain of Youth. Through the ages, man has tried to preserve youth, only nothing works."

"Really? What if I told you certain botanical herbs combined together are the real McCoy?" His eyes went to Lydia. "What if I told you Mrs. Krause would look as young as her daughter after taking this formula for six months?"

Silence reigned as everyone considered Steve's words. Lydia stared at him, trying to remember what Doris had told her about Claire's miracle compound. Had she stumbled upon the person who'd sold her the capsules, here in her daughter's home? It was possible. Very possible. Steve Thiergard stayed at Twin Lakes several days at a time.

She felt her son-in-law squeeze her shoulder as he spoke. "I, for one, think Lydia's perfect as she is."

"But what about the dangers?" Cerilla demanded. "There have to be side-effects. There are side-effects to every drug."

"Potential side-effects, yes, but we haven't seen any."

"Do you actually sell this stuff?" Jen asked.

"Not yet," Steve replied. "It's still in the testing stage."

Lydia wasn't prepared to call him a liar. After all, she had no proof that Steve Thiergard had sold the capsules to Claire, though it certainly looked that way. Instead she said, "I take it the company you work for will manufacture this wonder drug."

Steve cleared his throat. "My friend's company is working on this product and I've been helping him out. As for my paying job, I sell meds related to gastrointestinal problems."

He went on to extol the wonderful pharmaceutical products his company had on the market. Lydia decided bringing the conversation back to the herbal compound might raise his suspicions if he was Claire's supplier and if he had anything to do with her murder. Instead, she stood and began her good-byes. Jeff stood, too. "I'll get your coat," he offered.

"Thank you, Jeff, but Meredith can get it for me," she said in her best CEO tone.

Startled, Merry followed her into the hall where she retrieved Lydia's good wool coat from the hall closet.

"Thank you." Lydia put on her coat then kissed her

daughter's cheek. "Dinner was terrific."

"And your sweet potato pie and cakes were great. I'll speak to you soon."

Merry turned, eager to return to her guests when Lydia put a hand on her arm.

"Let's have brunch together on Sunday. Just you and me. I'm sure Jeff will be home then to watch the girls."

Meredith opened her mouth to dispute this high-handed arrangement, but one glance at her mother's expression changed her mind.

"Good," Lydia said. "Why don't I come for you at eleven? There's a restaurant not far from here I've been wanting to try. I'll see myself out after I say good-bye to the girls."

Home again, Lydia fed a hungry Reggie, then changed into jeans and an old sweater. She should call Sol Molina about Steve Thiergard, but too many strings held her back. She didn't want to disturb his family dinner with his daughter. Even more important, she resisted offering information connected to her daughter. Not that Meredith had anything to do with Steve's wonder capsule. It was the affair itself that kept her hand from dialing.

Peg called to see how her Thanksgiving dinner had gone. She'd eaten out in a lovely restaurant with a few single women friends. Then she mentioned that Marshall was very appreciative that Lydia was looking into Claire's death.

"Why did you tell him I had Lieutenant Molina's ear?" Lydia asked, finally venting her annoyance.

"Sorry, but Marshall was distraught, and that was all I could think of to make him feel better." When Lydia said nothing, Peg demanded, "Tell me! Have you learned something?"

"Possibly."

"Really? What?"

Lydia frowned. Her neighbor was the biggest yenta in Twin Lakes. Lydia never should have alluded to knowing anything in the first place. Besides, the only information she had involved herbal capsules, and they might have nothing to do with either death.

"Sorry, Peg, I'm not free to discuss it with you."

"Have you told Detective Molina?"

"I will, once I have proof."

She was beginning to sound like an addled fool. Having Merry so close to the person who might be involved somehow with Claire's death had upset her.

"I have to go now. See you, Peg."

Peg grumbled about Lydia not finishing what she'd started to say and hung up.

~ * ~

Saturday morning Lydia caught an early train into Manhattan. The cars were filled with riders off from work and school, intent on getting a head start on their holiday gift-buying. Not one of them, Lydia mused, had any connection with Twin Lakes, where two women had died and suspicions ran rampant.

She browsed in Lord & Taylor and Saks, buying cashmere sweater sets on sale—Chanukah gifts for

Meredith and Abbie. She tried on stretch jeans and tops and bought three of each, as well as two warmup suits. Her lifestyle was casual now. She had little use for the suits and silk blouses she used to wear to the office. Even now, on a visit to the city, she wore pants and a woolen poncho over a turtleneck sweater.

Today Abbie was the first to arrive at the restaurant, the same one where they'd dined weeks earlier. She and Todd sat close to one another, heads touching as they laughed over a private joke. The sight filled Lydia with joy and sadness. She was delighted her daughter had found someone to love, but the young lovers were a keen reminder of all she'd lost when Izzy died.

Abbie saw her. Todd immediately rose to his feet as Lydia went to join them.

"Hi, Mom," Abbie greeted her. She leaned over the table to kiss her. "This is Todd."

Lydia started to put out her hand, but Todd came around and gathered her in a bear hug. "I'm so pleased to finally meet you, Mrs. Krause."

"I'm happy to meet you, too, Todd," she answered, meaning it.

Abbie was grinning. "Surprise! Todd has none of the British reserve you hear so much about. It must be his Jewish roots."

So he was Jewish—her daughter's first Jewish boyfriend since she'd turned sixteen. Todd was compactly built and only inches taller than Abbie. He had brown hair and eyes, and good, even features that gave him a boyish look. In fact, he appeared to be eighteen years old. But after five minutes in his company, Lydia saw he was a sound and savvy young man who knew what he wanted in life and how to pursue it. Lydia quivered because it was clear he wanted Abbie.

"I understand you've moved into a new community and you've taken a new job," Todd said.

Lydia smiled. She found his accent delightful. "I'm doing my best to settle in." She glanced down at her packages. "Each time I come into the city I spend a fortune on furniture or clothing."

"If you'd rather stay home, you can order anything you like online," he said.

"I know that," Lydia said, grinning, "but I much prefer old-fashioned shopping."

Abbie laughed and rubbed the nape of Todd's neck. "Todd's permanently connected to the web. His machine runs on his blood instead of electricity."

"Computers—serving businesses, actually—are my livelihood and my passion." He winked at Abbie. "My only passion besides Abigail."

A man who speaks his mind and his heart, Lydia thought, warming to him even more.

"Any news about the two murders?" Abbie asked.

"Nothing really," Lydia said, "though Marshall Weill swears he had nothing to do with either of them."

"That's precisely what he would say if he killed them," Abbie said. "Be careful, Mom. There's a murderer wandering around that gated community of yours."

"Of course I'm careful, honey," Lydia reassured her.

Their waitress approached and they turned their attention to the menu.

After they ordered, Abbie asked, "Was Merry pissed because we didn't come to Thanksgiving dinner?"

"I don't think so. She didn't say anything to me," Lydia answered, thinking Meredith had other things on her mind.

"Well, that's good," Abbie said. "I hate when she projects her hurt feelings long distance. I wanted you and Todd to meet first, before making him face the rest of the family."

"You make your sister and her family sound like monsters," Lydia joked, though after the shock of meeting Steve Thiergard, she was glad Abbie and Todd had decided to visit his relatives instead of coming to Long Island.

"I'd be happy to meet them," Todd offered, "but we're very close to my cousins, and they invited us to Thanksgiving Day dinner last month."

"Oh," Lydia said. Things were more serious between her daughter and this young man than she'd thought.

She asked Todd what he was doing in Manhattan and he explained that he was here to make contacts for his computer company, which was something like Google but different in many ways.

"There's every kind of information on the web, available to everyone—if they know how to access the right sites. My job is to gather and facilitate the flow of information for businesses who hire our company. It's as simple as that."

"There's a lot about everyone on the internet," Abbie told her. "Even about you, Mom."

"Me?" Lydia asked, surprised.

"There are pages and pages about Lydia Krause. Articles about the company, articles you've written."

"Interesting," Lydia said. "I never realized."

"Everything ends up on the web," Todd said. "Check out Google and see for yourself."

"Maybe I will." Maybe she'd google Steve Thiergard and discover something really reprehensible about him, bad enough to persuade Merry to end their affair. Not very likely, she told herself.

Their food arrived and they chatted as they ate. When they were done, the waitress removed their plates and asked about dessert.

Lydia shook her head. "I'll just have more coffee."

"Please try the chocolate cake, even if you take but one bite," Todd said. He winked at the waitress. "It's the best in the city. I'm going to miss it when we leave."

"And we'll miss you guys," the waitress answered. She turned to Lydia. "The cake is very good. I'd say it's our most popular dessert."

Lydia didn't hear her. Her mind was four sentences behind as she turned to Abbie. "You're leaving? I thought you planned to stay in New York for several more months."

"Mom." Abbie stroked her mother's arm. "Share a

piece of chocolate cake with me, okay?"

Obediently, Lydia nodded.

"I'll have the raspberry custard tart," Todd said, "and refills of coffee and decaf all around."

When the waitress left, Lydia stared at Abbie. "Do you mind telling me what's going on?"

She hadn't meant to sound confrontational, but was only half sorry when Abbie flinched and Todd's arm went around her shoulders.

"We're getting married," Abbie said. "The first Saturday in January. The wedding's at Todd's cousins' house in Connecticut."

"Abbie!"

Joy, pain, relief and jealousy commingled and sparred for dominance in Lydia's heart. Why was Abbie telling her this now, after having made all her wedding plans? It wasn't like they were eloping. They were getting married in Todd's relatives' home.

She mustn't criticize or reprimand or question. Abbie had always taken her own path. Lydia forced a smile. "That's wonderful, dear! Though everything seems so sudden."

Abbie got up and put her arms around Lydia. Lydia sniffled and did her best not to burst into tears. Honestly! Her daughters were sending her emotions on a roller coaster ride.

"I didn't mean to spring it on you so suddenly," Abbie said, "but Todd just found out he has to return to England on January tenth, and we want to go there as a married couple. We decided to have the ceremony in the rabbi's study, then yesterday Karen—Todd's cousin—offered her house. I accepted since I didn't think you were up to making a wedding." Now she was sniffing. "Mom, I'm sorry if I've upset you."

Lydia blinked and tried to smile. "I am happy for you, Abbie. For you and Todd. It just takes some getting used to."

"We wanted to tell you first," Abbie said. "I'll call Merry Sunday night—I promise—and fill her in."

"After the wedding you'll leave for England," Lydia said, remembering the upsetting part of Abbie's news.

"We have to," Todd said quietly. "I've gotten a promotion, and they need me back in the main office before the other chap leaves. But you'll come and visit us, Mrs. Krause, just as soon and as often as you like."

Lydia nodded. She both liked and admired this young man who knew his priorities, and made no secret that they would shape his life.

"Thanks for the open invitation, Todd. I certainly will come and visit. And please call me Lydia."

"I'll do so with pleasure," he said, and stood to hug her.

Their care and concern made Lydia feel as though they were consoling her when she should be happy for them. She *was* happy for them, only everything had come as a surprise. They'd made their plans and she had no part in the planning.

She grew calmer once their desserts arrived and the

conversation turned to wedding arrangements. When it was time to go, Todd insisted on paying the bill. Abbie and Todd waited with her outside the restaurant for the taxi they'd called to take her to Penn Station.

It arrived too soon. Lydia clung to Abbie for a long good-bye. *They'll be happy,* she thought as she kissed them both. But once the cab started uptown, all reserve broke down.

"Oh, Izzy, how I'm going to miss her," Lydia whispered, and sobbed all the way to the station.

Twelve

When she got home, Lydia stifled her impulse to call Meredith to discuss Abbie's news and dialed her sister's number instead. Sammy was home, deep in her work. She was delighted to hear that Abbie was getting married.

"He's nice, doing well and Jewish! You must be thrilled."

"Of course I'm happy for her. I just wish she would let me host the wedding instead of having it at Todd's cousins' house."

"You said Todd lived with these cousins for three years, so they're really very close. Abbie probably figures you have enough to cope with these days. She doesn't want to burden you."

"I'm going to miss her, living far away in London," Lydia moaned.

"You never made a fuss when she took off for India or China months at a time."

"This is different. She's getting married. Soon she'll have children."

Sammy chuckled. "All the more reason to get on a plane and stay a month or two. How's Meredith?"

"Meredith?" Lydia's distress over Abbie's departure turned into a hot ball of anger at the mention of her older daughter's name. "She's carrying on an affair with a fellow whose uncle lives here at Twin Lakes. She had the absolute chutzpah to invite him over for dessert on Thursday, along with some friends."

Sammy let out a bark of laughter that sounded dangerously like admiration to Lydia's ears.

"It isn't funny! Think of Greta and Brittany. And poor Jeff, who adores my selfish daughter. I've decided to stop tiptoeing around her moods and give her a piece of my mind!"

"Do you think she'll listen to you?"

Lydia considered the question. "I don't know," she finally admitted. "My life has lost its continuity. Everything familiar is changing, spinning out of control. I wish Izzy were here."

"To share the experience," Sammy said softly, "not to change the course of your daughters' lives."

Lydia sighed. "I suppose. Thanks for listening, Sam."

"Hey, that's what sisters are for."

~*~

Saturday morning Lydia rose with the sun. She'd spent a restless night, then fallen into a deep sleep and dreamed she was a guest at a wedding in a foreign country and the rabbi was Marshall Weill. Though she felt strung out and tired, she decided a vigorous walk followed by a swim would do more for her than trying for two more hours of slumber. She dressed quickly, promising herself she wouldn't mull about her daughters. Abbie was going to be fine and Meredith—well, she'd deal with Meredith tomorrow.

She turned left, taking the longer route around the lake. As she reached the juncture where N Boulevard met Lake Boulevard, she remembered that beyond the woods lay the parcel of property the HOA was in the process of buying. The new additions they planned to build would be a plus to the community. Though Lydia didn't enjoy golf, she looked forward to playing on the miniature golf course with her granddaughters.

Impulsively, she forged a path through bushes and trees to peer through a crack in the stockade fence at the house that, come spring, would be razed to the ground. The siding was weatherbeaten, almost colorless from neglect, and a few shutters hung askew. The last owner had lived there until well into his nineties and had allowed the house to fall into disrepair. Still, it was sad that what had once been the home of various families for almost a century would soon to be destroyed.

Lydia resumed her walk down Lake Boulevard, greeting the few dog walkers she passed. She felt as though she'd come home after being away for some time. Her concerns about her daughters these last two days had pushed the tragic events into the far corner of her mind. Now they clamored for her attention.

She considered what she knew about the two dead

women, focusing on what they shared. Both Claire and Doris had a relationship with Marshall. Even more curious, he was possibly the last person each had seen before dying. Quite a coincidence for an innocent man.

Lydia's pulse quickened. Maybe not such a coincidence if the murderer hated Marshall with an intense passion that drove him to seek vengeance through insidious means. That was it! She had to discover who detested him enough to kill his wife and an innocent woman in order to frame him for the crimes. Excited by her premise, she formulated a plan. She'd ask Marshall for the names of everyone who might hold a grudge against him and eliminate them, one by one.

Lydia had the swimming pool to herself. After checking the pool cover switch to make sure it was indeed out of the reach of any fingers, she swam laps then showered and changed. Eager to carry out her project, she strode home along Lake Boulevard, intent on calling Marshall the moment she walked through the door.

The sound of shouting unnerved her. It came from Steve Thiergard's uncle's house, she realized. She recognized Marshall Weill's voice, though the familiar sardonic tone was gone as his anger spilled into the street, disturbing the peace of a Saturday morning.

Lydia stepped up to the screen door and peered inside. At the far end of the living room, Marshall screamed accusations and obscenities at Steve.

"You killed her! Just as sure as that car drove over her. You filled her body with dangerous drugs. Poisons never approved by the FDA."

"The botanical compound never harmed Claire," Steve answered. "Civilizations have been using youth-enhancing herbs for centuries."

"Really? For centuries?" Marshall loomed closer to Steve, his hands balled into fists. "Then why were you gouging Claire, charging her a thousand dollars for one lousy bottle?"

Steve, who was taller, broader and less than half Marshall's age, stood his ground. "The compound's expensive because it's made from ingredients difficult to harvest. One in particular. It comes from the bark of a rare tree in China."

"Bull shit!"

"No, really. You know what? The herbs were helping Claire feel more energetic. She looked great, which you would have seen if you had taken the time to notice."

"What's that supposed to mean?"

Marshall shook his fists in rage. His face was as red as a trumpet player's after three hours on the horn. Lydia, fearing another death—this time a heart attack—reached out to the door handle. It yielded to her touch.

"Cool it, man." Steve pushed Weill away. Marshall let out a gasp as he tottered backwards and landed on the sofa. Steve shook his head as he gazed down at him.

"What a piece of work you are, acting the grieving widower. Christ, everyone knows you neglected Claire. She only wanted some of the attention you spread around."

"I loved my wife!" Weill got to his feet and lowered his head to butt Steve in the stomach.

Lydia had seen enough. Any more of Marshall's shenanigans and Steve was likely to punch him out. She opened the door and spoke loudly as she entered the house.

"Hello, fellows. I could hear you from outside."

Steve turned to her, all apologies. "I'm sorry about that, Mrs. Krause. Marshall and I were having a discussion."

"He and his damn herbs put Claire's life in danger. If she wasn't so hopped up, she'd never have taken to running outside the community where it wasn't safe."

His logic was so skewed, Lydia didn't know what to say. Steve was determined to clear himself. He walked toward Lydia.

"Claire was fine before someone killed her." He tossed a glance at the glowering Marshall. "She told me she felt better than she had in years. Mrs. Krause, I swear the capsules I sold her aren't dangerous in any way."

"Was Mrs. Weill taking the herbal supplement you talked about at my daughter's house?"

"Of course not! It hasn't been thoroughly tested."

"They sound like one and the same to me," Lydia said.

"Well, they're not!"

He's lying, Lydia thought, but saw no point in arguing. Her immediate concern was convincing Marshall to leave.

"At any rate, the supplements didn't cause Claire's demise," she said as she gripped his upper arm. "Come,

Marshall, we need to talk. I've an idea how we might get to the bottom of what we were discussing the other day."

"If you insist," he said testily, shaking off her hand. He thrust back his shoulders and frowned at Steve. "You haven't heard the end of this. I'm sending the police over here. They'll want to know what kind of racket you're into, preying on innocent women."

Steve laughed. "Me preying on innocent people! That's good. Even the police will get a chuckle out of that one." He turned to Lydia. "Thanks for stopping by and collecting him."

Lydia ignored him as she followed Marshall out of the house. Her sympathies, erroneous though they no doubt were, lay with the apparent loser of this round.

Marshall walked slowly toward his black Mercedes. The altercation had sapped much of his energy. He appeared frail and foolish in his expensive hip clothes.

Once they were inside the car, he breathed deeply, then leaned back in his leather seat. "The little creep! He doesn't even live here, and he's set up a lucrative business for himself."

Lydia was astonished. "You mean other women are buying his herbs?"

"So I'm just beginning to find out. What great idea did you come up with?"

Lydia ignored his sarcasm. "First tell me how you found out it was Steve?"

"Your friend, Detective Molina, and I wondered if the substance found in Claire had any connection to the two cash withdrawals Claire had taken from her account for a thousand dollars each. Last night I went through her personal items. In her sewing basket I came upon pamphlets about herbal supplements and receipts with Thiergard's name on them."

"A thousand dollars a bottle," Lydia murmured. No wonder Steve could afford a Jaguar. The more she heard about her daughter's friend, the less she liked him. She forced herself to ask the next question because she dreaded hearing the answer.

"Are the capsules dangerous?"

"Molina says they've been implicated in heart attacks, but since this particular formula hasn't been sold on the American market, the FDA has no control over it."

"Oh." Lydia slumped against her seat. "Steve Thiergard was at my daughter's house Thanksgiving Day. He talked about the compound, insisted it was safe and beneficial, though it's still in the testing stage."

Marshall threw her a cynical look. "He's a liar, and he preys on older women."

"Reprehensible," Lydia murmured, distressed that her daughter was mixed up with the likes of Steve Thiergard.

"What did you want to tell me?"

Lydia struggled to change channels. She'd tell Meredith all about Steve Thiergard, and his vile side business tomorrow. Now she had to concentrate on the issue at hand.

"Two women are dead. Murdered, and you knew both of them."

"So did everyone else at Twin Lakes."

She ignored his interruption. "One was your wife. As for Doris Fein, she blamed you for financial losses, and you were the last person to see her alive. A bit too much of a coincidence, don't you think?"

Weill glared at her. "I thought you were going to help me."

"Which leads me to believe that someone here at Twin Lakes has it in for you, hates you enough to kill, and frame you for the murders."

After a minute he said, "The idea passed through my mind, but I decided it was too preposterous to give it any credence."

"The situation is preposterous," Lydia pointed out. "Who goes around murdering women in a retirement community?"

They studied each other. Lydia took a deep breath, and continued.

"So, I'd like you to draw up a list of all the Twin Lake residents to whom you've given financial advice or with whom you've had the slightest altercation—be it over a parking spot, a card game, anything."

He said nothing. Lydia pressed her lips together to keep from coaxing him. Either he'd agree or he wouldn't.

"You realize you're asking me to breach the confidentiality of people who have nothing to do with the murders?"

"At this point, I want general information. Did so-and-so invest a lot or a little? Did he lose money? Things like that."

"So-and-so might be totally innocent."

She threw him a scornful glance. "You claim you're innocent, but people here treat you like a pariah. Besides, don't you want to know who killed Claire?"

"Of course I do! Molina asked me similar questions about her relationships with other residents."

"See!" Lydia crowed. "That proves we're on the right track." *Only I'm one step ahead of you, Sol,* she thought.

Weill frowned suddenly, and shot her an angry scowl. "None of this would have happened if you hadn't opened the can of worms."

She cringed inwardly but answered him evenly. "Or if you hadn't put the worms there in the first place."

"Sorry," he muttered. "That was stupid."

He turned on the motor. "Do you want to come back to my house while I write out the list?"

It was her turn to hesitate. Marshall wasn't a murderer, she reminded herself, and he wouldn't dare make a pass at her. She needed that list of names to start her investigation. Investigation, hah! Lydia suddenly felt like a fool as she wondered how she was going to extract information from, and about her fellow residents. With Caroline, and Barbara's assistance, of course!

Marshall's mood lightened as soon as he entered his home. He excused himself to listen to phone messages, then insisted on preparing coffee, and putting a Danish on a plate for Lydia to nosh on while he checked through his records.

"I'll be in my office if you need me. There's today's

Newsday, and some magazines in the living room. Relax. Make yourself comfortable."

He switched on speakers, filling the house with light jazz, and left her in the kitchen. The house was beautifully decorated, in an understated way. Lydia admired the cherry wood cabinets, granite-covered counters, and chrome fixtures as she drank her coffee, and finished off her Danish. She used the bathroom, which was as luxurious as the kitchen, then ambled into the living room.

She stood before the sliding glass doors, and gazed out onto the lake. Marshall had an exceptionally large back lawn that sloped gently to the water's edge. Pine trees grew along both ends of the property, giving him considerable privacy. A bench faced the water about five feet from the shore. Nearby stood small stone statues of a boy, and a girl.

She sat on one of the two nubby beige sofas, and picked up the newspaper, but her eyes were drawn to the decor around her. Who would have thought that beige, brown, dark green, and a touch of turquoise would work so fabulously well together, keeping a room cozy yet exciting? The art work was interesting, too. Lydia got up to study the two large paintings over the sofa where she'd been sitting. They were oriental. Vietnamese, she guessed. The stone figures of musicians in the étagère were striking, and original.

She grew restless as the minutes passed.

"Sorry to be taking so long, but you wanted a complete list," Marshall called out.

"Yes, I do. Take your time."

She strolled over to admire the gold-leaf regent bombé chest. A white porcelain bowl, adorned with orange birds rested on the black granite top. Surrounding it were four photographs in elegant frames. One was of a smiling Claire, and Marshall, taken at least ten years earlier; another of Marshall alone, looking debonaire in a suit, and tie; the third was a wedding picture—no doubt of their daughter, and son-in-law; the fourth was a more recent picture of the young couple, and their baby.

Her fingers seemed to take on a life of their own as they pulled open the narrow top drawer of the chest. It was half-filled with napkin rings, and coasters, objects a hostess used when company came to dine. The middle drawer held three sets of place mats, and a folded tablecloth, and napkins for twelve.

To complete her investigation, Lydia tugged open the bottom drawer. More tablecloths, and napkins. She ran her hand among the folds of fabric—for what, she had no idea—and felt a surge of excitement when she touched the hard, slippery surface of a glossy envelope. She removed it from the drawer.

The envelope contained half a dozen photographs. Lydia stifled a gasp as she stared at more than she'd ever hoped to see of Viv Maguire. A shawl had been draped over one shoulder, discreetly hiding her bulging middle, and considerable thighs, while displaying one drooping breast. The smile, no doubt meant to be enticing, had a gruesome intensity that sent shivers down Lydia's back.

She shuffled through the remaining photos, which were more of the same. She nearly burst out laughing at the sight of Viv on her stomach, her puckered butt jutting into the air, a parody of a popular baby pose sixty years ago.

Lydia shoved the photos back into the envelope, and returned it to its hiding place amid the napery in the drawer. Whatever doubts she'd had about the extent of Marshall's involvement with Viv had been laid to rest. The question was, had their affair begun before Claire was murdered or after? If it was before... Lydia shuddered, hating to speculate further. But the thought pushed itself forward for consideration. If they'd been lovers before Claire was murdered, it stood to reason they might have conspired to kill her.

For love? Money?

The doorbell rang, jarring her from her hypothesis. Lydia leaped away from the chest, not wanting Marshall to see her next to it, and figure out what she'd been up to. But Marshall didn't appear, and she wondered if he'd heard the bell over the music. The bell rang again, more insistently. Lydia called out his name, and he came rushing from the den.

"I'll get that," he muttered.

She sat on the living room sofa, and flipped open the newspaper.

"Oh, hello, Viv," she heard him say, though she couldn't see either of them. "This is a pleasant surprise. I thought you were spending the day with your daughter."

Viv let out as phony a laugh as Lydia had ever heard.

"I am, and I'm on my way. I just happened to be driving in this direction, and when I noticed your car in the driveway I suddenly remembered you never told me what time we're going out this evening."

"My dear, it must have slipped your mind. I said I'd come for you at six-thirty. I look forward to seeing you then."

The phony laugh sounded again, making Lydia cringe. "Would you mind giving me a glass of water? I find I'm terribly thirsty."

Marshall's tone took on a brusque edge. "Certainly, though I can't entertain you any further, I'm afraid. I'm with a client. Now, if you'll wait here, I'll..."

Viv followed close on his heels, determined to catch a glimpse of his visitor. "I am sorry for being such a nudge. I'll take one sip of water, and be on my—oh! What are you doing here?"

Viv glared at Lydia, oblivious to the fact that her red-orange warmup suit had turned her into an overripe beef tomato. The absurdity of it all—Viv's chasing after Marshall, then finding her here, and assuming she was a rival, set Lydia off in a paroxysm of giggles.

"I'm—I'm—here to talk to Marshall," she said when she caught her breath.

"Shame on you!" Viv snorted. "It's a desperate woman indeed, who takes advantage of a man in mourning!"

"Me take advantage?" Lydia asked incredulously as another fit of giggles threatened to overtake her. "Let me tell you—"

But she had no opportunity to set Viv Maguire straight about anything, because Weill intervened, intent on damage control.

"Viv, I'm in the midst of helping Lydia resolve a minor business problem." He put an arm around his unexpected visitor, and escorted her back to the front hall. "You have a wonderful afternoon with your daughter, and her family, and I'll see you at six-thirty. We'll have a delightful evening as always."

Though Lydia strained her ears, she was unable to hear the whispered exchanges. Marshall's knowing laugh, and Viv's simpering response told her they were of a sexual nature. To her surprise, she felt a stab of envy. She certainly didn't want to have anything to do with Marshall that way, but she was beginning to miss the male-female component in her life.

The door closed, and Marshall reappeared. "Sorry about that. Viv gets kind of territorial. She considers me her charity project."

Lydia gave him an amused smile. "She considers you her territory, period."

Marshall's smile was enigmatic. "Sit tight. I'm almost finished."

A few minutes later he called out her name. Clearly, he expected her to come into his office.

The room, meant to be a den, had been set up as a fully equipped office. Lydia counted four tall file cabinets. Paper, and other supplies were piled high on open shelves in the space originally designed as a closet. The printer-copier-fax machine, and the sleek computer rested on a massive desk that encompassed most of the room. She had priced one like it once, then decided she didn't need an expensive status symbol for her papers, and phone. But desks were like cars to certain men, and Marshall wanted her to see his.

Lydia had no problem admiring the truly beautiful. She ran her hand along the edge of polished wood. "Real mahogany. Hand-crafted. Magnificent."

He laughed, delighted with her response. "I knew you were a woman of discerning taste." A wistful note crept into his voice. "Too bad you're not receptive to the desk's proprietor."

"You called me in to give me the list." She held out her hand as a teacher would demand a note that had been passed around the classroom.

"I'll have it for you just as soon as I make one addition."

Lydia glanced around the room as he wrote. A large abstract oil painting done in tones of brown, and beige adorned the wall behind the desk. Well-executed, no doubt, but what held her attention was the large ceramic bird set on a pedestal in the far corner. Lydia moved closer for better viewing. It was truly a work of art. The artist had captured the ebony beauty of the beak, and iridescent tail feathers, the plump white body, the expressively intelligent if malevolent eyes.

"It's a magpie," Marshall told her. "A most fascinating creature I've been studying these last few years."

"I didn't know you were a bird watcher."

Her comment struck Marshall as particularly amusing, and brought on a spate of laughter. When he could speak again, he said, "Magpies are noisy, gregarious birds. They kill songbirds, and are capable of pecking baby lambs, and calves to death. But to their credit, they help control garden pests. Many people find them amusing. Here's your list."

Lydia glanced at the list of names printed in bold letters. He caught her surprised expression, and laughed.

"Rather long, isn't it?" Marshall swiveled his desk chair to one side so he could stretch out his legs. "I want you to know that most of these people approached me once they discovered my financial background."

"Is that before or after you offered to manage the HOA's money?"

"Both, actually. I've invested for some on this list, merely offered advice to others. I swear I've done nothing illegal, though a few of the portfolios have decreased considerably because of the market. I'll tell you which ones, but I prefer that you not put anything in writing." He eyed her meaningfully. "I trust you'll keep our discussion confidential."

Lydia nodded her assent. The list included, andrew Varig, Peg DiMarco, Viv Maguire, and all the board members except Benny Lieberman.

"Who besides Doris has lost a lot of the money they'd invested with you?"

"George Linnett, the Board president, lost a bundle,

and it was his own fault. He insisted on buying stocks I didn't recommend."

She tried to imagine George Linnett running down Claire, but the image simply refused to take shape in her brain. Besides, George couldn't have killed Doris. He was conducting the meeting when she died.

"Anyone else?"

"Andrew Varig lost some. John Trevor a bit more."

"Steve's uncle? He's not on the list."

"Really? I haven't seen him for some time, which is probably why it slipped my mind."

"Was he angry over the loss?"

Marshall let out a humorless laugh. "Furious. He had the nerve to come here, and let me know it. The guy has more money than Trump, and keeps it safely invested in long-term annuities, and bonds. He felt like letting loose, and playing the volatile end of the market with a tiny fraction of his assets. He took a risk, and lost."

"Did he threaten you?"

He threw her a condescending look. "My dear, I closed my ears, and showed him the door."

The list presented possibilities, Lydia thought, but most of the residents named had been in the meeting room at the time of Doris's death or out of state. Unless her death had been an accident, and had nothing to do with Claire's murder.

"Who on this list has reason to hate you?"

"Let's see." Marshall reached across the desk for the sheet of paper. He seemed to be studying it, but Lydia got the feeling he was buying time.

"I often butt heads with Roger, our treasurer, because nothing he does is cost effective, and, Andrew Varig rues the day he ever told me about Twin Lakes." He looked up at her. "The man despises me, all right."

Yes, he did. "Anyone else?" Lydia prodded.

Marshall shook his head. "No one comes to mind, though it's safe to say except for Viv, Peg, and Sally, and Bob Marcus, the others would be delighted if I left, and never returned. Of course that will reverse itself once we prove my innocence."

Lydia admired his aplomb. It couldn't be easy going from popular community bigwig to outcast. She folded the list in half.

"I get the picture. I'll find out all I can about these people as discreetly as possible, and if I learn anything suspicious I'll call Detective Molina, and let him take it from there." She smiled. "This way no one can accuse either of us of pointing a finger."

Marshall took her hand between both of his. "Lydia, I appreciate what you're doing. Thanks for believing in me."

Lydia jerked her hand free, and made a beeline for the front door. She would never like or respect this man. "I want to see the murderer caught, too. How much I can accomplish remains to be seen."

"You're a clever woman. I have faith in your success." He stopped beside her in the small entranceway. "Shall I drive you home?"

"No, I'll walk."

"In that case, good-bye, and good luck. You are a treasure."

He opened the door. As she turned to say good-bye, the kiss she believed he'd intended for her cheek landed on her lips. Startled, she drew back, and collided with the outer glass door. She unlatched it, and stepped outside.

"I'll call when I've something to report."

"I look forward to hearing from you."

Lydia kept up a brisk pace as she headed for home. *Old lecher,* she thought heatedly. Trying to romance me as his next rich wife! Though he had seemed honestly appreciative of her help.

What was he really after? she wondered as she walked past the woods, and peered up at the house that would soon be torn down. She chuckled when she realized he was after both. Marshall Weill was the type of man who thrived on challenges, and taking risks. She was a woman who had dealt with all sorts of men in her business life. Forearmed with this knowledge, she promised herself to keep him in his place the next time they met.

Thirteen

Sunday morning, Lydia showered, and dressed on automatic as she practiced opening sentences for her discussion with Meredith. She had to persuade her daughter to end her relationship with Steve Thiergard, and the trick was to do it so that Merry didn't flare up, and shut down. Lydia put on her jacket, and gathered up her keys, and pocketbook. Reggie approached, rubbed against her legs, and meowed. She reached down to pet him.

"Thanks for your support, old pal. I'll need it."

She drove slowly toward her daughter's house, dreading the confrontation before her. Meredith had to promise to stop seeing this man. Not only for the sake of her husband, and children, but because Steve was a money-grubbing extortionist who took advantage of older women desperate enough to buy his untested miracle drug. Only then could Lydia set out with a clear mind to investigate the two murders.

Her heart thudded against her chest as she pulled into the driveway. She honked the horn instead of going inside. Seeing the children now would only complicate the issue looming in her mind.

Two minutes passed, and Lydia honked again. Where was that girl! Jeff came to the door with Brittany snuggled under his arm. They both waved to her.

"Merry will be out in a minute," Jeff called.

It was more like five minutes later when her daughter opened the passenger door, and slipped into the car on a waft of some delicious-smelling perfume. She looked stunning in forest green slacks, and a matching turtleneck sweater under her leather jacket.

"Hi, Mom." She leaned over to kiss Lydia. "This is a great idea. Where are we going?"

Lydia mentioned the restaurant where she'd made reservations for brunch, and took pleasure in watching her daughter's eyes light up.

"Cool! I hear their food is awesome. Jeff, and I tried to eat there one Saturday night, but couldn't get in. You need to call weeks in advance."

They drove south on Route 97, and chatted about the children. Lydia told Merry about her lunch with Abbie, and Todd, and their plans to get married, and live in England. "We'll be going to a wedding in January."

They stopped for a red light. Merry didn't speak for a moment. Then her beautiful face formed a scowl. "It would have been nice if Abbie told me this herself."

"It's all so new, and she's busy making wedding plans. I'm sure Abbie will be calling you tonight."

"You always defend her, no matter what she does! I

can't believe she didn't ask you to plan the wedding."

The light changed, and Lydia turned onto a narrow road that ran parallel to the water.

"I would have liked that," she admitted, "but Abbie said she didn't want to put me to any trouble. They planned to get married in a rabbi's study, then Todd's cousin offered them her house."

"Still," Meredith insisted, "she should have included you in their plans."

"What I really mind," Lydia said softly, "is her living all the way off in England. I'm happy for Abbie. Todd seems like a wonderful person, and he's crazy about her. Only everything's happening so quickly."

Merry let out a brittle laugh. "The naive little fool. She can't possibly know what she's in for."

"What do you mean?" Lydia asked, her voice rising with concern.

"Nothing specifically. Just that nothing ever turns out as planned."

Her daughter's cynicism almost caused Lydia to drive past the restaurant. She swerved, and pulled into the parking lot.

"Mom!" Merry complained.

"Sorry." Lydia parked then turned to her daughter. "Are you saying you, and Jeff aren't getting along?"

Merry shrugged. "We're not '*not* getting along'. Just wading through life side-by-side." She stepped out of the car, and marched ahead, putting an end to the discussion. Lydia sighed, and followed after her.

The restaurant's high ceiling gave it a spacious, airy feeling. Sunlight poured through the floor-to-ceiling windows facing the Great South Bay.

"Fantastic!" Merry murmured.

"Yes, it is," Lydia agreed. They followed a smiling young woman to a table with a water view.

"I see you haven't lost your knack for reserving the choice table," Merry teased.

"Only the best for my daughter," Lydia answered.

They leaned back into the well-padded chairs, and gazed out in companionable silence. Lydia sighed as the gentle, monotonous motion of the wavelets seemed to brush against her soul, releasing all tension.

"This is so relaxing, I could sit here all day," Meredith murmured.

"It's almost like being on an ocean liner. I've always wanted to sail on the Queen Mary—all the way to England."

"Do it, Mom, when you visit Abbie."

"You'll come with me," Lydia said. "In the evening we'll wear long dresses, and dine at least once at the captain's table."

"Won't that be fun!" Merry grinned impishly at Lydia. "When we dock in London, we'll kidnap Abbie from her love nest, and have a night on the town. Imagine that—the three Krause women living it up. We haven't done that in a long, long time."

"No, we haven't," Lydia agreed. In fact, the only time the three of them had gone out together was the evening of Abbie's college graduation. Surprisingly, Meredith had drunk too much, and was sick during the night.

Lydia was enjoying her daughter's company, and felt a pang of disappointment when their young waitress came over to ask what they'd like to drink, and to offer the list of specials. They ordered, and the waitress hurried back with their Bloody Marys. Meredith drank deeply from hers.

"It feels decadent, being away from the girls, and drinking before noon."

"Do you miss teaching?" Lydia asked.

Merry shrugged. "A bit. I feel as though my life has been put in dry dock like a winterized boat." She gave a little laugh. "I'm not sure how it's going to be once spring comes around."

Lydia shuddered as a chill snaked down her back. "Every woman's life changes when she has children. It's a fearsome responsibility, and you're often left to cope on your own during the day."

"Unless you go to work—as you did."

"Yes." Lydia met her daughter's eyes. "You were eight years old, and in third grade when I started working in your grandparents' company. They were running it into the ground. I discovered I had a knack for the business world. I came up with several ideas, and we managed to turn the company around. I liked working there. I was happy to take over the company when they asked me to. Your father was relieved because it meant he could concentrate on his sculpting." She lowered her voice. "I'm sorry I wasn't at home when you needed me."

"I hated when the school day ended, and I had to go home to a strange woman, knowing I wouldn't see you until dinner time."

"Your father was usually home by six."

"Watching TV in the den."

Lydia chortled. "That's rich! I don't see you sitting home with Brittany, and Greta every afternoon. I know because half the time I'm watching them!"

"Mom, please! Is this why you invited me out for brunch, so you can tell me what a terrible mother I am?"

"Of course not! It's just that I feel you're restless, and unhappy, and I want to help if I can."

"Here you are!" their waitress chirped, setting a huge platter of food in front of each of them. While Lydia welcomed the interruption, she suddenly had little appetite to tackle the Belgian waffle topped with strawberries, and cream.

Meredith ate in silence. When the waitress asked if everything was all right, she ordered another Bloody Mary. Oh, oh, Lydia worried. Is she turning into an alcoholic or is she upset? When she'd had enough of her shrimp salad, Meredith pushed her plate away.

"I'm not happy playing wife, and mother," she said.

"Playing?" Lydia echoed. "You are a wife, and a mother. Your children are small now, but they'll grow up, and become people in their own right."

"And Jeff?"

"He loves you. I suspect he'll be there—if you want him to stay."

Meredith looked away, but Lydia saw the tears in her eyes.

"Don't you love him anymore?"

"I don't know. We don't connect. The only things we have in common are the girls, and our house."

Lydia took a deep breath. It was now or never. She stretched out her hand to cover Merry's. "I think you should do your best to make it work. For everyone's sake. Steve Thiergard isn't the answer."

Meredith jerked her hand free. "Who said anything about Steve? He's only a friend!"

"Call him what you like. I think you've been seeing him on days I've come to watch the girls. I don't like being used so you can have some excitement in your life."

The blush started at Merry's neck, and rose to her ears.

"I'm not after excitement. We talk. Steve understands what I'm going through."

"What exactly are you going through?"

The tears rolled down her cheeks. This time she made no attempt to hide them. "I feel lonely all the time. I love Brittany, and Greta, but they always want, and need, and demand my time, and attention."

"And Jeff?"

Meredith's face hardened with anger. "I know you think he's perfect, but that's an act he puts on when you're around. Jeff feels overwhelmed by everything—the girls, the house, even me. He works more than he has to, to avoid us. At home he watches TV or goes on the computer."

"Are you sure about that?"

Merry nodded. "When I ran into Steve, and we got to talking, it was such a relief to laugh, and chat like I used to. Like I haven't in a long time. It only seemed natural for us to get together again."

"So you did know him in college."

"Oh, yes. It felt like a gift, running into him like that."

Some gift, Lydia thought grimly. More like an accident waiting to happen. The waitress took away their dishes. They ordered coffee, and apple pie a la mode. When she left, Lydia reached across the table, and squeezed Meredith's arm.

"You always felt things more than most people. But Steve Thiergard isn't the solution to your problems."

Merry's eyes glistened as she spoke. "Maybe he is, Mom. He's a genuinely sympathetic person. I remember that from when I went out with him in college."

"You did? I don't remember your mentioning his name."

Meredith shrugged. "We only saw each other for about a month. He pulled back because he felt we were getting too serious, and he needed his space." Reading Lydia's expression, she quickly added, "He's different now. More mature."

"Merry, you find him so appealing because you, and Jeff are weighted down by responsibilities, and the realities of children, home, and mortgage payments. You've no idea how Steve would react if he had to stay up all night with a feverish child."

Meredith gazed steadily into her mother's eyes. "I think I love him, Mom."

Lydia gasped as the ground seemed to shift beneath their table. The waitress set down their coffees with a smile. Lydia stared back as if she were a space alien.

"You're infatuated with a good-looking guy who listens to you complain about your husband. That's not love, Meredith."

Meredith gave a rueful laugh. "I'll take it over sitting in silence because you both know whatever words come out of your mouths will lead to an argument."

"What do you, and Jeff argue about?"

"Everything. A toy I want to buy for Greta. I want to throw out the old den couch you gave us, and get a new one. If you heard Jeff, you'd think we were poor. I keep telling him that's why we took out the home equity loan. So we can buy what we need."

"How much do you owe?"

Meredith shrugged. "Around fifty thousand dollars."

"And you have your monthly mortgage payments, which are hefty, if I remember correctly."

Meredith glared at her. "I'm not asking you to help out."

"I already have—with the down payment," Lydia reminded her. When Meredith didn't answer, Lydia continued, "I think you should take the offer to return to work next semester."

"Jeff told you! He had no right!"

"I don't know about that, but I think it's a good idea.

You've been too isolated staying at home. You're better off teaching, and socializing with your colleagues. Money will become less of a problem."

"Working's supposed to make me forget about Steve, and turn Jeff, and me into a happy couple? Get real, Mom. Things don't work that way."

Lydia sighed as she ventured into deeper waters. "Meredith, how well do you know Steve Thiergard?"

"Well enough. Why?"

"Did you know he's been selling dangerous herbs to older women desperate to regain their youth?"

Meredith hesitated, then said, "I knew he was selling them, but they're not dangerous."

"We don't know that because the tests haven't been completed. Steve said so himself on Thursday."

"Steve told me they've seen enough good results to put the compound on the market. It actually enhances a woman's appearance, and vitality. What's holding up production is some silly glitch involving filing or registration."

"The glitch is probably because the capsules have been implicated in causing heart attacks."

Meredith shook her head. "Not true. The compound is perfectly safe for healthy women. The three women who got sick during the trials had previous heart conditions. Steve told me the label on the bottle will read 'Contraindicated for anyone with heart disease' in big, bold letters."

She leaned forward, and her voice filled with emotion.

"Steve's totally dedicated to promoting this compound so older people can lead fuller lives. If anything, his intentions are altruistic."

"Now who's being naive?" Lydia demanded. "Your boyfriend's been peddling the stuff at Twin Lakes, and charging a small fortune for each bottle. Claire Weill was taking the compound before she was killed."

"Mom, you don't think Steve had anything to do with her murder!"

"No, I don't," Lydia admitted, "but Marshall Weill was furious with him once he learned he'd been selling the capsules to his wife, and Steve lied to me. He said they weren't the same capsules he was raving about on Thanksgiving, when I know damn well they are!" She grimaced. "Steve Thiergard's more devious than you know. It's probably how he managed to buy himself a Jaguar."

"He told me he'd inherited money from a great-uncle," Meredith said softly.

The waitress stopped by to offer coffee refills. Lydia asked for the check. They drove home in silence. A few times Lydia opened her mouth to urge Meredith to end her relationship with Steve, then closed it again, sensing that any more motherly advice would infuriate her daughter. She'd spoken her mind, and expressed her outrage regarding Steve's shady dealings. Meredith had turned him into her savior. On the other hand, her daughter had a good head on her shoulders. Lydia sighed. She'd done all she could. The rest was up to Meredith.

She pulled into Merry's driveway, and was surprised when her daughter turned to hug her. "Thanks for listening, Mom, and for not telling me what an awful person I am."

Lydia stroked her daughter's sleek hair. "Of course you're not an awful person, Merry, but I hate to see you do something foolish that will destroy your family. Seriously consider working next semester. I'll watch the girls the afternoons I'm free, and help pay for a woman the other three days."

Merry gave her a rueful smile. "Thanks for your kind offer. I'll think it over, and let you know."

Lydia drove home slowly, musing about the fragility of life. It wasn't only grave illness, and accidents that changed people's lives suddenly, and irrevocably. Fraying relationships—especially between husband, and wife—caused misery to everyone involved. Relationships had to be nurtured or they withered, and died.

She'd been unfair to Merry, thinking she was the root of all her marital problems. Of course there had to be discord between her, and Jeff for her to go willingly into the arms of another man. Her fondness for her son-in-law had blinded her to his part in their strained relations. Lydia shook her head as she passed the security gate, and entered Twin Lakes. Repairing the damage wasn't going to be easy, either. Relationships were much too complex to expect a quick, and simple solution.

~ * ~

She knew something was wrong the moment she entered the house. Reggie came barreling toward her, wailing his complaint. Lydia took him into her arms, and nestled her face in his fur as she walked cautiously through the kitchen. *Nothing untoward here,* she thought, moving on through the dining area to the living room. The damage was to the long side window—a hole that had scattered pieces of glass over the carpet. Shocked, she nearly dropped Reggie, causing him to yowl in complaint. She set him down gingerly before approaching the rock that had landed obscenely on a sofa. Her hands trembled as she removed the note from the string that kept it in place.

"This is a warning," it said. "Keep your nose out of other people's affairs or something bad will happen to you."

She giggled with nervous laugher as she sank back against the other sofa, hugging a cushion to her chest. Someone had vandalized her home! Fear tempered her fury, and she tried to make light of her growing terror. The gesture was ridiculous, the note's wording over the top. Lydia shuddered as reality asserted itself. Melodramatic or not, there had been two murders, and the pool cover incident to prove that danger lurked in Twin Lakes. She'd be a fool not to take the threat seriously.

What exactly was it referring to? Her helping Marshall Weill prove his innocence? The affair between her daughter, and Steve Thiergard? Exposure of Steve's herbal capsule business? Or the fact that she was trying to discover who had murdered Claire Weill, and Doris Fein?

Lydia had no idea, nor did she know who was warning her off in such a crude, and childish manner. She knew, however, it was time to call Detective Sol Molina to inform him what had happened.

Fourteen

Sol Molina was pissed. His displeasure came through loud, and clear as he paced up, and down Lydia's kitchen floor, berating her in the coldest, most formal of tones, for being the most foolish—no!—the most arrogant, irresponsible woman on Long Island for offering to help Marshall Weill clear his name.

What was she thinking? Where were her wits? Her common sense? Didn't she realize that by poking around, and not leaving the police work to him, and his men she was antagonizing the murderer, who undoubtedly had thrown the rock?

"But I haven't questioned anyone about Marshall," she insisted. Frantically, she racked her brain to come up with a plausible alternative. "Maybe someone threw the rock for another reason."

"Name one!" he snapped.

His anger flustered her, and for a moment Lydia's mind went blank.

"Viv Maguire's the most logical suspect. She was

furious to see me at Marshall's house yesterday when she stopped by."

"Why the hell were you there?"

Lydia squirmed under his scrutiny. Why was he so enraged?

"We were talking. What else? I told Marshall if he didn't kill his wife, and Doris, then someone might have wanted to make it look like he did. I asked him for a list of everyone who might have it in for him."

"Where is this list?"

"In my den. Do you want to see it?"

"Please, and if you have a copier, I'd appreciate your making a duplicate for me."

She left, and returned a minute later, a copy of the list in hand. Molina dropped into a chair to study the names. He stretched out his legs. They were slender but strong, Lydia noticed. Nicely shaped. She imagined he'd look good in a bathing suit or...

Blushing, she concentrated on answering his questions about the people Marshall had listed. As she spoke, the detective jotted down notes.

When they were finished, he said, "We still don't know if Mrs. Fein's death was a homicide. The ME's leaning toward a coronary, and running tests. Her medical records indicate she had a weak heart. However," he gazed meaningfully at her, "they found traces of the same herbal compound in her system that Mrs. Weill had taken."

"Oh, no!" If Doris had heart problems, the capsules may very well have caused her coronary. In which case—

Lydia pressed her hands together to stop them from trembling—Steve may have caused her death.

Molina fixed a stern eye on her. "What's going through that overactive brain of yours?"

She couldn't meet his gaze. "I was just wondering if there's another tie-in with the two deaths, that's all."

"Our thought precisely. Believe me, we're checking out every lead."

He stood abruptly, and reached for the rock, and the note he'd placed inside separate plastic bags. He was about to leave. Lydia felt obliged to tell him about Steve Thiergard, and his herbal capsules, but the words wouldn't come. She dreaded mentioning his name for fear the police would find out about his affair with Meredith. In which case, Jeff would hear about it, and he'd divorce her. Two women were dead but Meredith, and her family were alive. They needed her protection. However, Steve couldn't be allowed to continue peddling those pills, and put more lives in danger.

Not to worry. The police would find out about Steve eventually. If he severed his relationship with Meredith now, it need never be mentioned in any of their reports. The solution to everything, she realized as she showed the detective to the door, was to deal with Steve Thiergard on her own.

Molina gave her the first smile of the afternoon. "I wish you'd go to Florida for the next few months. I don't like having to worry about you."

Her heart lurched. "I won't do anything rash."

"Then throw away that list, and promise me you won't go around asking questions."

She shrugged.

He studied her for a minute. "Lydia, you don't owe Marshall Weill the time of day, much less the obligation of proving his innocence—if he is innocent."

"I know, but I've done my share of upsetting his life."

He cleared his throat. "I hate to think you've come under his spell like all those foolish women."

Lydia burst out laughing. "Contrary to what you think, I am not a foolish woman."

"I'm delighted to hear that." He bent down, and brushed his lips against hers. Then he opened the door, and stepped outside, letting in a blast of wintry air. He turned, and winked.

"Take care of yourself, and call a glazier to put in a new window. My men are questioning your neighbors to find out if they've seen anything, and I'll have a chat with Mrs. Maguire."

She nodded, and, too flushed with happiness to feel the cold, watched him get into his car.

"Meow."

Reggie brushed against Lydia's leg to announce he was hungry. He wove around her feet, but she continued to ignore him. What was wrong with his mistress, standing at the open door with a dopey grin on her face? Didn't she care that he was starving, and needed nourishment? Disgusted, Reggie nipped her ankle.

Lydia yelped at the stinging pain that snapped her out

of her reverie. She fed Reggie then cleaned up the broken glass she'd left as Sol had instructed her to so he could view the scene. Careful not to cut herself, she gathered up the larger pieces, then vacuumed the carpet, and the sofa several times.

All the while her mind whirled like a fan in high gear. She had ruffled someone's feathers. The question was whose? The doorbell rang, interrupting her speculations. Lydia wasn't surprised to find Peg on her doorstep, the brown rabbity eyes blinking with a blend of commiseration, and excitement. She thrust a piece of paper at Lydia.

"Sorry to hear what happened. Here's the name of a glazier I've used. He's good, and he's reasonable."

"Thanks, Peg. I can't believe someone did this in broad daylight."

Peg gave her a baleful look. "Oh, I can. As I told the detective who came to my house, once the weather turns cold, and grim, people stay indoors. I didn't notice anyone skulking about." She glanced toward the broken window. "Of course I never saw who threw the rock since that window faces the Winslows' house."

"They're away in Arizona," Lydia commented, suddenly feeling vulnerable.

"Need any help cleaning up the mess?"

"No, thanks, I've taken care of that. I'll call the glazier."

"Put a towel or a piece of cardboard over the window to keep out the draft. Any idea who did this?"

Lydia shook her head. "None whatsoever."

Peg shrugged. "Things were quiet here, until you stirred them up. Not that I'm blaming you," she quickly added. "Marshall's past was bound to come out, one way or another."

"You sound as if you knew about it before I broke the news."

Peg shrugged. "He told me about it one day when we were discussing investments."

"Then other people must have known as well," Lydia said slowly.

"Probably a few." Peg reached out to squeeze Lydia's arm. "Be careful. An evil force is loose in Twin Lakes. You don't want to get caught in its grip."

Lydia watched Peg walk across the lawn, and enter her house through the garage. What was that all about? It sounded like a cryptic warning. Was Peg, in her unique, and peculiar manner, offering her solace, or was she advising her to lay low?

She telephoned the glazier, who said he'd come by at eleven the next morning to make the repair. That accomplished, Lydia draped an old quilt over the curtain rods, and secured it so it cut down much of the frigid chill permeating the house.

But when the sun went down, she put aside the novel she couldn't focus on, and faced her dark thoughts. Where had she found the chutzpah to tell Marshall to draw up a list of potential enemies from which she'd try to deduce who had murdered his wife? The idea would be laughable if it weren't deadly serious.

She started for the kitchen, intent on boiling water for tea, but found herself staring at the quilt that covered the shattered window. The rock thrower had, in one fell swoop, both vandalized her home, and rendered her vulnerable. Lydia shuddered, knowing she wouldn't sleep a wink that night until the damaged pane was replaced. She dialed Barbara's number, and smiled with relief when her friend picked up on the third ring.

"Hello there!" Barbara was in good spirits. "I got back from my son's house an hour ago. It was fun but hectic. I'll be happy to spend a quiet evening in front of the TV. How was your weekend?"

Lydia gave her an abbreviated version of all that had transpired since Thanksgiving morning.

"Whew!" Barbara exclaimed when she'd finished. "I'm exhausted just listening to everything that's happened. Your life sounds like an action-packed movie."

"They're fun to watch, not live through. Actually, I feel kind of creepy staying here knowing anyone can push his way through the broken glass. Do you mind if I come over?"

"Of course come over!" Barbara exclaimed. "Stay the night. The guest room's made up, and I've plenty of Thanksgiving leftovers, courtesy of my daughter-in-law."

"I don't think I can eat anything."

"Maybe not now, but you'll be hungry later. Pack your nightgown, and toothbrush. I'll leave the garage door open for you."

~ * ~

Hours later, having been fed, and cosseted by Barbara, Lydia felt the calm of a convalescent recovering from a debilitating illness. As they chatted over decaf coffee in Barbara's cozy den, she reveled in the tranquility that had settled about her like a worn cardigan. Murders, and rock-thrown threats were incidents one read about in the newspaper.

"How lovely to babble about trivial matters," she mused. "I'd forgotten the simple joys of everyday living."

"Something you haven't enjoyed in quite some time," Barbara observed.

"Not since Izzy took sick. But I refuse to dwell on that any more. I'll tell Marshall I can't help him, and leave solving the murder or murders to Sol Molina." *Who kissed me, kind of, but I'll keep that to myself.*

"Good for you!" Barbara said. "You've one happy *simcha* ahead of you—Abbie's marriage."

"Oh yes," Lydia agreed. "Todd's perfect for her. He's motivated, and clever, adoring, and kind. But then I thought Merry, and Jeff would live happily ever after, and look at them now."

"They're no different from thousands of other young couples overwhelmed by having to care for kids and responsibilities." Barbara patted Lydia's arm. "Don't imagine the worst case scenario. Things may very well work out."

"I don't know. Merry thinks she's in love with Steve Thiergard." Lydia grimaced. "Given her state of mind, this was an affair waiting to happen. A gorgeous hunk of a man appears from her past, and offers her affection, and sympathy—for problems real or imagined." She groaned. "She must stop seeing him or her family will suffer. My granddaughters will be traumatized. Poor Jeff will be devastated."

"From what you told me, I got the feeling Meredith was receptive to your advice."

Lydia sighed. "I certainly hope so. I have to get it through her stubborn head Steve Thiergard isn't the answer to her problems. It didn't faze her one bit when I told her he's selling potentially dangerous capsules to older women. Now Doris is dead, possibly of a coronary. Brought on, no doubt, by those damn capsules Steve sold her."

"Didn't Merry tell you the compound's contraindicated for women with heart conditions? If Steve told her that, he must have made it very clear to anyone asking to buy the capsules."

"Maybe," Lydia reluctantly conceded, "but Steve's been underhanded about this entire business, and charging a thousand dollars a bottle is gouging, any way you look at it."

She remained silent as an idea took shape inside her head. "I'd love to hire a professional to investigate this miracle capsule, and Steve Thiergard so I could prove to my daughter her boy friend is less than perfect. What I want more than anything is immediate proof."

Barbara stood suddenly, and tossed Lydia an impish

grin. "In that case, let's google Steve Thiergard, and his herbal compound."

Lydia laughed. "Funny, that's precisely what my future son-in-law advised me to do if I need information."

Barbara booted up her computer, and typed in Steve's name. They ignored the other articles, and sites related to people with the same name—Stephen Franklin Thiergard, a Texan rancher, and aviator, and Professor Steven Thiergard, authority on California migrant workers from 1940 until 1948. There were only a few articles about Steven Daniel Thiergard.

Barbara printed out two similar articles he'd written in praise of the botanical compound. Lydia highlighted the individual herbs with the intention of reading about them later, then she studied the articles with care. Steve referred to earlier tests of two groups of people, each taking one of the two principal herbs. Most claimed to have more energy after ingesting the herb on a daily basis.

Testimonials from people who had taken the herbal compound were more dramatic. Over ninety per cent insisted they had more vitality, and enjoyed better health after two weeks of use. Steve made it very clear that the compound was not for anyone with heart problems. Everything appeared technical, and aboveboard—and dull.

"Here's an article about Hadley Health Products, the company that created, and will distribute this compound," Barbara said above the sound of her laser printer. "It has a bio of its CEO, Paul Hadley. Gee, he's young."

"Steve said he's a friend of his," Lydia said, picking up the printouts.

"Hmm, all these other articles are about the other Steve Thiergards. No, here's one from three years ago. It's a wedding announcement." Barbara clicked on the article. Lydia read it aloud.

"'Mr, and Mrs. Patrick Hadley of North Caldwell, New Jersey, are pleased to announce the wedding of their beloved daughter, Marigold Catherine, to Steven Daniel Thiergard.'" Blood rushed to her face as she scanned down several lines to a quote from Paul Hadley.

"'I'm as happy as Marigold regarding this marriage. Steve's been my best friend these last five years, and now he's going to be my brother-in-law.'"

Stricken, Lydia gaped at Barbara. "My God, the louse is married!"

Barbara burst out laughing.

"It isn't funny! I know Merry's married, but she has no idea that Steve is."

"Maybe he isn't any longer. Some of these kids marry, and divorce in the few years it takes other people to buy a new car."

Lydia shook her head. "I don't think he'd be involved with his brother-in-law's company if he'd divorced his sister." She marched to the coat closet, and pulled on her jacket. "God knows where he'll be off to tomorrow morning. I'll speak to him now."

"Now?" Barbara glanced at her watch. "It's almost ten-thirty."

"I'm not going far. I'll be back soon." Lydia started for the door.

"I'll come with you."

"No, you stay here. If I'm not back in an hour, call Molina."

Fifteen

Pinpoints of light escaped above the drawn drapes at John Trevor's house. Lydia parked in the driveway, and rang the doorbell. Steve, dressed in jeans, and a sweatshirt, came to open the door in his stockinged feet. When he saw her, he grinned.

"Lydia—Mrs. Krause! What a pleasant surprise!"

"I'm glad to find you're still at your uncle's. I wanted to speak to you but was afraid you'd gone home."

"I'm here through Friday, then I'll be gone for a month. Come on in."

Without waiting, he turned left,, into the den, where canned laughter emitted from the TV. Lydia squelched the urge to dash back to her car, and the comforting warmth of Barbara's home. She was about to do something she despised. At best she'd be considered an interfering mother; at worst she'd be facing a murderer in his lair.

Don't be melodramatic! she chided herself. Steve didn't kill Claire or Doris. At least not intentionally.

She forced one foot in front of the other until she stood

in the middle of the now silent den. It was a man's room, furnished with a maroon leather couch, and matching leather armchairs. A deer's head with large antlers topped the fireplace.

Steve stood beside one of the chairs. "Please sit down. Can I get you something? A drink?"

His manner was hospitable, and friendly, but she detected tension in his hunched-up broad shoulders.

"Nothing, thanks. I'm sorry to bother you so late. This won't take much of your time."

"Be my guest." He gestured toward the couch, and sat in the armchair opposite her. "What would you like to talk about?"

She decided to be straightforward. "I'm not happy that you, and my daughter, Meredith, are involved. I'd like you to stop this relationship now, before anyone gets hurt."

Steve nodded as though he were considering her request. "I see. What does Merry have to say about this?"

"She's in a confused state, and doesn't know her own mind. I told her an affair wasn't the answer to her problems."

"Confused or not, it's Merry's call. It's Merry's life."

"Don't give me that! Merry's behavior affects my granddaughters, and my son-in-law. I don't want their family destroyed because Merry's going through a difficult period, and you—a former boyfriend—happened to come along, and made her feel better."

"I'm sorry you see it that way. Merry, and I give one

another emotional support."

"I see." She eyed him balefully. "Do you love my daughter?"

"I care about her a great deal."

Which wasn't the same as love. Lydia slapped her thigh in frustration. This was getting nowhere!

"If you care about Meredith, you must realize you're not helping her. You're only making matters worse."

Steve said nothing. Lydia's anger dissolved, replaced by a heart-pounding panic.

"Please, I beg you to end the affair. If you break it off, I won't tell the police you supplied both murdered women with those herbal capsules."

Steve stared at her in amazement. "Do you imagine for one minute I had anything to do with their deaths?"

He leaped to his feet then paced up, and down the length of the room. "I'd stake my life on that herbal compound. In fact, I've sunk most of my own money into the product, and I expect it to make me a wealthy man in a few years."

"You lied about it, didn't you? You told me the herbal compound wasn't what you'd sold to Claire, and Doris."

"I'm sorry. I didn't..." His eyes widened as the full impact of her words sank in. "How did you find out about Doris?"

"Detective Molina told me."

"Oh, no!" He sat in his chair, and covered his face with his hands. Moments passed before he was calm enough to continue. "My uncle mentioned the herbal supplement to a few women at Twin Lakes. Claire, and Doris approached me. I explained it wasn't yet on the market, and would be terribly expensive, but they insisted on buying it ASAP. I swear I made it very clear the capsules were not to be taken by anyone with a heart condition. Obviously, Doris lied to me."

Stunned, Lydia asked, "How do you know?"

"Because when the police questioned me, they asked me if I knew Doris had a weak heart."

Lydia was puzzled. "The police questioned you?"

"They aren't completely incompetent, you know. Twin Lakes is a close-knit community. People talk. Besides, I never swore anyone to secrecy. I didn't have to."

He returned to his seat, and leaned forward. His voice took on the eager, enthusiastic tone he'd used when speaking about the compound on Thanksgiving Day. "Taken properly, these capsules are beneficial. They're neither lethal nor illegal. I don't appreciate your threatening me, Mrs. Krause."

Lydia felt her ears redden with shame. What she was doing was contemptible. If Steve told Meredith about this conversation, her daughter would probably never speak to her again! But more was at stake than her feelings or Merry's. She had to make one more stab at ending this relationship. She stood.

"Does Meredith know you're a married man?"

His eyes widened. He opened his mouth to speak, then closed it again.

Lydia pursed her lips. "I see. You forgot to mention that small fact."

Steve shook his head, his face suddenly grim. "My wife suffers from severe depression. She's been at a clinic since last May, and isn't making progress." He lowered his voice so Lydia could barely hear what he was saying. "They give her so many meds, she sleeps most of the time. I'm not happy about this, but since our insurance ran out, and her father's footing the bill, he calls the shots."

Lydia moved toward him, and, before she realized what she was doing, touched his arm. "I am sorry, Steve. How awful for you!"

He nodded, blinking back tears. "It's worse for Marigold. She's a wonderful girl, and I love her. We knew each other for six months when we married. I had no idea she'd suffered from depression during her teenage years. The miscarriage set it off again, worse than ever."

Lydia's heart went out to him. "Merry said you've been very supportive of her. Her problems are nothing compared to what you've been going through."

Steve gave a joyless laugh. "Being with Merry keeps me from thinking of Marigold—if you can understand what I'm saying."

"Certainly I do, but Merry knows nothing about your wife's existence. She thinks she might have a happy life with you."

All color drained from his face. "That can't be! We never talked about being together in the future. I swear I didn't lead her on!"

Lydia gave him a bittersweet smile. "Didn't you know?

As soon as a woman's involved with a man, she thinks about the future."

Dazed, Steve got to his feet. "Your coming here is so weird. Merry, and I aren't two kids, you know."

"She has two kids," Lydia said softly.

"I understand. The last thing I'd want to do is hurt Merry or her children."

Lydia reached up, and kissed his wet cheek. "Thank you."

She drove slowly back to Barbara's, her sense of relief mingling with sadness. Real life was never black, and white, but a wide spectrum of grays. Steve Thiergard had turned out to be a decent young man struggling under a heavy burden her daughter knew nothing about. He'd deceived Meredith by not telling her he was married, and had been genuinely shocked to hear that Meredith was considering a future with him. Steve loved his wife, and wasn't thinking divorce—at least right now he wasn't. The idyllic fantasy world he'd created with Merry to escape from the pain in his life had imploded. Lydia had no doubt he'd let her daughter down gently.

~ * ~

Lydia told Barbara about her visit with Steve then went straight to bed. She slept soundly, and woke up refreshed, and in good spirits. After breakfast, she thanked Barbara for her hospitality, and returned home to call her insurance agent, and to wait for the glazier.

By one o'clock, the new window was installed. With her house restored to order, Lydia felt her apprehension ebb away. After all, she reasoned with herself, the stone thrower might not be the murderer but someone who had seen her with Marshall, and didn't like her befriending a suspected killer. Or it might have been Viv, jealous at having found her in Marshall's home. The more Lydia considered it, the more likely it seemed that Viv had thrown the stone. As infuriating as that was, at least a woman like Viv wasn't capable of murder!

Her fear behind her, her resolution to forgo the investigation forgotten, Lydia reached for the list of names Marshall had drawn up, and concentrated on remembering everything he'd said about each person. The investors seemed to fall into two categories. Most, like Peg, and Sally, and Bob Marcus, were making slow, and steady gains with their investments. The big losers, aside from Doris, were George Linnett, andrew Varig, and John Trevor. George, and, andrew had been at the meeting in full view of everyone just before Doris died, and couldn't have been involved in her death, and it was possible Doris had died of natural causes.

But Claire sure as hell hadn't. Lydia had no idea if George resented Marshall enough to murder his wife, andrew had expressed his dislike of the man, both to her, and by posting his let's-get-rid-of-Weill notice on the bulletin board. But, andrew was a physician, sworn to save lives. Would he actually go so far as to kill Claire to take revenge on her husband?

If Weill was the runaround Lydia knew him to be, he was bound to his marriage more by his wife's purse strings than heart strings. If a disgruntled investor had killed Claire to wreak revenge on her husband, he'd be getting back at Marshall in the pocketbook where it hurt. Which implied the murderer knew that once Claire was dead, Marshall had no claim to her estate. The murderer, being a resident of Twin Lakes, would have known that Claire's death would hurt Marshall both emotionally, and financially. Lydia shook her head. She was getting nowhere fast.

What about the absent John Trevor? Everyone said he was in Florida, but that didn't mean he was there. He could have returned to Twin Lakes, hidden his car in his garage, killed Claire, then left again. Did he hate Weill all that much to plot the murder months in advance?

Her pulse quickened. Trevor had been furious with Marshall because he'd lost money on investments made at Marshall's recommendation. His anger must have been stirred up further when he learned Marshall had stolen money from clients in the past. Stirred him up sufficiently to commit murder?

It was possible. Lydia shook her head at the strange behavior of her fellow humans. She had recently read in the newspaper that a woman spurned by her lover had taken her lover's son out of school, and begun beating him. She probably would have killed him if the police hadn't gotten wind of it, and rescued the poor child, tied up, and bleeding in a basement.

"Enough!" she shouted, causing Reggie to cock his head, and stare at her quizzically. "I'm going out! I've groceries to buy, and errands to run, and tonight I must call Abbie, and Todd's cousin, and take part in the wedding festivities, whether they expect me to or not!"

She rummaged in her pocketbook to make sure she had both keys, and sunglasses, and was putting on her jacket when the doorbell rang. She flung open the door, and suppressed a gasp when she saw Detective Sol Molina grinning down at her.

"Hi, Lydia. Coming in or going out?"

"Going out to run a few errands. They can wait."

He squinted his bright green eyes, his entire face a question. "Are you sure? I meant to call after what happened yesterday, but I've been on the go all day, and didn't have a free second."

"As you can see, both the window, and I are now fine."

She ushered him into the living room, where he scrutinized the glass replacement. "The fellow did a nice job."

"I think so. Have you eaten lunch?"

"Coffee, and doughnuts, yes. Lunch, no."

She headed into the kitchen, and called after him. "I'm low on supplies, but I can offer you a bagel cheese sandwich."

"That sounds terrific."

Lydia pulled out cheese, mayonnaise, and a ripe tomato from the refrigerator, and asked Sol what he'd like to drink.

"Tea."

She laughed as she cut the sandwich in half. "I didn't know cops drank tea."

"This one does when he's had his fill of coffee."

She boiled water, then sat, and watched Sol devour his sandwich. He ate neatly, and efficiently, learned no doubt, from working on the run. When he'd finished every crumb, he told her, "Mmm, that was delicious. I'm glad I stopped by."

"So am I," she admitted. "I was kind of shook up yesterday. I took your advice, and spent the night at Barbara's place. Did you find out who threw the rock?"

"I'm sorry to say we haven't, though we're working on it. Along with every other aspect of the Twin Lakes case."

"Is that what you call it?"

He grinned. "One of the names."

"Do you think the incident's related to the murders?"

"Murder. Singular. Doris Fein definitely died of a coronary."

Lydia paused, then asked anxiously, "Are the herbal capsules she was taking implicated in her death?"

"The ME doesn't think so. Doris was under great strain for weeks before her death, and she was extremely agitated when she fled from the meeting."

"Steve will be relieved. Last night he—"

"You spoke to Thiergard last night?" Molina's voice grew louder with each word. "After the killer or some crackpot told you in no uncertain terms to stop nosing around? What the hell's wrong with you, Lydia Krause? Do you have a death wish or something?"

"Of course not!"

He sighed. "I thought you were going to stop playing

Miss Marple, and leave the investigating to us."

She hesitated, then decided she had no choice but to tell him. "I went to talk to Steve because he, and my daughter have been seeing one another. She's married with a wonderful family. This affair could destroy everything if it doesn't end now."

Molina stared at her in disbelief, then threw back his head, and roared. Lydia resisted the impulse to place her fingers around his neck, and squeeze.

"It isn't funny!"

The laughter waned, and finally died down. "You're damn right it isn't. I know because it happened to me."

"Oh? Is that why you, and your wife divorced?"

"It was the final spin of a marriage spiraling down. It didn't help that the guy was another cop on the force." He made a gruff sound that passed for an ironic laugh.

"I'm sorry."

"Don't be. I wasn't home much—the usual cop story—and she wasn't who I thought she was. My only regret is now my daughter lives far away. But you were telling me about yours."

Amazing how smoothly he switched channels. "Yes, it turns out my older daughter, Meredith, went to school with Steve Thiergard. She's out of sorts with herself, and her life. He appeared on the scene in time to play the good friend, and sympathetic listener. Steve has his own marital problems," she added.

"Were you successful in breaking up this soulful relationship?"

Lydia grimaced. "I think so. Now Steve knows Merry's taking their relationship seriously, which doesn't suit his plans. I hope Merry comes to her senses." She gave him a winsome smile. "I also hope she never finds out I talked to him. She'd kill me if she knew."

"You did it out of love." He leaned over, and kissed her lips. "Now I'd better leave. Thanks for lunch—and for your company."

She followed him to the front door. He turned to face her.

"When this is over, I'd like to take you to dinner."

"I'd like that," she answered serenely, as though she were used to being invited out by men.

He pressed his palm to her cheek. "Take care, Lydia. I don't want anything bad to happen to you."

She smiled. "I'll keep that in mind."

Sixteen

Lydia sang along to the silly lyrics blasting on her car radio. "I'll love you forever!" she crooned.

Amazing that all three Krause women were in love! Of course she wasn't in love, just a bit infatuated with the first man who'd made her feel alive, and happy since Izzy died. Abbie was in love with Todd, and Merry thought she was in love with Steve but really loved her husband—or so Lydia prayed.

She slowed down, not wanting one of Sol's fellow Men in Blue to pull her over, and issue a ticket. Sorry, Officer, I was daydreaming about Detective Sol Molina. Do you happen to know him? She laughed as she lowered the volume, and switched to her favorite talk station.

Lydia zipped through her errands, then called Barbara on her cell phone from the supermarket parking lot, and invited her to dinner.

"You're in a good mood," Barbara commented. "Did a certain detective happen to stop by?"

"As a matter of fact, he did. I fed him lunch."

"That's progress."

"Come for dinner. Would you like chicken or meatballs, and pasta?"

"Either is fine, as long as I'm not cooking."

"In that case, leave it to me. Come over at six-thirty."

"I'll be there, along with a nice Chardonnay."

~ * ~

After dinner, Lydia, and Barbara carried their coffee mugs into the living room where they kicked off their shoes, and curled up on facing sofas.

Barbara let out a sigh of contentment. "That was delicious."

"Thank you."

"You'll notice my restraint. I haven't mentioned the murders all evening."

Lydia laughed. "Until now. For your information, it's one murder, singular. Sol told me that Doris died of a heart attack."

Barbara rolled her eyes. "So now it's 'Sol,' is it?"

"Uh huh."

"Anything else you'd like to share with me?"

Lydia grinned. "Not at this moment."

Barbara winked, but didn't press her. "Any word from Meredith?"

"She called before to ask if I'd watch the girls this weekend. She's made reservations for Jeff, and herself at a bed, and breakfast in Pennsylvania."

"Sounds promising," Barbara said.

"At least she's making an attempt to get her marriage

back on the right track. I hope she's not merely going through the motions."

"Don't be negative. What's new with Abbie?"

"All's well. She phoned to say Todd's cousin would like to talk to me to discuss plans for the wedding."

"You'll be busy with that the next few weeks. Too busy to get into trouble investigating."

Lydia sipped her coffee. "There's nothing more I can do. I've thought about who might have killed Claire, and why. The only new possibility is John Trevor. Marshall said he was angry after losing a bundle on some investments he'd touted."

Barbara shrugged. "I doubt John would kill someone's wife over a few thousand dollars he could easily write off as a tax loss. He's an amiable sort of man."

"You never know what fury rages inside a person who feels he's been taken."

"Kind of like a woman scorned."

"Kind of," Lydia agreed.

"And he's been in Florida since the beginning of October."

"So we've been led to believe."

Barbara laughed. "Have you shared this suspicion with Molina?"

Lydia shook her head.

"That's good. I don't want him to get the impression you're a loon."

"I have no brilliant ideas on the subject. I'll wait a few days, then tell Marshall I can't help him."

"Good. Keep out of trouble so no one will get the urge to throw more rocks. Concentrate on your family."

"That's precisely what I intend to do."

Todd's cousin, Karen, was delighted to hear from Lydia. She invited her to come for an overnight visit so they could get to know one another, and arrange wedding plans.

Lydia accepted with alacrity. She'd take the ferry to Connecticut Wednesday morning, and be back home Thursday night. She'd explain to Len that a family affair had called her out of state. Lydia giggled, eager to set out. A break from Twin Lakes was exactly what she needed.

Karen, a tall, large-boned woman with four grown children living in four different states, worked for a computer firm on a part-time basis. Her husband had just flown off to the Far East for a three-week business trip, leaving her on her own in their rambling twelve-room colonial home.

The two women took to each other immediately. They talked nonstop about their families, their outlook on life, and, of course, the wedding. Karen outlined her plans, and said she was open to suggestions. Lydia liked the simplicity, and good taste of her arrangements, and offered a few minor alterations, which Karen welcomed as strokes of genius. After an hour, Lydia finally gave up trying to coax Karen to accept her offer to share the wedding expenses.

"I consider Todd my fifth child. He's lived with us for

years. I want to do this for him, and Abbie."

"All right," Lydia agreed, "but when they return to the U. S. for a visit, the party's at my place."

"Agreed," Karen said, offering her hand.

Thursday afternoon, as Lydia hugged Karen, and thanked her for her hospitality, she felt she was saying good-bye to a dear friend.

At home she made a big fuss over Reggie, who needed much soothing for having been left alone. She called Meredith, and Barbara to let them know she'd arrived safely. Nothing of importance had transpired while she was gone, Barbara told her. Quiet as a grave. She waited until Abbie was home from work, then called to say she, and Karen had become fast friends, and the wedding plans were coming along.

"Today was my last day at work," Abbie told her. "Can you come into the city tomorrow? I really want you to help me find a dress."

"A dress? You mean a wedding dress? It's kind of late, honey, with the wedding a month away."

"Not a formal wedding dress," Abbie explained. "Something Laura Ashley-ish. If you can't make it... " She sounded forlorn.

Len would be furious when she called to say she was taking another day off from work, and she didn't blame him. But her daughter was getting married! Even if she'd still owned her company, Lydia would have set aside time to shop with Abbie before her wedding.

"Of course I'll help you find a dress!" she exclaimed.

"I'll come in early, and meet you at Lord & Taylor. They have the absolute best selection of dresses for special occasions. I've always had luck there."

"Great! What train will you be taking?"

As Lydia consulted the timetable, she considered asking Abbie if she'd like to invite Meredith to join them, then decided not to. If Abbie had wanted her sister's company, she would have said so. They set a time, and place to meet, and Lydia hung up the phone feeling just a bit harried.

"My daughters are keeping me hopping," she told Reggie. "I don't have the time to help Marshall find his wife's murderer even if I had some leads."

"Meow," Reggie agreed.

"I'll tell him I'm stymied, and that will be the end of that. Won't Sol be pleased?" She lifted the phone. "Now to tell Len what he won't be happy hearing."

~ * ~

Finding a dress for Abbie proved to be more difficult than Lydia had anticipated. Five-three, and small-boned, Abbie squawked about looking in the Petites' section.

"Why, honey?" Lydia asked. "You are petite."

"I hate that kind of labeling. I always get my clothes in juniors." After a pause, she added, "except for my pants, and tee-shirts."

"Where do you buy those?"

"Mostly in the boys' department."

Lydia forced an encouraging smile. "Come on. Let's give the Petites' section a shot."

Abbie tried on several dresses. Though most fit her, she discarded one after the other, proclaiming them either too frilly or simply too awful for words.

"It's just not me," she complained as she climbed out of the ninth, and last dress they'd brought into the dressing room.

Lydia let out a sigh of exasperation. "One's wedding dress is meant to be a bit formal. It's a statement that you're taking part in an important life ritual."

Abbie put on her stubborn camel look, but two try-ons later, she declared this one "wasn't too bad."

It suited her perfectly. The ivory-colored silk dress had a beautiful heart-shaped neckline; the slim skirt ended just below her knees.

"Doesn't need shortening," the middle-aged saleswoman commented.

"We'll take it," Lydia said. "Right, honey?" she added quickly when the stubborn camel look threatened to reappear.

Abbie nodded, and they followed the saleswoman to the register where Lydia paid for the dress.

"Thanks, Mom." Miraculously, Abbie's sunny nature reappeared, and she bussed her mother on the cheek. "I'm glad that's over."

"Not quite," Lydia informed her. "Next we get you matching shoes, and a small purse. But first let's have some lunch."

They spent the rest of the day shopping for Abbie. Once the shoes, and purse were out of the way, Lydia bought her an outrageously expensive apricot-colored negligee, and matching robe. In Sportswear, she had Abbie try on sweaters, silk turtleneck tops, jeans, and slacks. If an article fit well, she added it to the growing pile.

"Your trousseau," she explained.

"Oh, Mom!"

"Don't 'oh, Mom,' me! I want you to have pretty things to wear over in England."

Abbie pursed her lips. "All right. If it makes you happy."

Lydia kissed her daughter's cheek. "It makes me ecstatically happy."

Abbie loosened up as the afternoon wore on, and by the time they stopped for a coffee break, she, and Lydia were joking around in their usual manner.

It was after five when they left the store. *Just in time for rush hour,* Lydia thought, but it was worth it. She'd always treasure this day. Carrying some of the packages, she walked to a corner with Abbie, hoping to snare her daughter a taxi. They were in luck. Within five minutes, a yellow cab zoomed to a stop in front of them.

Abbie tossed her new purchases into the back seat, and instead of getting in, suddenly grabbed Lydia's hand. "You're going to come visit us soon, aren't you, Mom?"

"Of course I am."

"Promise?"

"I promise."

As Lydia watched her daughter's taxi head downtown,

it dawned on her that she'd been incredibly obtuse! Abbie was nervous! That's why she'd carried on about the wedding dress, and everything else. Lydia walked through the crowded streets to Penn Station, her daughter never leaving her thoughts. Abbie, for all her certainty that Todd was the man for her, had qualms about leaving her family, her country, and everything familiar behind. Lydia smiled. Abbie's former world-traveling days would help her adjust, and she'd be just fine living in England, and she intended to visit her, and Todd as soon as they were settled in their new home.

~ * ~

The phone was ringing as Lydia unlocked the front door. It was Meredith.

"I've been calling, and calling! Your cell phone was off!"

"I don't leave it on," Lydia said. "I keep it in the car, in case of an emergency."

"I was worried something had happened to you."

"Sorry, dear. I just this moment stepped into the house. I was in the city shopping with Abbie." She bent down to pet Reggie, who was weaving between her legs.

"I wish you would have told me!"

Lydia felt a pang of guilt. "You would have wanted to come along?"

"Of course not. I've too much to do here before we go away. I meant about your disappearing without letting me know where you'd gone. I even called your friend Barbara, and she didn't know where you were."

"I don't make a habit of checking in with someone before I go out for the day! Honestly, Meredith, I'm not in the mood for an interrogation. It's almost eight o'clock, and I'm thoroughly exhausted." She wedged the phone between shoulder, and neck, and set down a bowl of food for her starving cat.

Meredith tone softened. "Sorry, Mom. I didn't mean to come on like gang busters. I'm worried because of everything that's been happening at Twin Lakes."

Reggie gobbled down his food. *Like a dog would,* Lydia thought. She shrugged out of her jacket, and sat in a kitchen chair.

"I'm here, and I'm fine. What's up?"

"I convinced Jeff not to work tomorrow morning, and he suggested we get an early start. Could you be here at nine instead of at noon?"

Lydia sighed. "I don't think so, Merry. I've been running around these last few days, and I need to wind down. I was hoping to sleep late, and get in a swim before I came over."

"Mo-om, please!" Meredith lowered her voice. "You know how important this weekend is. Couldn't you please come early this one time?"

"I can't be there at nine. I must get some sleep or I'll be irritable, and my granddaughters don't need a grumpy grandma. The best I can say is ten-thirty."

"Thanks, Mom! Ten-thirty's perfect!"

Merry's jubilance told Lydia she'd been angling after ten-thirty all along. But this was an important weekend,

Lydia reminded herself as she scrambled eggs for her dinner omelet. Her way of helping was to watch her granddaughters while Meredith came to her senses. If she came to her senses. Because even if Steve backed out of the affair, which she believed he would, Merry had to want to remain in her marriage to make it work. Lydia hoped fervently that Merry, and Jeff would reconnect this weekend. Hoping was all she could do.

After dinner, Lydia glanced through the newspaper, too tired to read more than the headlines. She decided to make an early night of it. As she slipped between the covers, her thoughts returned to Merry, and Abbie. Though her daughters were adults, lately they required a good deal of her time, and maternal attention.

She awoke at nine the next morning, refreshed, and in good spirits. Much as she would have loved to swim laps, she hadn't enough time. A brisk walk would have to suffice. She opened the blinds, and blinked at the bright sunlight. Yes, a walk around Lake Nissaquage would be perfect on this lovely fall morning. She dressed in a warmup suit, and sneakers, downed a glass of orange juice, then turned left on N Boulevard, in the direction of the rear of the property, which ran parallel to the woods.

Though the temperature was in the mid-forties, there was no wind, and Lydia was able to maintain a brisk pace. As she walked, she made a mental list of what she had to do before leaving for Merry's. That done, she began a tentative list of wedding guests who had to be notified ASAP.

Lydia frowned as she suddenly remembered she had to call Marshall to let him know she could no longer help him. The thought had no sooner crossed her mind when she heard him speak. She stopped in her tracks, hand pressed against her thumping heart. Was she hallucinating? Could thinking about the man have conjured up the sound of his voice inside her head?

Only the burst of Marshall's condescending laughter was no figment of her imagination. Though Lydia listened keenly, she couldn't make out what he was saying. She glanced around, and saw she stood almost at the point where N Boulevard ran into Lake Boulevard. Marshall's voice was coming from the parcel of land on the other side of the woods that the HOA had recently purchased.

Another man spoke. Lydia suspected they were there for nefarious reasons. She had to find out what they were discussing. She moved through the trees, and underbrush, careful not to step on a branch or dry leaves, and give away her presence. She crouched down behind a large bush, and peered through a crack in the fence.

Marshall, and the board's treasurer, Roger Patterson, stood at the side of the house. Though she couldn't hear every word they exchanged, from the fanfare of smiles, back pats, and recap of points of agreement, she gathered their discussion was drawing to an end. At one point Marshall took out a tiny calculator to tally up some figures.

"Seventy-five thousand each!" he crowed. "Sounds good to me."

"It will sound even nicer after I cash in on your information."

"Buy yourself a Ferrari, if that's your pleasure."

The men burst into laughter.

Lydia ground her teeth. She was witnessing a pact between thieves! Roger was cutting Marshall in on padded contractors, and landscapers' fees in return for insider trading information to which Marshall, no doubt, had access through his old connections.

Her temples throbbed with fury. How dare they steal from their friends, and neighbors! People with whom they played cards, dined out, and visited in their homes!

It was immoral. It was criminal! It was disgusting!

She longed to crash through the fence, and give them a piece of her mind! Especially Marshall. He'd lied when he said he'd given up his thieving ways to live an honest life. He was amoral. Totally without principles.

A shiver ran down her back. If he'd lied about this, what other lies had he told her? About her sister, Allison? Claire's murder?

Lydia stood, eager to leave this scene of iniquity, but crouched down again as Marshall slowly turned toward her, his outstretched arm encompassing the house, and its property.

"Just think, by next year, this will be the most beautifully developed, sought after, and well-utilized asset of Twin Lakes."

Roger grinned. "Definitely, since we're going to make sure we have the best contractors, and workmen on the job. The best costs more, and who's to begrudge us our small share of the profits?"

Marshall threw an arm around Roger's shoulders. "No one, my friend. Besides, our affluent neighbors can well afford the slight difference it will make in the cost."

They strolled along. Lydia held her breath as they passed her, barely a foot away on the other side of the fence.

"Of course they can. Each household will contribute a small seven hundred dollar fee, and never be the wiser."

"A mere pittance."

"A pebble in the bucket."

Their self-satisfied laughter stoked her fury. She'd see them both in jail before they stole as much as one cent from the Twin Lakes residents!

When they reached the end of the property closest to Lake M, they passed through an opening in the fence, crossed the woods, and got into their cars. Lydia waited until they drove out of sight before she started for home.

She marched straight to the kitchen phone, and called Marshall, determined to denounce him as a thief who would always be a thief, and knew nothing about decency, honesty or truth. His phone rang, the tape came on, advising her to leave her name, but she didn't.

She considered calling Sol Molina, and decided not to. She had no proof of what she'd overheard—no tape recording or video of their felonious plans. No information to offer regarding Claire's murder except the revelation of her husband's totally venal character. She'd tell Sol about it eventually, but there was no urgency to call him now.

Instead, she tried Weill again. This time she got a busy signal. Disgusted, Lydia concentrated on getting ready for her overnight with her granddaughters. She fed Reggie, cleaned his kitty litter box, and saw she was running late. Still, she was determined to speak to Marshall. She dialed his number, and heard the phone ring, and ring. Dammit, he'd come in, and now he was gone! When the tape switched on, she slammed down the receiver, and grabbed her overnight bag.

She backed out of her driveway, and waved to Peg, and their neighbor across the street. Peg moved toward the car so Lydia had to stop. She opened her window.

"Where are you off to this time?" Peg asked.

"I'm babysitting this weekend."

"Have fun."

"I will." She drove away wondering what Peg would think of her friend, Marshall Weill, if she knew what he was up to.

Seventeen

Lydia's breathing slowed to normal as she drove away from Twin Lakes. She put her concerns about Marshall, and Roger's chicanery on hold, and gave her complete attention to Brittany, and Greta. Since Meredith had been clever enough to present Grammy's visit as a special treat, the girls were in good spirits, and behaved like angels. Saturday afternoon, Lydia dropped Brittany off at a birthday party, and took Greta to see a movie. Her small granddaughter sat enthralled, while Lydia's thoughts returned to the morning's revelations.

First thing Monday morning, she'd contact George, and Benny, and the other Board members to let them know what Marshall, and Roger were scheming. The Board would probably resist hearing more bad news coming from her. No doubt they'd insist on talking to Roger, and Marshall to get their side of the story. The two men were wily enough to concoct a tale that might deceive the others, at least temporarily.

She'd better speak to Caroline, and Barbara first.

They'd believe her, and would help convince the Board that, at the very least, any expenses incurred while Roger was still treasurer had to be checked, and counterchecked by the other Board members.

It was fortuitous that she hadn't managed to speak to Marshall, after all. Lydia shuddered as she considered the consequences had she vented her fury at this incorrigible, amoral thief. If he'd lied to her about his intentions to lead an honest life, he might very well have lied about killing his wife. She frowned, thinking how stupid she'd been to go with him to his house while he drew up a list of suspects. Suspects! He must have had a good laugh over that.

She had to face the fact that he'd managed to bamboozle her despite everything she'd known about him. Face it, then put it out of her mind. She'd let the police deal with the likes of Marshall Weill.

A small hand clutched her arm. "Look at that, Grammy!"

"Awesome," Lydia whispered.

She focused on the funny chase scene, then found herself speculating about Marshall, and Roger Patterson. What had driven them to commit felonies? She didn't have access to their bank accounts, but she doubted that either Marshall or Roger lacked for funds. They enjoyed a lifestyle of luxury, as did many of the others she read about almost daily—people in high positions who embezzled, and stole from clients, coworkers and the companies they worked for.

Maybe they loved the power that money endowed. Maybe they wanted more expensive possessions—a kind of keeping up with the Joneses. Because, as Lydia well knew, no matter how much money one had, there were always people who had more.

How did they reconcile their consciences with stealing from people they knew, people with whom they lived? Even worse, people whom they were supposed to be helping? What rationale did they concoct that allowed them to live with themselves?

Lydia had seen her share of trickery, and thievery in her years of running Krause Gifts, and Furnishings. It angered her as much as it pained her the few times she'd encountered employees cashing in on a crooked deal or shortchanging the company, and she'd seen to it those employees were punished to the full extent of the law. Even when Carley, her beloved secretary of four years, cried, and apologized over, and over for skimming money off five months of orders, and swore she'd make restitution, Lydia remained firm, and prosecuted. In her heart, she was glad Carley had managed to repay some of what she'd taken, and that she got off with a fine, and a suspended sentence, but she would never have the woman anywhere near her company again. In this world, people had to rely on one another's ethics, and good will. Without honesty there was no trust, and a world without trust was a scary place indeed.

Lydia took the girls out for an early dinner, then played games with them until it was time for bed. Sunday, she made them waffles for breakfast, and let them put ice cream on top. Then they went shopping at the mall, where she bought them each a toy. Meredith called to say that she, and Jeff would be a little late—they'd be arriving home around nine. The sound of her daughter's happy voice squelched the retort about to leap off the tip of her tongue. Spending a few extra hours with her granddaughters was well worth the price of saving their parents' marriage.

She sang along with the radio as she drove home, thrilled by the way things had turned out. She'd been right to confront Meredith about the affair. Thank God her daughter had come to her senses, and was back where she belonged—in the center of her family. Watching Meredith, and Jeff bump rears as they laughed over a silly joke made Greta cackle with delight, and Brittany shout "stop acting silly!" *One less thing to worry about,* she thought as she turned onto Bellewood Road. Now to persuade Merry to return to school ASAP. She'd offer to pay for a nanny three days a week, and watch the girls the other two days herself. She was willing—no, happy—to help ensure the smooth running of Meredith's household. Merry, Jeff, and the girls were an important part of her life.

A police car blocked the visitors' lane of the Twin Lakes' gate house. Lydia's heart began to pound. Something was wrong, terribly wrong. She inched up to the residents' electric eye, then stopped when a young police officer stepped out of the car, and held up his hand.

He asked her name, and address, then glanced at his clipboard.

"Are you going home now, Mrs. Krause?"

Fear formed a ball in Lydia throat. She had difficulty swallowing. "I was planning to. Why?"

"I'll follow you, if you don't mind."

She gripped her hands together to stop them from trembling. "What's wrong, Officer? What's happened?"

"There's been another death. Lieutenant Molina told me to escort you home when you arrived."

The shivering was now uncontrollable. "Who is it this time?"

"A resident named Marshall Weill."

"Oh, no!" To her astonishment, and his dismay, tears streamed down her face, spilling onto her corduroy jeans.

"Are you all right, Mrs. Krause? Would you like me to drive you home?"

Lydia wiped her face with the back of her gloves. "Give me a minute, I'll be fine." She sniffed. "When did it happen? How?"

"This morning a neighbor thought he noticed something odd near the tall grass growing along the lake back of Mr. Weill's house. When it was still there at noontime, he walked over, and discovered Mr. Weill face down in the water."

She shivered. "Was he murdered?"

The officer shrugged. "Too early to say. Lieutenant Molina will fill you in. Do you feel up to driving now?"

Then it struck her. "Why does Lieutenant Molina want

you to escort me home? Am I in danger?"

"We're taking precautions with everyone who knew the Weills."

She nodded, too numb to speak.

"Fine. I'll follow you, and see you into the house."

When they pulled into the driveway, the officer insisted on checking out every room before he allowed her to enter the house.

"All right, Mrs. Krause. Please don't open the door to anyone, and I mean anyone, except the lou. I just spoke to him. He'll be along in about fifteen minutes."

She collapsed onto a living room sofa, too shaken to feed Reggie. Someone had murdered Marshall Weill! This took some getting used to. For all his venal ways, Marshall had been a vibrant, charismatic figure. Now he was dead like his wife, killed by someone he'd offended.

Lydia shook her head, refusing to speculate about who that someone might be. She took some deep breaths, then went into the kitchen to feed Reggie, and call Barbara.

"Lydia, I'm so glad you're home! Did you hear the news?"

Lydia sank into the comfort of Barbara's concern. "I just heard. I'm still reeling from it."

"I called you at Meredith's this afternoon, but you were out. I didn't leave a message as I didn't want to upset you. Detective Molina agreed."

"Oh?"

Her suspicion, and jealousy must have come through, because Barbara laughed. "Don't worry, we're not carrying on behind your back. He stopped by after they finished going over the crime scene to ask me when I'd last seen Marshall, etcetera. He asked if I knew where you were, and when you were expected back. I told him I thought around eight tonight."

"Merry, and Jeff were delayed. The weekend was a success. They're happy with each other."

"They can thank you for that."

"Who killed him, Barb? I get dizzy running through the many possibilities, and you can add Roger Patterson to the list."

"Really? I know they didn't especially like each other, but I never heard they quarreled."

"When they were plotting to rip us off, they were the best of friends. But a falling out among thieves is a strong motive for murder."

"What on earth are you talking about?" Barbara exclaimed.

Lydia told her about the conversation she'd overheard on Saturday morning. "I considered calling Sol to tell him, but didn't think it was relevant to Claire's murder."

"Maybe not, but the Board has to be informed."

Lydia sighed. "Oh, I'll inform them all right. Once I catch my breath."

"Lie down. Take it easy. I'll speak to you tomorrow," Barbara said, and hung up.

Lydia stretched out on the sofa, and closed her eyes. She dozed until the doorbell rang, startling her awake. She bolted upright, and moved to open the door. Too late, she remembered the police officer's warning, but there was no need to worry. Detective Sol Molina stood before her. She wanted to throw herself in his arms, have him hold her close, stroke her head, and promise everything would be all right.

His hazel eyes were bloodshot with fatigue. The half-smile he offered was more of a grimace as he stepped inside the hall.

"Sorry to be so long," he said. "You look like you just woke up."

"And you look like you could use some sleep."

He nodded. "Marshall Weill is dead, and I'd like to ask you a few questions."

"Come into the kitchen. I'll put up some coffee."

"None for me, thanks."

Puzzled, she led the way to the living room. "Fine. We'll talk in here."

She sat on the sofa where she'd been sleeping, and puffed up the cushions. He perched, tense, and upright, on a nearby chair, notepad, and pen in hand.

"When was the last time you saw Mr. Weill?"

Mr. Weill? "Yesterday morning."

"Where?"

"He, and Roger Patterson were conversing on property the HOA's in the process of buying." She pointed. "Over there, beyond the woods. They were making plans to pad building expenses, expenses that would go directly into their pockets."

"Ah."

She watched him jot down what she'd said, disappointed that he didn't seem at all surprised. No doubt he'd found notes or figures on Marshall's desk, and had a good idea what they meant. Still, she couldn't understand why he was acting so distant, and formal. Almost as though he were angry with her.

"Did you speak to either man at the time?"

"No."

"Did either Mr. Weill or Mr. Patterson notice your presence?"

"Of course not. They certainly wouldn't have spoken so freely if they had."

"How did you happen to overhear their conversation at that particular time?"

She glared at him. Did he suppose she was tracking Marshall Weill, for God's sake? "I was taking a walk. I often take the route that passes by the new property. When I heard voices, I went up to the fence to see who was there."

He sighed, exasperated. "And afterward?"

Lydia pressed her lips together. "I got furious, and called Marshall."

"Why?"

"To let him know what I thought of him. To tell him what a despicable person he was, and that I had every intention of informing the Board of what he, and Roger Patterson were up to."

Sol Molina slapped his knee. "Brilliant! Absolutely brilliant!" he said sarcastically. "The man's a convicted felon. You overhear him arranging another crime so you decide to call to let him know you're on to his scheme. If that isn't a death wish, I don't know what it is."

"I—" Lydia began, but he gave her no opportunity to explain herself.

"Then there's the small matter that he might have arranged his wife's murder. Remember we discussed that the spouse is always the first suspect?"

Lydia nodded, but Sol didn't notice. His eyes narrowed to slits as he demanded, "Or are you one of those women who were half in love with Weill, and willing to use any pretext to call him?"

"Of course I'm not! What a ridiculous idea."

"I'm relieved to hear that."

He was relieved, she noted with some pleasure watching his shoulders relax.

"What did he say when you told him off?"

"Nothing," Lydia said. "I called three times, and got his tape. No, once the line was busy. Anyway, I gave up, and left to babysit my granddaughters for the weekend."

He nodded, a smile on his lips. His smugness made her want to smack him.

"But you know all that, don't you? My calls must have registered with Marshall's Caller ID, even though I left no message, and Barbara told you where I was."

"Regardless, it's always refreshing to hear verification from the interviewee. What time did you return to Twin Lakes?"

"You know to the minute. Your officer called you as soon as I drove through the gate."

"You didn't come back here last night?"

"Certainly not. Why do you ask? Do you suspect me of murdering Marshall Weill?"

Sol shook his head, and leaned back into the chair. "Of course I don't. But, as you pointed out, his caller ID showed you tried to contact him repeatedly yesterday. It's my job to question everyone who had contact with the victim over the last forty-eight hours of his life." He gave her a wry smile. "And, in your case, wonder why you didn't consider this important enough to tell me."

She felt the blood rush to her ears, no doubt turning them beet red. He had asked her to keep him informed of anything important that happened which might have bearing upon his murder investigation. She'd let him down.

"I was going to call to tell you what I overheard, then realized I had no proof on which you could act."

"How kind of you to anticipate my response to the situation."

"It—it was larceny, not murder. Oh!" Her hand flew to her mouth. "It is now."

Sol shook his head as he rose to his feet. "Sorry, Lydia. I don't mean to browbeat you. I haven't slept in thirty-eight hours, though God knows that's no excuse."

"I'm sorry, too." She stood up. "The truth is, I was afraid to call, and come across as a pest."

He touched her arm, sending shivers through her body. "Please believe me, you're never a pest." He yawned, and rubbed his eyes with both hands.

"Care to change your mind about the coffee? My second, and last offer."

"I'll take it. I need to drive back to the station, and write up a report."

He followed her into the kitchen, and took his usual seat, the one against the wall facing the sink. She filled the coffee carafe, then put out cheese, and crackers. He was already devouring them when she sat down.

"Do you think Roger Patterson killed Marshall? They were the best of friends after their meeting."

He shrugged, and spoke when his mouth was clear of food. "Who knows? Either could have reneged or tried to change the terms of their agreement. Anything could have soured the deal."

"How did Marshall die?"

"We're not sure yet. His lungs were filled with water, and there's evidence of a blow to the back of his head. The ME thinks he was drugged, too."

"Wow, sounds to me like overkill." Lydia bit her lower lip. "Oops, sorry. Bad choice of words."

Molina cast her an amused glance. "That's the kind of comment I get from my men."

"Who else saw Marshall yesterday, or is that top secret?"

"Besides the murderer, you mean? We're working on that. It's common knowledge he was out with Mrs. Maguire last night."

"I'm not surprised. They had a date the Saturday night after Thanksgiving."

He nodded. "What's your take on their relationship?"

"Marshall received plenty of female attention after Claire's death. He zeroed in on Viv." Lydia frowned. "I got the feeling he was more attracted to her bank account than to her personally. Though that could be my own attitude toward Marshall coming through."

"And Mrs. Maguire?"

"Viv was besotted. I told you she was ablaze with jealousy that time she found me sitting in Marshall's living room waiting for him to finish his list of suspects."

"Small wonder," he murmured, eying her.

She smiled, pleased by his compliment, then returned to his question.

"Marshall played her like a fish, and he knew how to reel her in." She hesitated, aware of the flush reddening her ears. "I—er happened to come across some photos he'd taken of Viv."

Sol Molina burst out laughing. "Couldn't resist sleuthing, eh, Lydia?"

"Well, I—er—no."

"You must admit, Weill had an artistic touch with that drape."

She shrugged, refusing to meet his eye.

"Mrs. Maguire was frantic when I interviewed her, framing her questions as to whether we'd come upon some 'artistic photographs'—as she put it—in the most circuitous manner. When I told her we'd found them, she begged me to rip them up. I told her we had to keep them as evidence for now, but not to worry. They would remain in a safe place away from prying eyes."

"Is Viv a suspect?"

"Everyone's a suspect." He downed another cheese-laden cracker. "Except you, that is."

"Well, thanks. When did the murder take place?"

"Roughly, between one, and three in the morning."

She stared at him. "I suppose Viv has no way to prove she was home asleep. Then again, why would she kill Marshall?"

"Who knows? Hypothetically speaking, if Weill said he wasn't going to see her any more, she could have been hurt, and angry enough to murder him. People kill for all sorts of reasons."

"Could Viv have killed him? How could a woman manage it?"

"A strong woman might be able to, especially if she drugged him first."

"Has Viv said anything to make you suspect her?"

"Not really. Her story is they had dinner, spent a brief while on her living room sofa being affectionate, as she put it, then he left her at eleven o'clock." He winked. "Even though she tried to get him to spend the night. Now that isn't for anyone else's ears, including those of your friends, Mrs. Taylor, and Mrs. Lieberman."

She liked that he knew who her friends were. "You cover all bases, don't you?"

"I have to. I'm a cop."

"Did you ever question her about the rock thrown through my window?"

"Of course I did, immediately after the incident. She denies having done it, and we've no witness or prints to prove otherwise."

"Hmm," Lydia mused. "There's no way to prove she didn't do it."

"That, too."

She poured them each a mug of coffee, and sat. He added sugar, and drank his black, then finished off the crackers, and cheese.

"Would you like something else to eat?"

"No, thanks, this is fine." He glanced up to meet her gaze. "Just a reminder. If you're going to consort with cops, or a specific cop, you're going to hear plenty of things that aren't for other people to know. Think you can manage that?"

"I think so."

"Good." He got to his feet. "Thanks for everything."

This time the kiss was deeper. "See you soon. Keep your doors locked."

"I will," she promised. Her heart sang as she watched him get into his car, and drive off into the night.

Eighteen

The following morning Lydia turned on the local TV news channel, and was startled to see an exhausted Sol Molina being interviewed by a pert blonde reporter. He grimly acknowledged that as of yet no one had been apprehended for the murder of Marshall Weill, but the police were working on the case around the clock.

Feeling unsettled, she drove to the clubhouse for her daily swim. She walked past the police car parked in the semicircle, and nodded to Officer McKlusky. He, and another policeman were deep in conversation with Margie, the office manager.

When she got home, her answering machine was blinking. The Twin Lakes' Board was holding a homeowners' meeting that evening at seven-thirty sharp. All residents were requested to attend. She had no sooner made note of the meeting on her calendar when the phone rang. It was Merry, sounding frantic.

"Mom, I just heard about Marshall Weill's murder! How awful! Are you all right?"

"Of course I'm all right. It happened while I was at your house."

"I wish you'd come, and stay with us until they find the person who did it."

"Meredith, Weill had a long history of stealing money from clients. No doubt one of them got angry enough to kill him, and his wife. I'm not in any danger."

Merry's voice sounded teary. "I don't want anything to happen to you."

Touched, Lydia smiled. "Nothing will happen."

"Promise me you won't go anywhere alone. Turn your cell phone on when you go out, so I can always reach you."

Lydia gave a little laugh. "Meredith, disconnecting my ear from my cell phone is one of the perks of retirement. I usually leave it in the car for emergencies."

"Mom, make sure it's charged. Keep it on, and with you when you leave the house. If I can't reach you, I'll call the police!"

"Merry, dear, calm down. If it will make you feel better, I promise to take the phone with me wherever I go."

After repeating her promise two more times, Lydia managed to end the conversation. She gazed down at Reggie.

"That girl needs a sense of proportion! Either she's sulking, and secretive or her anxiety is driving me mad. Nothing personal, Reggie darling, but between Meredith, and the murders, I need to get out of here!"

Lydia grabbed her groceries list, and made a mad dash for her car. She'd no sooner backed into the street, when Peg came out of her house, and waved her down. She wore a bathrobe, and slippers. Dark smudges underlined her rabbity eyes. Lydia grumbled silently as she braked to a stop.

"Hi, Lydia. Going to the meeting tonight?"

"I think I should."

"Would you like to ride over there with me?"

"Sure, thanks."

"No, thank you. I'm so stressed out, I hardly slept a wink last night. I don't want to go anywhere alone. Not after what happened to Marshall."

Lydia suddenly remembered. "You must be terribly upset about his death. I gather he was a special friend of yours."

Peg drew back. "We were friends, but I'm not sure what you mean by 'special.'"

"Sorry. Someone told me you, and Marshall often discussed investments. I just thought you might have known him from Chicago."

"I'm from Indiana."

"Oh."

Peg let out a sardonic laugh. "I hope you're not confusing me with Viv Maguire."

"Why would I? You're both petite, but you don't look at all alike."

"I should hope not! Viv's a blimp, and as plain as white bread—despite all the work she had done on her face."

Viv was a homely woman, but why the animosity?

Peg went on. "The Weills, and the Maguires are old friends from the Windy City."

"Sorry. I must have misunderstood."

"No biggie. By the way, I hear your friend will be addressing the residents tonight at the meeting."

"My friend? Oh, you mean Sol—Detective Molina." It irked Lydia that Peg got wind of every new development that transpired at Twin Lakes. Irked her even more when that included news about Sol Molina.

"No doubt coming to warn us to keep our doors locked, and not to wander off alone in the dark," Peg said mockingly.

"I've no idea."

"He sure as hell isn't going to reveal his list of suspects to the Twin Lakes residents. By the way, have you seen it?"

"Seen what?"

Peg sighed, exasperated. "His list of suspects. Did he drop any hints when he stopped by yesterday?"

Damn that woman! Did she ever stop prying? "No, not a one." As if she'd share anything Sol told her with Peg.

But her neighbor was already moving on to another topic. "The Kreigels have put their house on the market."

"Because of the murders?" Lydia asked.

"Natch. I bet there's a rush of people trying to unload now. I'm considering doing the same. My blood pressure's shot up, and I feel edgy all the time."

"Where would you go?"

Peg shrugged. "I don't know. I might give Florida a try."

"Let's hope the police find the person who murdered the Weills."

"Let's hope it's before anyone else gets killed." Peg backed away from the car. "Be here five to, okay? So we can get a seat up front. They expect a full turnout."

~ * ~

Every seat in the meeting room was occupied by seven-twenty. Four of the Board members chatted quietly among themselves on the dais. Roger Patterson was missing. Caroline had told Lydia he'd resigned earlier in the day claiming overwhelming personal obligations. Roger knew from both the police, and an irate president of the Board that he'd been overheard making plans to scam the very people he was supposed to be serving. There was a good chance he'd be brought up on charges.

At precisely seven-thirty, George Linnett called the meeting to order. "We are here because of the sad event of Marshall Weill's death. The police believe he was deliberately struck down. Detective Molina would like to say a few words to the residents."

Sol winked at Lydia as he passed on his way to the raised platform. He introduced himself, and spoke about the need each person had to remain on guard, as this was the second murder to occur in Twin Lakes, and evidence indicated the murderer might very well be a homeowner.

Andrew Varig raised his hand. "If the murderer is one of us, how can we protect ourselves?"

"A very good question, though we don't know for certain that a resident has committed the murders. The assailant might be someone who has access to Twin Lakes—a relative or good friend of someone who lives here. Which is why we're asking for your help. On the sheet of paper each of you receives, please write your name, address, and phone number. Then indicate first, your list of people automatically allowed access past the gate, and second, a list of people who have visited you these last two weeks. Provide dates, names, addresses—whatever you can. Put down if they're friends, relatives, workmen or whatever. If you're not certain of the time or date someone came to your home, indicate this."

A dozen hands shot up as three men in uniform distributed paper. Sol fielded questions, in essence repeating his original instructions. A tiny, white-haired woman with regal bearing stood to speak.

"I'm sure the names we're supplying are important, Lieutenant, but please address Dr. Varig's question: how are we to protect ourselves if one of us is potentially, and probably the murderer?"

What sounded like a swarm of angry bees filled the room. Lydia gave a start when she caught Viv Maguire glaring at her from the other side of the room. The woman really hated her! Peg murmured, "If looks could kill, you'd be a dead duck." Lydia shuddered, and forced herself to attend to what Sol Molina was saying.

"I advise you to be cautious at all times. Lock your doors when you go out; don't go off walking on your own, but stay with your spouse or friends. We're employing all our manpower, and technical knowhow to solve these crimes.

"It might ease some of your worry when I share with you our belief that this is not the work of a serial murderer but of a person who held a serious grudge against both Claire, and Marshall Weill. For the next week or so, a police officer will be stationed on the premises for a good part of every day."

"What did I tell you?" Peg whispered.

He went on to say they were interviewing everyone who knew the Weills, and requested that whoever saw or heard anything in the vicinity of the Weills' home on Saturday night come, and speak to him.

After the papers were filled out, and collected, George took the floor to announce that the residents' security patrol was ready to roll into action. A car manned by two homeowners would patrol the grounds to make sure nothing else happened. All volunteers were welcome. Shifts were four hours long.

A woman suggested the Twin Lakes community have a memorial service for Claire, and Marshall Weill, andrew Varig objected, declaring he would neither support nor attend a service for Marshall Weill, considering the kind of person he had been.

"He was as crooked as they come,", andrew said, "and we still don't know if he killed his wife."

On the dais, Sally Marcus rose to her feet. "Regardless of the mistakes Marshall made, he's dead, killed by some evil person. I think that's proof enough he didn't murder Claire."

"An erroneous, and emotional assumption!", andrew thundered. "The police have yet to discover who killed Claire Weill."

Conversations sprang up, and were immediately quelled by a wail of anguish. All eyes fixed on Viv Maguire.

"You people! Don't you understand? Marshall is dead. Whoever killed him is one of us, and lives right here."

Viv ran from the room. Lydia shuddered, remembering how Doris had fled an earlier meeting in tears, and died minutes later.

George ended the meeting, saying there would be another in a week's time to discuss the latest developments in the police investigation. The residents broke into small groups to air private opinions of how the case was being handled. Sol had departed, Lydia surmised, to avoid being badgered with the same questions he'd answered earlier in the evening.

She chatted with Barbara, Caroline, and a few other women about the Women's Club's outing scheduled for Friday evening until Peg tapped her arm. There was a flurry of good-byes. Caroline told Lydia she'd pick her up at five, then Lydia left the clubhouse with Peg.

"Lots of yakking, and nothing accomplished," Peg commented as she drove out of the parking spot.

"I think the purpose of the meeting was to give residents a chance to vent their anxieties. Let's face it, no one can feel safe until the murders are solved."

Peg braked at a Stop sign. In the dappled light, she turned to Lydia. "Who do you think killed the Weills?"

Lydia shook her head. "I've no idea. Maybe Marshall killed Claire. Even if he didn't, there could be two murderers running loose."

"And if it's one person?"

"I haven't a clue. Though I agree with Detective Molina. The murderer acted from very strong emotions."

"You mean, maybe someone took revenge because Marshall gave them bad financial advice?" Peg's voice was scornful. "That's over the top, wouldn't you say?"

"Someone hated Marshall enough to kill him. Could be that person first killed Claire in order to hurt him."

"Like who?, andrew Varig?" Peg drove slowly home.

"Maybe, andrew disliked Marshall, and was sorry he'd introduced him to Twin Lakes. He also held Marshall responsible for heavy losses in the stock market." Oops, she shouldn't have let that out. "The question is, did he hate Marshall enough to kill him?"

"I don't know." Peg glanced at Lydia. "Does your friend, the detective, have any clues?"

"None that I know of."

As they rode, Lydia's thoughts turned to Viv Maguire. "I wonder if it was a woman."

"Come on. Most women adored Marshall."

"True," Lydia agreed. "He had a certain magnetism, a way of flattering that made a woman feel special. I think it worked wonders on vulnerable females."

Peg snorted. "Don't tell me you were immune to his charms."

"I suppose I was flattered when he asked me to help find his wife's killer. I thought there was something decent, even heroic, about his determination to discover who killed Claire. Only Marshall didn't have an honest bone in his body. I knew that as soon as I heard..." She stopped, sorry she'd said as much.

"Heard what?" prompted Peg.

"It doesn't matter now. The point is, he was totally amoral." She rushed on, driven by the need to rid herself of the subject once, and for all. "He was a despicable human being where women were concerned. He used them—for sex, for money, for laughs. I bet he never loved anyone but himself."

Peg's laugh sounded brittle. "What a bizarre analysis."

Lydia turned to face her. "I hope you weren't one of his victims."

"Hardly."

"I'm glad to hear that." They approached their homes in silence. Lydia said, "You saw Viv Maguire, how distraught she was over his death."

"I saw." Peg slowed down, and turned into her driveway.

Lydia spoke slowly as an idea dawned on her. "What if she really was upset, but also performing at the same time?"

"What on earth do you mean?"

"What if she loved Marshall, and wanted to marry him,

but that night he told her he was breaking off their relationship. She went berserk, killed him, then cried over the fact that he was gone—still loving him."

Peg ripped up the emergency brake. "Sounds plausible. Was that why she sent you dirty looks—because she thought Marshall was after you?"

Lydia felt her ears grow warm under Peg's scrutiny in the dim light. "She was furious to find me at his house one afternoon when she stopped by."

"When was this?"

"Thanksgiving weekend."

Peg's rabbity eyes widened. "Hey, isn't that when someone threw a rock through your window?"

"The following day, in fact." Lydia sighed. "But Viv left no evidence, and no one saw her do it, so she was never charged."

"Viv Maguire, Claire's bosom pal," Peg said thoughtfully. "Now I wonder if she was after Marshall all this time, and bumped off Claire to get at him. Only he dumped her in the end."

Lydia shivered. "What an awful idea!"

"Well, someone killed the two of them, and this is the only scenario that makes any sense. I'd mention it to your friend, the detective, if I were you."

Lydia stepped out of the car. "I'll ask my sister who lives in Chicago to find out what she can about Viv Maguire."

"Why bother? Everyone knows Viv's husband died under mysterious circumstances. She was a suspect for a while, but the investigation came up with zilch. Viv walked away a wealthy widow."

Lydia gave a start. "I had no idea."

"Life holds many surprises."

They said good night. Lydia glanced nervously around as she walked across the lawn to her front door, which she double locked behind her. For the first time, she wondered if she'd been a fool to scoff at Meredith's offer to stay over until the murders were solved.

Nineteen

Lydia sipped the scalding tea, then pressed the mug against her chest to warm her racing heart. Peg's news about Viv Maguire's husband's death both shocked, and frightened her. Viv, she knew, was a woman of strong emotions. Was she more than that—a madwoman who struck out at anyone who crossed her? Had she killed Claire because she wanted Marshall, then did the same to Marshall when he refused to marry her?

That was one ferocious look look Viv had given her at the meeting! Lydia shivered. If Viv were deranged, she'd view Lydia as a siren who had stolen Marshall's affections. Following her skewed logic, Viv would blame her for Marshall's death.

"Think with your brain, not with your nerves," Lydia scolded herself aloud. She was building up a case against Viv when there was no proof that she was the killer.

The sound of her voice must have reached Reggie wherever he was dozing, because he swaggered into the kitchen to demand a snack. Lydia swept him up in her arms, and nuzzled her face in his fur until he squawked his complaint. She reached for his treats, and spilled some into a bowl.

Watching him gobble up the dried food as he purred noisily had a calming effect. Viv wasn't necessarily the person to watch out for, but Lydia would be on her guard. She'd keep her doors, and windows locked, and not go anywhere alone.

She was slipping into her nightgown when the phone rang. It was Meredith sounding frantic.

"Mom! Thank God you're there! I was about to call your friend at the police department to send out a search party."

"If by my 'friend' you're referring to Sol Molina, he was here at Twin Lakes addressing the meeting I just attended."

"I asked you to keep your cell phone on, and you turned it off."

"Sorry, honey. George, our Board president, asked us to shut off all cell phones, and I did. I'll turn it on first thing in the morning."

"Have the police arrested anyone yet for the murders?"

"Not yet, but they're working on it."

Meredith let out a grunt of dissatisfaction. "I wish you'd pack your bag, and stay with us a few days. Jeff does too."

Lydia opened her mouth to say she'd come, then reconsidered. Her earlier fear had passed, now that she was safely ensconced in her own home, and there was the matter of Reggie. Besides, she hated to give up her inner sanctum for Merry's boisterous household.

"How are you, and Jeff doing?"

There was a pause. When Meredith spoke again, Lydia knew she was cupping the receiver with her hand. "We're okay. I told Jeff I resent all the hours he works. He promised to cut back if I cut down on spending."

"Sounds fair to me."

"It is fair. Only I miss Steve."

"Well, of course you do. That's natural," Lydia said.

"Really?" Merry's relief came through loud, and clear. "I was afraid I'd crossed a line of no return."

"Nope, you can return. It will take time, though."

"I'm glad to hear that." Merry paused a moment. "Mom," she said hesitantly, "do you know all this from personal experience?"

Lydia let loose a hoot of laughter. "No, I was always true to your father. Two friends of mine had affairs of the heart, which they ended when they chose to stay with their husbands. Their marriages were better afterward."

"Really? Which friends?"

"Can't say. I was sworn to secrecy."

"Drats!"

Lydia smiled at the expression Meredith used as a child when she was frustrated. She heard Jeff's voice in the background.

"Talk to you tomorrow." Merry lowered her voice to a whisper. "Thanks, Mom. I'd have screwed up everyone's life if you hadn't stopped me."

"I think this must be a first—a daughter telling her mother she did something right."

"You do practically everything right. Good-night, Mom. I love you."

Lydia smiled as she put down the receiver. Merry was finally growing up.

A few minutes later she called Barbara.

"I would have phoned you," Barbara informed her, "but I thought your 'special friend' might be there."

"No, he isn't. I believe Sol left right after he spoke."

"No doubt to question Roger. He went to the police station early in the evening, accompanied by his lawyer."

"I suppose Sol wants to question Roger about Marshall's murder. I wonder if the Board is pressing charges."

Barbara chuckled. "Either way, our ex-treasurer won't be showing his face around here. The Board's in the process of hiring an accounting firm to review every one of his transactions, involving HOA money. Caroline said we'll hear more about this at next week's special meeting."

"Do you think Roger killed Marshall?" Lydia asked.

"I've no idea. At any rate, he's a thief—like our dearly departed. It's a good thing we have you around to sniff out the criminal element."

"Frankly, I wish someone else did the sniffing. Barbara, didn't you tell me Viv came from Chicago, and knew Marshall, and Claire from way back when?"

"I think so."

"Can you remember who gave you that piece of information?"

"I think it was your neighbor, Peg."

"Peg?" Lydia was so startled, she nearly dropped the phone. Instead, she sank into a kitchen chair. "Viv's from Chicago, isn't she?"

"Yes, I believe the Weills, and Viv, and her husband traveled in the same social circle, and saw quite a bit of each other. Until Viv became a widow."

"Peg just told me her husband died under mysterious circumstances."

Barbara paused. "Gee, I thought that was a deep, dark secret. Claire told me about it in confidence."

"Nothing remains a deep, dark secret in Twin Lakes."

"True enough. Besides, it's something your friend should know."

Her friend. There was that expression again. "If Sol doesn't already. Tell me the details, if you remember them," Lydia said.

"About four years ago Martin, Viv's husband, bought a sailboat to celebrate their fortieth anniversary. Though he had little boating experience, he insisted on taking it out alone, just the two of them. An unexpected storm made the lake extremely rough. Martin fell overboard, and drowned. The boat nearly capsized, but Viv, who used to sail as a child, managed to bring it back to the marina. Claire said Viv never forgave herself for going along with his plans. She'd done so because she hadn't wanted to hurt his feelings."

"Summary: Martin Maguire died, leaving Viv a rich widow," Lydia said. "The question is: did he fall or was he pushed?"

Barbara gasped. "Come on, Lydia. Viv's opinionated, and she's been openly hostile toward you because she sensed Marshall had the hots for you—which he probably did. But basically she's a good soul. You're not suggesting Viv killed Claire then knocked off Marshall?"

"If she killed her husband, she'd have no compunction about killing again."

"A very big if. People do die in accidents, and from illness, as we both know first-hand."

"Of course." Lydia thought a moment. "And Viv knew the Weills from Chicago."

"I wonder if Peg did, too."

Lydia's pulse quickened. "What makes you say that?"

"A group of us was gabbing in the clubhouse. Peg made a sarcastic comment, as she usually does. After she left, Viv let out a hoot, and said she hadn't heard that expression since she left Chicago."

"Peg told me she comes from Indiana. Maybe they use the same expression there." Lydia thought a minute. "Come to think of it, I've never seen Viv, and Peg together. Peg's made some digs about her—to me, anyway. Which could mean either they simply don't like each other or they were once friends, and now they don't speak."

Barbara yawned. "No more detective talk. My brain is turning to mush. I'm going to sleep, and I suggest you do the same. Read something dull enough to lull you off to dreamland. This business has all our nerves in an uproar."

"Yes, dear," Lydia agreed in dulcet tones. She'd shelve the subject, and call it a night, after one more phone call.

Samantha picked up on the fourth ring.

"Hi, Lyd. Sorry, I was on another line. How are things?"

"You mean since Marshall Weill got himself killed, and our HOA treasurer's been questioned as the possible murderer?"

"Wow! It must have been on the news, but I've been too busy working to find out what's happening in the rest of the world. Did Marshall give the treasurer a bad stock tip or something?"

"From what I overheard, they were instant partners in crime."

"You overheard? Lydia, why are you suddenly in the middle of murder, and mayhem? Why all the killings at your place?"

Lydia let out a mirthless laugh. "Believe me, I don't go looking for it. Actually, I spent a quiet weekend with my granddaughters while their parents were away sharing quality time. They both came home beaming. Thank God, their marriage appears to be intact."

"Thanks to you, in large part. You must be relieved."

"Oh, I am."

"Getting back to Weill's murder, why do the cops think your HOA treasurer killed him?"

"He's one of many suspects. I overheard him, and Weill forming a thieves' alliance to rip off Twin Lakes residents. Our treasurer's contribution was padding contractors' bills for the new construction on land the HOA recently acquired."

Sam laughed. "And I thought I was the sister who dealt with the criminal class."

"Believe me, any exposure I have to the criminal class is not of my choosing. Which reminds me—I'd appreciate it if you'd do some checking on two women who were very friendly with Marshall. One is Vivian Maguire. Her husband, Martin, died in a boating accident four years ago. They were the only two aboard. I'm curious if the police considered her a serious suspect."

"Will do," Samantha said abruptly, which meant she was writing. "And the other?"

"My next-door neighbor, Peg DiMarco. She's divorced, so I don't know if DiMarco is her married name or her maiden name. Someone—Viv Maguire, in fact—thought an expression Peg used sounded like something they'd say in Chicago."

"What expression?"

"I've no idea, but when I said something about her coming from Chicago, Peg insisted she was from Indiana."

"Indiana shares a border with Illinois. Like New York, and New Jersey."

"Really? I didn't realize. My sense of geography west of Pennsylvania is a bit sketchy."

"So was mine, till I moved here. Does Peg stand for Margaret?"

"I would imagine. Doesn't it always?"

"Who knows. Nicknames are an interesting phenomenon. For example, nicknames for Margaret can be Meg, Maggie, Peg, Peggy, Mag. Even Greta, and Marjorie are derivatives of Margaret."

Lydia yawned. "Very interesting."

"I'll find out what I can, but I wish you'd leave the police work to the cops."

"I won't act on what you dig up, I promise. I'll merely hand over the information to Detective Molina."

"How is Detective Molina?" Sam asked in a provocative tone.

"He looked fine when he spoke at our residents' meeting tonight. Told us to be careful, and all that."

"Take his advice, Big Sister, and don't do anything reckless."

"Of course not. I'll watch some TV, and get to sleep early. I have to work tomorrow, thank God."

~ * ~

Wednesday started out as a chilly, rainy day. Lydia woke up in a glum mood, and drove to the clubhouse for her daily swim. Though the activity left her physically invigorated, her spirits remained as gloomy as the weather. It was a downer, living in a place where every other resident was a potential murderer or thief, or harbored a deep, dark secret. Her mood changed remarkably when she caught sight of Sol Molina's car outside her house. He waited for her to pull into the garage, then he parked in the driveway, and followed her into the house.

"Good morning! Any chance a copper can get some decent coffee around here?"

"Come right this way," Lydia instructed, pleased that she'd showered, and changed into well-fitting jeans, and a sweater in the locker room instead of her usual sweatsuit.

Sol sank into a kitchen chair, and yawned. He rubbed his eyes, making them even more bloodshot than they'd been. "When this case is closed, I'm going to sleep forty-eight hours straight."

Lydia ground beans, and measured out coffee. "What's happening?"

"Nothing earth-shattering. We're checking through Weill's papers, and interviewing everyone connected to the Weills. Incidentally, that list he drew up for you came in handy."

"Glad to be of service." Lydia plunked down two mugs, and placed cookies on a plate. "Any suspects?"

He ran a hand through his wiry salt-and-pepper hair. "A few possibilities. Unfortunately we've nothing solid—yet." He bit into a chocolate-chip cookie. "Mmm, good."

Over the sound of water filling the carafe, she asked, "Did you learn anything interesting from Roger Patterson?"

"You mean aside from the fact that he's tried the same funny business before?"

"Really! Did he serve time?"

"No. Made restitution, and paid a fine. I don't know if he'll be arraigned this time, either, since he hadn't gone much beyond the planning stage."

"That's too bad," Lydia said. "It's too bad so many con men prey on retirees, assuming we're easy pickings."

Sol winked. "I wouldn't worry. By now all con men must have gotten the word to steer clear of the formidable Lydia Krause at Twin Lakes."

She smiled, and said nothing, but inwardly she savored his compliment. It was a salutation to the take-action kind of person she was. If Sol viewed her involvement with the Weill murders as interference, their future relationship didn't have a ghost of a chance.

Relationship? Suddenly nervous, she poured coffee into both mugs, and sat.

Sol said, "As for the murder, Patterson has a pretty good alibi if everything checks out. He says he drove to his girlfriend's home in the afternoon, and in the evening they attended a family party. Then they went back to her house, where he spent the night. He claims it's a forty minute drive from here. One of my men is interviewing her, and timing the drive. But hey, that's our job—to check, and recheck."

She watched him down half his mug of coffee, and devour two more cookies. "Anything on, andrew Varig?"

"Interestingly enough, he had words with Weill Saturday evening, according to Mrs. Maguire."

"Did she hear what it was about?"

"She only heard Weill's side of the conversation. She, and Weill were on their way to a restaurant when Varig called Weill on his cell phone. He shouted loud enough for her to hear the word 'restitution' repeated several times."

"That's interesting." She told him what Barbara had told her about Viv's husband's death, and the fact that Peg came from Indiana, which wasn't far from Chicago.

He smiled. "Uh huh. We've got all that."

"Oh."

He laughed at her crestfallen expression. "Did you imagine we spent our time checking out footprints with magnifying glasses? We've all sorts of newfangled tests, and equipment, and we're in communication with every police force in the nation. Not to mention the FBI, the armed forces, Interpol, and—"

Embarrassed, Lydia reached over to cover his mouth to stem the flow of words. He took her hand, and kissed the palm.

"Did I mention that once this is over we'll go out for a nice, romantic dinner?"

She shivered. "Mmmm, yes."

He kissed the veins pulsing on the inside of her wrist. "We'll do some other things as well."

Flustered, she said, "That sounds—interesting."

Sol's cell phone rang. He released Lydia's hand, and spoke to one of his men.

"Right! Great! Be right there."

"What did they find?" Lydia asked.

Instead of answering, he strode to the front door, and she scrambled to follow after him. "Have to check something out. Remember, don't play Miss Marple."

"Miss Marple?" she echoed, not at all pleased with his choice of sleuths. But Sol was opening his car door, his mind focused on whatever new developments she wasn't privy to.

Still, she noted as she watched him drive away, the sun had come out, and her mood was considerably improved.

She spent the next two hours waiting for a furniture delivery. Abbie called with an update on the wedding plans. Then Peg phoned, her voice weak, and raspy.

"I woke up with this awful sore throat," she told Lydia.

"I can hear it. Do you need anything from the store? Though I can't run out right now. I'm expecting a furniture delivery within the hour."

"I could use a few cans of soup. Chicken or tomato would be terrific."

Lydia laughed. "No problem. I'll bring over a few cans. Anything else?

"No, thanks," Peg croaked. "Just the soup will be fine."

"I'll come over as soon as I've phoned the security guard at the gatehouse to have him call me at your house if the delivery men should arrive."

Peg's laugh turned into a cough. "You sure you want to give him such complicated instructions? Some of the bozos they've hired get everything wrong. Either they phone you about guests you've instructed are to be let in, or they call another resident about your delivery."

"In which case, I'll call, and give the guard my cell number, and bring the phone with me."

"Good idea. I'm in bed, but the door to the garage is unlocked. Do you remember my garage door code?"

"No, but I've written it down. Be over in a few minutes."

Twenty

Lydia filled a bag with four cans of soup, a few bagels, and several slices of cheese, and turkey, and carried it across the lawn to Peg's house. She waved at the security patrol car as it slowly drove by. The driver—she couldn't make out who it was—waved back. Personally, Lydia considered the volunteer patrol a waste of time, and gasoline, though it served some purpose if it gave nervous residents peace of mind.

She punched in Peg's six digit code on the pad beside her garage door. The great thing about living in a gated community—when one didn't have to worry about murder, and getting fleeced by the Board treasurer—was the freedom to go for a walk or visit a neighbor without having to shlep along a pocketbook or keys. Until the recent tragedies, many Twin Lakes' residents left their garage doors up, and the connecting door to the house unlocked, at least during the day.

"Hi, Peg, I'm here," she announced.

"I'm in bed. Come on in."

Lydia left the bag of food on a kitchen counter, and walked through the narrow hallway to the rear of the house. Peg's unit was smaller than hers. It had two bedrooms instead of three, and each room was scaled down in size. Propped up against the headboard of her queen-sized bed, Peg appeared small, and pale in the dim light. Had Lydia ever been in this room? No, she would have remembered the hideous maroon, and beige walls, drapes, and matching bed linens, totally oppressive, and contrary to Peg's lively personality.

Peg flicked off the TV, and turned on a lamp as Lydia entered the room.

"Hi, there. It's so nice to see a human face."

"Would you like me to heat up some soup?"

"No, thanks, but I'd love a cup of tea with milk, and sugar," Peg said wistfully. "And bread lightly toasted, if you wouldn't mind. It's in the freezer."

"Of course," Lydia said. "Shall I open the drapes?"

"Please."

Sunlight spilled past the venetian blinds, striping the bed.

"Have you called your doctor?" Lydia asked.

"He said half his practice has this sore throat. He called in a prescription at the drug store."

"I'll pick it up for you if you like."

Peg smiled. "You are too kind."

"Not at all." Now that the room was light, Lydia observed that Peg didn't look well. Her face was drawn; her eyes, and nose were red as if she'd been crying.

"Be right back," she announced, and went into the kitchen to prepare the tea, and toast.

Minutes later she returned with a tray she'd found in Peg's narrow pantry. Peg offered a wan smile. "What a treat! It's like a picnic."

"I put cheese, and turkey in the refrigerator for later."

"Bless you."

Lydia leaned against the armrest of the corner chair, also upholstered in the hideous maroon, and beige fabric, while Peg finished off the three pieces of toast. The poor thing must have been starving, and too ill to get out of bed. Peg sipped her tea. "Mmm, strong, and sweet, just the way I like it."

Lydia glanced around the room. Three framed photos on the shelf above the TV caught her attention. She picked up one of them.

"That's my son, his wife, and their children."

"A nice-looking family," Lydia mused, gazing at the two laughing children, a girl around eight, and a boy some years younger.

"They were, several years ago when that photo was taken. Since then my daughter-in-law has blown up to a size eighteen."

Not knowing what to say to that, Lydia replaced the picture, and feigned an interest in the small ceramic birds crowding the surface of the long bureau.

"You have quite a collection of magpies," she commented.

"They come from all over the world." Peg sounded

more proud of her collection than she had of her own family. "How did you know they're magpies?"

"Marshall kept a large statue of a magpie in his office. When I admired it, he told me quite a bit about the species—how they're a menace to other birds but help control garden pests." Lydia gave a little laugh. "But then you've probably seen it."

"Why do you say that?"

"I thought since he handled your finances—" Lydia stopped, wishing she could call back her words. She knew from Marshall, not Peg, that he'd been managing her money.

Peg gave a dismissive wave of her hand. "Yes, he showed it to me once. I thought it was a monstrosity that looked more like a crow than a magpie."

"I wouldn't know. This one is beautiful." Lydia reached out to pick up a yellow-billed magpie. Peg's voice cut across the room.

"Put that down—please!"

The fierceness of her tone startled Lydia, and she almost dropped the little bird.

"Sorry! It's just that they're delicate, and I don't like anyone to touch them." Peg let out a brittle little laugh. "Actually, I'm thinking of selling them. A new broom sweeps clean, and all that."

"Yes, I can understand," Lydia said, though she had no idea what Peg was talking about. In fact, Peg was acting weirder by the minute. "I'll get rid of these." She retrieved the tray of dirty dishes, glad for an excuse to leave the bedroom.

As Lydia stacked the dishes in the dishwasher, she recalled the broken pieces of a bird she'd seen in the garbage some weeks ago. The figure must have belonged to Peg! There had been a dedication of some sort on the base, though now she couldn't remember the words. Something romantic. Had Peg gotten nervous when she'd picked up the figurine for fear Lydia would see an inscription on the base?

When Lydia returned to the bedroom, Peg was nowhere to be seen. A toilet flushed behind the closed bathroom door. Curious now, Lydia lifted the bird closest to her, and read the dark scrawl at the bottom: "To My Magpie from Her Hawk." She set it down, and was standing in the doorway when Peg opened the bathroom door.

"I'll be on my way, then," she said, hoping Peg wouldn't notice how breathless she sounded.

"Any news of the murder investigation? Has anyone been arrested?" Peg asked as she climbed into bed.

"No." Lydia wouldn't tell her, andrew Varig had argued with Marshall the night of his death or that Roger Patterson was an old hand at fraud, and embezzlement. It wasn't her information to share. "The police are checking out every possible lead. I'm sure they'll find the murderer soon."

"Did you tell Detective Molina your suspicions regarding Viv Maguire?"

"I didn't get a chance," she admitted.

"Any word from your sister?"

"Not yet. Samantha's so busy with her own work, I

doubt I'll hear from her for another few days."

Peg let out a harsh laugh. "I wouldn't bother pestering her, if I were you. You already know Viv's from Chicago, that she might have killed her husband, and she was after Marshall to marry her."

"Which doesn't mean she killed Claire, and Marshall."

"Are you defending her?" Peg demanded.

"Of course not!" Lydia retorted. "I dislike the woman, but I've no proof she's a murderer."

"Use your common sense!"

Lydia had had enough. She'd come over to be a good neighbor, but she refused to put up with abuse. She eyed Peg sternly. "Do you know something about Viv, and Marshall you haven't told me?"

Peg lowered her gaze. "No, not really."

"Because if you do, it's your responsibility to tell the police."

"I thank you for telling me my civic duty."

"I think I have that right since you've tried to make me your messenger girl!"

Peg's rabbity eyes widened in astonishment. She'd never seen this side of Lydia. "Sorry," she mumbled. "I'm feeling awful."

Was being sick making Peg overreact to everything? Or had she seen something connected to the murders, and was afraid to tell the police? Come to think of it, she'd been terribly jumpy these last few days. Lydia remembered Barbara's words about Peg's changeable moods, and decided it was time to leave.

"I'll let you rest now. Which drugstore is filling your prescription? I'll pick it up for you."

"Don't bother. I'll have it delivered. Thanks for your help."

Lydia opened her mouth to repeat her offer, but her neighbor's closed expression warned her it wouldn't be welcome.

"Okay, then. Feel better."

Lydia shivered as she hurried home. Peg DiMarco was a strange bird, all right, with a collection of magpies given to her by a lover. Who was her lover? Lydia racked her brain, but couldn't remember ever seeing her neighbor act romantically with any man at Twin Lakes. The man Peg cared for, and occasionally saw probably lived back in Indiana.

~ * ~

December was a busy month for holiday parties, and Carrington House was doing a brisk business. Thursday, and Friday Lydia found herself hopping from one festive affair to another when she wasn't making phone calls, and trying to make a dent in her pile of paperwork. She barely had time to nibble on a few appetizers for lunch, let alone spare a thought for the dire events at Twin Lakes. As though to make up for this neglect, the murders filled her mind with the force of a gale wind as she drove home Friday afternoon. Home? Lydia frowned. Twin Lakes certainly wasn't the secure, and quiet haven she'd hoped it would be. She looked forward to the Women's Club outing that evening.

Caroline called to say she'd be coming by for Lydia in half an hour.

"I'm looking forward to seeing the film," Lydia said. "It got wonderful reviews."

"I'm glad we're seeing a comedy. It will take our minds off the murders," Caroline said. "Speaking of which, we're forming a telephone chain for residents who live alone, and anyone else who's interested. Would you like to be part of it?"

"Probably. Tell me more."

"Everyone calls three residents between seven, and ten each evening. Between ten, and ten-thirty each caller reports back to 'headquarters.' If you can't reach a party, someone else will try after that. If you plan to go out in the evening, like tonight, you'll have a number to call before, and after you go out."

"Sure, I'll be part of the chain," Lydia said. "It sounds like a practical plan."

Caroline laughed. "I'm glad you approve. It's my baby." She gave Lydia the name of three women to call. "However, they're all coming to the movies, and out to dinner with us tonight, so you start this tomorrow evening."

Barbara, and Shari Morgan were in the car with Caroline when she pulled into Lydia's driveway. A police car drove by as Lydia exited through her garage door. Officer McKlusky waved, and called out, "Enjoy your evening, Mrs. Krause."

"How nice to have an in with our local police," Barbara commented.

Caroline, and Shari laughed knowingly. Lydia grinned, and said nothing as she climbed into the backseat. Their teasing made her feel years younger. She was grateful to her new friends for including her in their circle. Over the years, her demanding work schedule had caused her to lose touch with most of her female friends. She vowed not to let that happen again.

Caroline stopped in the circular driveway in front of the horse statue. "We'll wait for the others to come. We're four cars, sixteen women."

"A nice-sized group," Shari commented.

"A few more would have come," Barbara said, "but they have difficulty reading the subtitles."

"A few others won't leave home because of the murders," Caroline said.

"You'd think they'd welcome the chance to get away from Twin Lakes," Lydia said.

"Katherine's pulling in behind us," Barbara said. "And June is right behind her."

"Did you remember to get the cell phone numbers of someone in each car?" Shari asked.

"Natch," Barbara affirmed. "I have them all. Here comes Dorothy. We can leave now."

It was a twenty minute drive to the town where the movie was being shown. The four women discussed the upcoming Twin Lakes holiday party. As their car joined the fast-moving traffic of the Long Island Expressway, Caroline said, "The police told the Board we're losing our police car patrol after tonight. They don't have the manpower to keep it up."

"No big loss," Barbara said. "I don't think a cop car circling the grounds can prevent another murder."

"I'd say it's a deterring factor, in conjunction with our own patrol car making rounds day, and night." Caroline moved into the middle lane, then added, "If I were the murderer, the patrol cars would make me think twice before I offed another victim."

"Stop scaring me!" Shari said. "What makes you think more people will be killed?"

"I don't think any of us is in danger," Lydia said, more to calm Shari's fear than because she was certain the killing was over. "The murderer must have had a grudge against the Weills."

"Is that what your handsome detective told you?" Barbara asked. "Fill us in."

Sol was handsome, but he was far from being hers. "If you're referring to Detective Molina, he hasn't told me anything. I'm as much in the dark as you are."

There was a minute's silence, then Caroline said, "Keep this to yourselves, and I'm not saying Viv Maguire did it, but the police brought her in for questioning today."

Lydia's heart began to race. Maybe it would all be over soon. "What new evidence have they found?"

"Our neighbors, Tony, and Rose, left early Sunday morning for some sort of retreat, so they first found out about Marshall when they returned home Wednesday night. Tony told the police he saw Viv speed by in her car late Saturday night when he was out walking the dog. She was driving toward Marshall's house. He waved as she passed, but she ignored him."

"She was out with Marshall that evening," Lydia said, "but he cut their date short because he had to meet someone."

Barbara laughed. "It sounds fishy, and I bet Viv didn't like it one bit. She must have gone over to check out her competition."

The other women nodded.

Shari said, "One of three things happened: Viv killed Marshall, she saw him being killed, or she came upon the body, and ran away."

"There's the chance she peered through a window, couldn't see anything, and left," Lydia added.

"Maybe," Caroline said. "There's also the possibility she heard Marshall, and the murderer talking outside his house."

Lydia thought for a minute. "In which case, she would have seen him."

"Or at least noticed an unfamiliar car in the driveway," Barbara suggested.

"There wouldn't be any car," Shari said. "Whoever planned to murder Marshall would have come on foot."

"Or would have gotten Marshall to pick him or her up. But then why did they go back to Marshall's house?" Barbara asked.

"Because the murderer didn't want the body or traces of the crime found at his house, silly," Caroline said.

"Well, excuse me," Barbara said. "I'm not used to thinking like a murderer."

The others laughed. The topic of conversation turned to holiday plans. Lydia said little. Barbara's comment about not thinking like a murderer echoed in her head. Someone in Twin Lakes was now a murderer, and thought like a murderer. Claire's murder had involved the use of her car, which meant the plan had occurred to the killer sometime that evening. Marshall's demise had been plotted with care. The hint of an idea niggled at the edge of her thoughts, but try as she might, it remained beyond her mind's reach.

Twenty-one

Lydia reclined against the well-cushioned seat of the movie theatre, and gave herself up to the soothing darkness. A lassitude overtook her once the previews began. Surrounded by fellow members of the Women's Club, their cell phones shut off as requested by the management, she felt snug, and safe from the upsetting events at Twin Lakes. She sighed as the accumulated tension of the last few weeks fell away from her neck, and shoulders.

The movie, a clever French romantic mystery, captured her attention with the discovery of a corpse in the opening scene. When the handsome detective appeared, Barbara nudged her, and made her smile. Of course, Jeanne, the heroine, was gorgeous, and young—of her daughters' generation. The foolish girl kept putting herself into dangerous situations. At one point she nearly got herself killed doing something Lydia considered an act of downright stupidity. But for the most part, she admired Jeanne's spunk, and smarts. She was clever, the way she tricked the murderer into revealing a small but important fact that linked him to the crime.

That was it! The incident in the movie triggered what she'd overlooked—the nugget of information pointing to the identity of the Twin Lakes' killer. Lydia gasped at the realization. Barbara threw her a questioning glance, which she dismissed with a shake of her head. The connecting factor wasn't something the murderer had slipped up on, but one Marshall had inadvertently revealed.

She'd noticed it at the time, of course, but then it had no meaning. Now, knowing what she knew...

She whispered to Barbara she was going to the ladies' room, and slipped out of her seat. She had to tell Sol what she suspected. If she was right, the police would be able to prevent another murder.

In the deserted lobby, she called his cell phone, and got instructions to leave a message.

"Hi, it's me, Lydia. I'm at the movies now with the Women's Club, and something in the film we're watching made me realize..." She paused, not wanting to ramble on unnecessarily. "Anyway, if you look at the list of names that Marshall gave me you'll see—" Her voice suddenly sounded different. The tiny box in the right-hand corner of her phone screen held one bar, indicating her phone had little power. The "call ending" sign appeared. Damn! She'd remembered to leave her phone on for Merry's sake, but had forgotten to recharge it.

Lydia glanced down at her watch. The movie was ending in fifteen minutes. She returned to her seat. Surely, nothing would occur between now, and the time she got back to Twin Lakes. She'd call Sol the moment she walked through the door.

Afterward, the women lined up to use the ladies' room, then gathered in the lobby to review directions to the restaurant several blocks away. Once again in Caroline's car, the four women discussed the film as they rode along. Though Shari drew a parallel between the murder in the film, and those at Twin Lakes, no one pursued the subject.

Surprisingly enough, Lydia relaxed, and enjoyed herself over dinner. The restaurant, which served northern Italian cuisine, was decorated like an outdoor café, reminding her of the delightful repasts she, and Izzy had shared when they'd toured Italy.

She ordered a salad, and a veal dish, and found herself chatting with two elderly women she'd never met. They were lively, and highly entertaining as they regaled her with wild stories of their European adventures. When it was her turn, Lydia enjoyed watching their eyes widen with admiration then crinkle with laughter as she related a few tales of her own. Bella, the elder of the two women—a slip of a thing close to eighty—mentioned she'd be leaving for Florida in a few weeks, and invited Lydia to stay with her at her condo.

"Well, thank you. I may very well take you up on that, Bella," she answered in jest.

"Please do. This is a genuine offer. I've a beautiful guest room, don't I, Dorothy?"

Her friend nodded enthusiastically.

"I have plenty of friends, young, and old." Bella eyed Lydia appreciatively. "Believe me, all the men will be dying to meet you."

To Lydia's relief, no one brought up the subject of the murders. It was as though the sixteen women had made an unspoken pact to thoroughly enjoy their evening out, and not think about the terrifying events in their midst.

If I'm right, Lydia thought, it will soon be over. Twin Lakes will regain its tranquility, and the biggest decision a resident will have to make is whether to spend the evening playing cards or going to the movies. She smiled, anticipating her special treat when the case was closed—a date with Sol Molina.

After dessert, and coffee refills, they called it a night. Caroline ordered the bill, did the addition, and collected everyone's share. A few women drifted off to the ladies' room. Finally, they all rose, some unsteadily, and bid each other good night as they walked out into the chilly night air, and climbed into the four cars for the return trip to Twin Lakes.

In Caroline's car, silence reigned for the first five minutes of the ride. Then Barbara yawned. "It's not even nine-thirty, and I'm falling asleep."

"It's the wine," Lydia told her. "Tonight was wonderful, Caroline. What's scheduled for next month?"

"We have a lecturer coming to lead a discussion about current events."

They fell silent again. Barbara spoke. "I wonder if the police have charged Viv for the murders."

"I hope they solve this case soon," Shari said, "or I'm going to fly down to Florida, and spend a few weeks with my sister."

Lydia wondered if Sol Molina would answer his cell phone when she called him the minute she arrived home.

The Twin Lakes' patrol car cruised past her house as Caroline dropped her off. Lydia thanked her, and wished everyone a good night, then punched in the numbers on the pad beside her garage door. The three women called out their "good-nights" as the door closed down behind her.

Lydia walked through the small washer-dryer room calling, "Reggie, Reggie," but her cat remained out of sight.

How very odd, she thought. He always ran to greet her after she'd been out, whether to express his annoyance for having been left alone or to demand food.

In the kitchen, Lydia kicked off her shoes, and reached for the phone.

"Put that down!"

Stunned, Lydia dropped the phone, which clattered to the ceramic tile floor. The voice had come from the unlit dining room. Lydia gasped as Peg DiMarco appeared, her outstretched hand pointing a pistol.

"Get in here, away from the window!"

Lydia eyed the bay window, and the curtains she'd forgotten to draw.

"Hurry, or I'll shoot your precious cat!"

"Don't hurt him. I'm coming."

Lydia moved slowly to give herself time to gather her wits. How could she have forgotten Peg knew the combination to her garage door just as she knew Peg's? She must have said something during one of their conversations to make Peg believe she'd figured out Peg was the murderer when, in fact, she hadn't the slightest idea at the time.

Damn it, she should have borrowed a cell phone to call Sol everywhere—at the police station, on his cell—until she reached him! On his list, Marshall had crossed out letters before Peg's name. Undoubtedly, they were part of his special nickname for her or the name Peg had used when he knew her before they'd both moved to Twin Lakes. Not that it mattered. Now Lydia had to focus on getting out of this alive.

Peg waved her toward the living room. "Sit down there!"

Her brand new sofa. Lydia perched on the edge of the cushion, and stared at the small pistol that followed her every move. Her anxiety grew when she noticed Peg's arm was trembling. Peg was on medication, and extremely agitated. There was the horrible possibility she'd press the trigger by accident.

"This is all your fault, Miss CEO. You had to stick your nose where it didn't belong, and rake up the past. You turned everyone against Warren."

"Warren?" For a moment, Lydia had forgotten Weill's original name, which infuriated Peg even more.

"Warren Mannes, you moron! My Hawk. My life." A

heartrending groan rose up from the core of the bantam-sized woman holding her hostage, moving Lydia to pity. It was quickly replaced by repulsion.

"You took my car, and mowed down poor Claire Weill!"

"Poor Claire, my ass. She had everything she wanted, including Warren. He loved me. Warren, and I were a team. We belonged together."

"You helped him steal from the company you worked for," Lydia said slowly as she pieced it all together.

"I sure did, and was happy to do it." Peg's voice quavered with fury. "I was a damn good bookkeeper, but that wasn't enough for the bastard I worked for. He had me perform unmentionable acts. This was before anyone heard of suing for sexual harassment at the workplace, and I needed that job."

I'm not going there, Lydia thought, but didn't say out loud. "Your boss had to have known you were involved with the embezzlement, yet he didn't blow the whistle on you."

Peg curled her lip into an ugly grimace. "I had enough on him to send him away for twenty years. I earned that money! Even Warren agreed. He paid back most of what he'd taken from the company, including what he'd given me as my part of the deal. He looked after me."

"Afterward, he moved to Twin Lakes, and you did too."

Peg perched on the chair beside Izzy's statue of "Family." "He promised he'd divorce Claire, and we'd get married. We could pretend we met here. No one knew about us. Any time he came to the office, we hardly spoke. We always met in secret. Everything was going fine until that nosy—no matter."

Lydia stared at her. "You killed Frank Fuller."

Peg shrugged. "The guy was always creeping around taking photos. When I realized he'd shot a few of Warren, and me, I had to destroy them, and fix him for good."

Peg was insane. Ice-cold terror crept up Lydia's spine, threatening to paralyze her. She had to keep Peg talking. "Only Warren didn't keep his part of the bargain."

Peg shook her head. "He had trouble keeping up his end of any bargain. Warren found he liked living at Twin Lakes. He decided he'd stay married to Claire, and continue to see me—like old times."

"Did he know you killed Claire?"

Peg snorted. "Smart as he was, my Hawk wore blinders when life turned raw, and ugly. I swore I had nothing to do with Claire's death, and he believed me. He had to, you see, if we were to live happily ever after."

She paused then snorted again. "Only there was no happily ever after. The fool never knew when to stop."

The gun, Lydia noticed, no longer pointed at her but rested on Peg's lap. Now would be the moment to distract Peg then fling the keys she still gripped in her hand at Peg's face.

Unfortunately, Peg seemed to read her thoughts. She leveled the gun at Lydia's chest. A look of pure hatred colored her face.

"I saw how he looked at you, despite the mud you threw at him. Figured he could have a new wife who was both pretty, and rich, and keep his magpie on the side, as usual."

"But I never—"

"Shut up!"

Peg eyed the sculpture beside her. "Lucky Lydia, who had such a wonderful, and loving husband. An artist instead of a drunken, gambling bum. Two lovely daughters."

With both hands, she shoved the sculpture from its pedestal. Lydia screamed as it fell to the ground, the head of the father figure breaking off. Peg's glare warned her to stay where she was.

"Only you weren't vulnerable, as you put it." Her laughter turned maniacal. "Too good for the likes of Warren. So he decided to go after money alone."

"Viv," Lydia murmured.

"Yes, Viv, that ugly humped-back dwarf! I asked him how he could even think of making love to her, and he said it was easy—he closed his eyes, and thought of me."

"Is that when you decided to kill him?"

Peg cast her a look of respect. "As a matter of fact, it was. I went over there, promising myself I'd forgive him if he agreed we'd get married. When he told me he was going to marry Viv, I carried on a bit then agreed to spend the night with him. I prepared his favorite tea with enough drops to knock him out in ten minutes. He got groggy. I insisted we go out back so he could get some air. When he was weak enough, I hit him on the head with a statue, then put him face down in the water. I went home, and cried all night."

Lydia heard a muffled meow. "Where's Reggie? What did you do to him?"

"Your annoying cat's in the bathroom." Peg threw her a malevolent grin. "Don't worry. I'm sure some kind person will adopt him."

"What do you mean?" she asked, her heart thudding against her ribs.

"Did you really think I was going to let you live? I saw that bulb light up in your brain when you spotted my magpies, and asked if I'd ever seen Warren's."

"But I didn't know then," Lydia protested.

"Sure you did." Peg sniggered. "Only it gave you the willies to admit it was your helpful next-door neighbor who'd killed all those people."

Maybe, Lydia agreed silently, not that it mattered anymore. What mattered was disarming Peg before she shot her.

"Get up!" Peg ordered. "Slowly."

Lydia stood. Peg circled around the coffee table so that she stood between the living room, and the dining room.

"Now, unlock the back door, and we'll go outside."

Lydia's eyes flew to the door. She could have sworn she heard a sound coming from that direction. "I don't have shoes on!"

"You won't need any shoes. Go on!"

Her hesitation earned her a prod from the gun. Peg was

that close. Close wasn't good. Lydia took two tentative steps, and turned her head to keep Peg within sight. Peg hadn't moved. She took two more steps then veered suddenly into the darkened hallway that led to the bedrooms, and baths.

"Hey! What do you think—!" A bullet whizzed by.

Lydia crouched to the floor. She reached up, and turned the knob of the door closest to her. A blur of red fur zoomed past her as she tumbled into the guest bathroom. She turned, ready to slam the door shut, when she saw Reggie scamper between Peg's legs. Peg stumbled backward, her left hand out to break her fall.

Damn it, she still held the gun in her other hand.

"Lydia!" Peg screamed. "You can't get away from me!"

Lydia locked the bathroom door. A temporary reprieve. In a matter of seconds, her homicidal neighbor would be shooting off the handle. She threw open the window, and saw cars parked helter-skelter on her lawn. Help had come but she couldn't afford to wait five seconds, not with Peg on her tail. She pushed out the screen, and was halfway through the window when the sound of shattering glass made her pause.

She opened the door a crack, and peered out. Detective Sol Molina stood in the police stance she knew well from TV, and movies—a semi crouch, both hands on his gun. It was pointed at a now whimpering Peg.

"Place the gun on the floor," he ordered.

Peg did as she was told.

"Now walk toward me. That's right."

Sol clicked handcuffs on Peg. Lydia stood just inside the bathroom, and stared as uniformed officers filled the house. Two approached Peg, and ushered her out the front door. Lydia felt as though she were watching a movie. What was happening couldn't be taking place in her house, in her life.

I'm safe. I can leave the bathroom, she told herself. She stepped into the hall, and stumbled. She would have fallen if Sol hadn't rushed over to lend his support. He helped her into the dining room where she sank into a chair.

"Are you okay?"

She nodded. "Only I feel totally discombobulated."

"Delayed reaction. Shock, actually." He strode off to the nearest bedroom, and brought back a quilt, which he wrapped around her. "Be back soon as I can."

The house filled with more people. Benny Lieberman, and another man came toward her. Benny put an arm around her. "Are you all right, Lydia?"

"I think so." To her dismay, she burst into tears.

Benny settled her on a sofa as if she were an invalid, then he phoned his wife, and Barbara. Her two friends fluttered around her like handmaidens, bringing pillows, and doing everything they could think of to make her comfortable. Caroline prepared a mug of steaming tea, and brandy, which she swore was the very thing Lydia needed. Sipping the hot drink helped soothe her rattled nerves, and helped her to realize her horrible ordeal was over. She was safe.

When Sol returned, her two friends faded into the kitchen to give them privacy. Sol knelt beside her. For a moment, he just gazed into her eyes. "Thank God we stopped her in time."

Lydia nodded, too full of emotion to speak.

"We're leaving now. I'll be down at the station, taking your neighbor's statement, and doing paper work for a good part of the night. I'll come by tomorrow to take your statement."

The spin he'd put on the last sentence set her heart racing.

"I look forward to it," she said demurely.

His knowing laughter was loud enough to bring Barbara into view. She gave Lydia a wink.

"Just one thing," he said, "call your daughter when you're up to it, and thank her for saving your life."

"Merry?"

"That's right. She phoned me sounding frantic because she couldn't get you on your cell phone. She insisted something was wrong or you would have picked up."

Lydia cast a guilty glance toward the kitchen, where her uncharged cell phone lay in the bottom of her pocketbook.

Sol went on. "I was on my way over here when she called. I had my suspicions about your neighbor. After I got your aborted message, I took another look at Weill's list, saw the scratched-out 'MAG,', and managed to put it all together."

She gazed into his eyes. Now they were green.

Definitely green. "You saved my life, you know."

He winked. "All in the line of duty, ma'am," he said, then lowered his voice. "I better get the hell out of here while I still can."

She watched his retreat to the door, not noticing that Barbara, and Caroline had taken his place.

"That's some hunk of man," Caroline commented. "I hope you're not letting him out of your life."

Lydia grinned. "He's coming back tomorrow to ask me questions."

"Make sure you give him the right answers."

The phone rang. Barbara went into the kitchen to answer it. She returned a minute later, holding the phone out to Lydia. "It's your daughter."

"Hi, Merry," she began.

"It's me, Mom," Abbie said. "Are you all right?"

"I'm fine—now."

"Good. Merry was worried because you went out, and she couldn't get you on your cell phone. I told her you probably just forgot to turn it on."

"That's kind of what happened."

Lydia heard sniffling. Her traumatized brain finally understood that something serious was troubling her normally placid daughter. "What's wrong, Abbie?"

"Oh, Mom, it's simply awful!" Abbie began to sob.

"Try to calm down, honey, and tell me about it."

"All right." Abbie blew her nose, and let out a very deep sigh. "My wedding's scheduled in three, and a half weeks, and suddenly Todd's cousin, Karen, can't have it at her house. Can you believe it?"

Lydia's pulse, which had just resumed its normal rate, started racing again as her daughter explained that a piece of a plane had simply fallen from the sky, and damaged two of the upstairs bedrooms. Karen, and her husband had to move out until the repairs were made, which could take months, and months, maybe a year.

"And the invitations have all gone out!" Abbie finished with a wail.

"Don't worry," Lydia reassured her. "How many people have you invited?"

"Seventy-five. But only about sixty are coming."

"Sixty guests," Lydia mused. "Carrington House has a beautiful room that would be perfect. I'll check tomorrow, see if it's free."

She glanced up at Barbara, and Caroline, who were nodding enthusiastically, their eyes lit up with the anticipation of planning a wedding.

"Oh, Mom! You're the best! I should have asked you to take over in the first place."

Yes, you should have, Lydia thought. "I'll handle everything, but once I sign for the place, you'll be responsible for informing your guests of the new wedding location."

"Will do. Todd's cousin's canceling the caterer."

Lydia yawned, suddenly overcome by fatigue. "Abbie, let's talk about this tomorrow. I've had a very tiring day."

"Sure, Mom. By the way, what's the latest on the murderer at your place?"

"She's been caught, and is now in custody at the police station."

"She?" Abbie exclaimed. "Wow, it was a woman?"

"I'll tell you all about it tomorrow, I promise, and do me a favor, and call Merry. Tell her I'm all right, and I'll speak to her tomorrow."

Getting rid of Barbara, and Caroline wasn't as easy. Barbara wanted to stay over, in case Lydia had a delayed reaction, and needed human company.

"Don't worry," Lydia said as she stroked Reggie stretched out beside her. 'I have Reggie. Tomorrow I'll call on both of you to help plan Abbie's wedding."

They started spouting names of musicians, and florists until Lydia threw up her hands.

"We'll talk about it tomorrow," she said, herding them to the door. She felt a bit wobbly but, strangely enough, she was eager to be alone. Alone except for Reggie.

"Meow!" Reggie declared, tail in the air as he led the way into the kitchen.

"Exactly!" Lydia agreed, and fed him.

She changed into her nightgown, and got ready for bed. She intended to go right to sleep for some much-needed rest. Tomorrow was another day, and she had much do—give her statement to Sol, talk to her daughters, and friends, and settle on a place for Abbie's wedding. Her life was full, she suddenly realized, full of people she loved, though she'd met some of them only a short while ago.

Lydia sighed as she snuggled under the quilt. That was how life was: it took away, and it gave back—as long as you kept an open heart, and a willing mind. She suddenly thought of the white stallion in the fountain that faced the clubhouse, rearing up on his back legs ready to charge ahead into the unknown future. Kind of like what she was doing now.

Best of all, she, and her fellow residents were safe. That Peg DiMarco had killed the Weills, and intended to kill her was something Lydia hadn't even begun to absorb, much less understand. It would take time for her to get over the shock of it all. But now she had friends at Twin Lakes. Good friends, and there was Sol.

Lydia closed her eyes, and wondered if her forest green suede pants, and a white silk blouse were too dressy an outfit to wear when he came over. On second thought, she'd save it for their first dinner date. Smiling, she drifted off to sleep.

Meet

Marilyn Levinson

Marilyn Levinson is a former Spanish teacher, and the author of several books for children, and young adults. RUFUS, and MAGIC RUN AMOK was selected by the International Reading Association, and the Children's Book Council for "Children's Choices for 2002." NO BOYS ALLOWED has been in print since 1993, and has sold over 200,000 copies.

A MURDERER AMONG US is her first published adult mystery. MURDER A LA CHRISTIE was a finalist in the 2010 Malice Domestic contest. She is a member of The Authors Guild, RWA, The Mystery Writers of America, Sisters in Crime, the Guppies, and is president, and co-founder the Long Island chapter of Sisters in Crime. She lives on Long Island with her husband, Bernie aand their cat, Sammy.

*VISIT OUR WEBSITE
FOR THE FULL INVENTORY
OF QUALITY BOOKS:*

http://www.wings-press.com

*Quality trade paperbacks, and downloads
in multiple formats,
in genres ranging from light romantic
comedy to general fiction, and horror.
Wings has something
for every reader's taste.
Visit the website, then bookmark it.
We add new titles each month!*